Beware the Cuckoo

JULIE NEWMAN

URBANE
Publications

urbanepublications.com

First published in Great Britain in 2017
by Urbane Publications Ltd
Suite 3, Brown Europe House, 33/34 Gleaming Wood Drive,
Chatham, Kent ME5 8RZ
Copyright © Julie Newman, 2017

A CIP catalogue record for this book is available
from the British Library.

ISBN 978-1-911129-91-2
MOBI 978-1-911129-93-6
EPUB 978-1-911129-92-9

Design and Typeset by Michelle Morgan

Cover by Michelle Morgan

Printed and bound by CPI Group (UK) Ltd, Croydon, CR0 4YY

urbanepublications.com

Beware the cuckoo! By what name
You call her, she is still the same.
And, if you must admire her art,
Keep a wing over your heart.

Beware the Cuckoo *by Ernest G. Moll*

For Tom & Hayleigh

PROLOGUE

September 1961

The woman leans over the girl and strokes the hair from her tear streaked face. She gently kisses her forehead, as she does the girl opens her eyes and stares straight at her; she is exhausted and then she remembers.

"Where is my baby?" she asks.

"I'm sorry darling, she died before she entered this world."

"I heard a cry."

"No, she is gone, God has her now."

"But Mama, I heard a cry, I heard my baby."

"Sleep now."

"I heard her," she protests. "Mama, I heard my baby. Where is she? Please Mama." The girl tries to rise, pushing her mother's hands away from her. Her mother holds her firm, pushing her back into the bed, she nods at the nurse who swiftly injects the prone girl. "I heard her, I heard…"

Sleep takes her.

❂

He hears the crunching of tyres on the gravel, then headlights illuminate the room as a car sweeps along the drive. She is here. He goes out onto the veranda; watching, waiting. The rear door of the car opens and a woman gets out, she stands there looking at him for a moment, impassive, expressionless; she holds his gaze before turning back to the car. She reaches into the back seat, lifting out a basket. She walks toward him and hands the basket to him.

"How is…?"

Before he can finish his sentence the woman raises her hand putting one finger across his lips.

"You will never speak her name. You will never see her. You will never touch her, ever again. To you, she is gone, dead. From this moment on, my daughter is dead. Do you understand?"

He nods his accord without speaking.

The woman returns to the car pausing a moment before getting in then she turns and looks straight at him.

"You are very lucky that I have not informed the authorities, but my daughter is still a child and I do not want her life blighted because of your sin. However, every action provokes a reaction, every deed spawns a consequence and that is yours," she said, pointing at the basket. "I will be watching you, God will be watching you so do right by her and I pray that in her future she does not encounter a man like you."

He watched the car until its rear lights were no more than tiny red dots. As he turned to go back inside the house, something in the basket stirred.

She was awake.

2010

K aren read the letter once more before sliding it back into its envelope and pushing it to the bottom of her handbag. So, Bill Davids is dead; but why would anyone think I would want to go to his funeral, she mused.

◉

As she pulled into the car park Karen was surprised at how few cars there were. The last time she had come to St. Luke's church she had to park in the supermarket car park several streets away. Although that had been for a wedding and it was a Saturday, but she was surprised nonetheless. She entered the church and looked around; she was beginning to worry she had the wrong day as there were only a handful of people inside. It was a large church so she didn't expect it to be full, but certainly she thought there would be more people than this. After all, we're talking about Bill Davids; he knew everyone and more importantly everyone knew him. Karen supposed that many of his friends may have passed away before him or perhaps they had moved away; Bill himself had moved back to South Africa. She wondered why he had ended up back in the U.K. After scanning the pews Karen decided to sit alongside a couple that were a few rows from the back. At least she wouldn't stick out and if necessary it offered her a quick getaway. She sat down pulling her coat tightly around her as she did. Why are churches always so damn cold? The couple beside her looked up, gave a brief smile and nod of the head before both refocusing on their feet. God, what am I doing here? Karen asked herself. Until this morning she'd had no intention of coming, but when she woke it was the first thing she thought of and she knew she had to come. This sudden compulsion had not gone down well with Andrew, especially as it meant he would have to collect the boys from school.

"What is the point of running your own business, if you can't take a couple of hours off?"

Andrew decided not to argue with her and just agreed to pick them up. It was obvious it wasn't the school run that was the problem. No, what really bothered him, was the fact that she would see Sandra again, a fact that was beginning to bother her too if she was honest. As that thought began to properly sink in there was movement behind her. She turned and through the open church door she could see that the hearse had arrived, any notion of escape was pointless now. Music began to filter through the church as the sparse congregation rose.

Karen walked back to her car, the shock of Sandra not being at her father's funeral gave way to relief. After all what would they have said, it had been years since they last saw one another, they didn't even exchange Christmas cards anymore. She got into the car and as the engine turned over so the depressing tones of Leonard Cohen filled her ears.

"Something more cheerful please," she muttered to herself. She tried other radio stations; interviews – boring, traffic reports - no, an advert for a well-known tyre and exhaust centre - no thank you. She leant across the passenger seat and opened the glove compartment, as she began rifling through the CDs someone tapped on the window making her jump and drop Now (that's what I call music) 100 & whatever and Billy Joel's greatest hits into the foot well. She turned to the window and was shocked to see Sandra standing there.

Karen got out of the car and as she did Sandra threw her arms around her, almost knocking her back in again. This redoubled the shock Karen was already feeling as the Sandra she remembered was not demonstrative or emotional at all.

"This is such a surprise," said Sandra. "You are the last person I expected to see here. How are you?"

"You missed your Dad's funeral," said Karen ignoring Sandra's question.

"I was here, I just couldn't go in there," she said, nodding towards the church. "How was it?"

"Quiet."

"That's no surprise really. He alienated a lot of people over the years and then when the Alzheimer's took hold, the few friends he had left found him increasingly difficult to cope with."

"I'm sorry, I didn't realise he had Alzheimer's."

"Yes, the man I knew, my Dad, I lost a long time ago."

As Sandra spoke her eyes moistened, Karen gently put a hand on Sandra's arm but Sandra pulled it away pretending to look at her watch.

"Goodness, is that the time? I haven't even checked into my hotel yet."

"Yes, and I need to collect the boys from school," Karen lied.

"Listen," said Sandra. "Let's have dinner. It'll be good to catch up. I'll book a table at my hotel, about eight. I'm staying at the Regent, just off the ring road," she shouted as she walked away.

And before Karen could reply, she was gone.

"Shit," said Karen, a little too loudly, as she got back into her car. "Shit, shit, shit," she kept repeating louder and louder as she drove away; a crescendo of curses. "Why didn't you just say no?" she questioned herself. Perhaps she could come up with an excuse and cancel. She wouldn't even need to speak to Sandra, she could just leave a message at the hotel reception; but she wouldn't do that. Karen never let anyone down. If she said she would do something, then she would do it, whether she wanted to or not. Andrew says that her desire to please everyone and inability to say no is both her best and worst attribute.

When she got home, she went straight upstairs to her bedroom and threw open the cupboard doors. She stared at the dull muted tones that formed her wardrobe. What on earth am I going to wear? Sandra will no doubt look stunning, she thought. As she rummaged through her clothes the feeling of inadequacy she encountered as a teenager began creeping over her. Sandra was even able to make the school uniform look chic. As her mind wandered back to her schooldays, Karen recalled an end of year disco or party where Sandra had upset her. As she remembered the details of that evening she was rescued from her thoughts by the sound of the back door opening. Andrew and the boys were home. She went downstairs, the boys were scavenging in the food cupboard and Andrew was standing by the sink, filling the kettle.

"I thought you weren't going to be back until later," he said without looking up.

"I didn't think I would be, but the service was short and there wasn't a wake."

Andrew looked up at her without speaking, his eyes enquiring. She knew what his silence was asking. Was she there? The silence dragged on for a few seconds more, then he spoke.

"Fancy Chinese tonight? You probably haven't had time to think about dinner."

Bugger, she thought. She knew what she was about to say would not go down well.

"Well actually, I'm having dinner with Sandra tonight," she said as casually as possible.

"You're what?" Replied Andrew.

"I'm having dinner with Sandra," she repeated. "She's just lost her Dad, I could hardly say no," she continued, trying to justify herself. "You and the boys have Chinese."

"Fine," said Andrew as he brushed past her and went upstairs.

It wasn't quite 7.30 when Karen arrived at the hotel. She had left home earlier than necessary to avoid Andrew's sulking, she knew he didn't want her to go and she knew why. Karen would rather he actually say what was on his mind, she couldn't cope with the silent treatment. Yes, they would have argued, yes, she would still have gone and he probably knew that, yet still she wished he had said what he was thinking; but that wasn't his way. No shouting, screaming or banging, just scowls and sulky expressions that eventually gave way to a silent fury that permeated everything and everyone. His anger would spread throughout the house leaving each room feeling dark and airless. She had felt momentarily guilty about leaving the boys with him, but knew once they had switched on the X-Box they would be oblivious to the gloom surrounding them. The worst of it is he is probably right; meeting Sandra is a bad idea.

Karen pushed through the revolving door and entered the hotel lobby. It was an open plan design; large leather chairs were arranged in straight lines. The primary colour was a greyish brown or maybe a brownish grey. The designer probably described it as taupe or fawn. The austere surroundings made the space feel cold and cheerless; fine for business travellers, who were probably the mainstay of the hotel, but Karen didn't feel the hotel lived up to the Regent's reputation or indeed it's 5* rating. She located the restaurant and peered in, as far as she could see only a couple of tables were occupied and neither of them by Sandra. A waiter approached and asked if he could help her. Yes, she thought, show me the quickest way out of here.

"I'm meeting a friend for dinner, Miss Davids, Sandra Davids." As she said this she suddenly wondered if that was still her name, she could have married for all she knew, she hadn't thought to ask when they met earlier. "I'm a little early though," she added.

The waiter thumbed through the reservations book.

"Yes, you are, early that is, perhaps you would care to wait for her in the lounge," he suggested, politely but firmly.

"Thank-you," replied Karen, "I can see you're busy in here," she muttered sarcastically.

The waiter escorted her to the lounge, which was a much nicer room. You could easily think you were in a completely different hotel to the one the lobby represented. It was decorated in an art-deco style with a beautiful grand piano at its centre. The bar was beautifully ornate with huge mirrors behind it that reflected the subtle lighting. This room alone was worth the five stars. It was busier than the restaurant but Karen managed to find a table that gave her a perfect view of the door, she did not want Sandra surprising her again. She ordered a gin and tonic and sat and waited. About ten minutes or so passed and then Sandra made her entrance; she always did that. Most people just walk into a room, some you may notice, most you don't, but not Sandra. When she entered a room, she was making a statement, I'm here, look at me and sure enough everyone did. She paused in the doorway, just long enough for people to take her in and wonder about her.

As always, she looked immaculate, polished; she was wearing a long cream skirt and dark jacket with contrasting trim, simple, yet elegant. Karen had opted for a sage green trouser suit and floral blouse which had earned her compliments on previous occasions, but now she was starting to feel a little uncomfortable. Sandra went to the bar first, ordered herself a drink then came and sat at the table with Karen.

"Have you been waiting long?" she asked eyeing Karen's almost empty glass.

"No, just a few minutes," replied Karen. "You look great," she added.

"Thank-you," said Sandra, without returning the compliment. "Not bad for someone who has been travelling for eighteen hours out of the last twenty-four."

Before Karen could respond the barman brought Sandra's drink over.

"Cheers," said Sandra raising her glass.

"Cheers," repeated Karen. "Here's to your Dad."

Sandra paused and briefly stared at Karen before emptying her glass in one large gulp. Sandra raised her hand and signalled to the barman to bring her another drink.

"Another?" She asked Karen.

"No, I'm fine, thank you."

Sandra's second drink only lasted marginally longer than the first and Karen was beginning to feel a little apprehensive about the evening that lay ahead.

"We may as well go through to the restaurant now," said Sandra as she put down her glass.

Karen stood up, finishing her drink as she followed Sandra through the crowded lounge. The same grumpy waiter from earlier greeted them and showed them to their table. As they sat down, Sandra ordered a bottle of Shiraz, South African Shiraz.

"A taste of home."

The waiter returned with the wine, poured a large glass for each of them and handed them menus, telling them the specials and what wasn't available all in one breath. Sandra drank her wine as if it were a glass of iced water on a hot summer's day. She poured herself another, had a small sip then looked at Karen and asked,

"So, how's what's his face; Alan, Adam…?"

"Andrew, his name is Andrew. He's fine. He sends his love."

"Oh, I'm sure he doesn't." Sandra replied tersely.

Karen smiled nervously and decided not to argue, it was clear that Sandra's lack of sleep or consumption of alcohol was aiding her belligerence. The waiter brought over a basket of bread which Sandra pounced on almost before it was placed on the table. As she bit into a roll so her demeanour seemed to soften.

"Thank-you for coming today; to the funeral I mean."

"Oh, you're welcome" said Karen. "I'm glad I went."

"Why did you come?"

Karen was taken aback by the question and initially didn't know how to respond. She thought for a second before replying.

"I, erm, I remembered how your Dad rescued me from that grotty bedsit."

"Goodness, I'd forgotten about that; that place was awful. Then you moved into my house with Yvonne and me."

Karen couldn't help but notice how Sandra emphasised the word my when talking about the house - the house that was actually a flat, although Karen decided against correcting her - for it was hers, well her Dad's, which probably amounted to the same thing, but strange she felt the need to remind her.

September 1974

"Karen, Karen. Are you up yet? Hurry up or you'll be late for school," screeched her Mum up the stairs.

She was up, she'd been awake for quite a while and was now sitting at her dressing table, staring in the mirror at the enormous spot that had taken up residence on her forehead overnight. She had tried to cover it up, but there it was, red and angry like a mini Mount Vesuvius on the verge of eruption. This is so unfair, she thought. Why today? Not one bloody spot all summer, not a single one, and now first day back at school, there it is. She was going to be the target yet again; she so wanted this year to be different, she'd had enough of being the butt of everyone's jokes.

Karen hated school, the only good thing to happen last year was meeting Yvonne. It was their friendship that had sustained Karen and kept her strong, but still she didn't think that she could take another year of being tormented, even with Yvonne by her side. She stood up, went to her wardrobe, took out her uniform and began to get dressed. She had to breath in to get the skirt done up. Why did Mum insist on buying new school uniform at the beginning of the holidays? It was just plain stupid, after all you had six weeks of eating and drinking whatever you liked, (well almost) ahead of you. School holidays were the only time that Karen and her younger brothers and sister were allowed fizzy drinks and junk food. The rest of the time their Mum was extremely fussy about their diet. Karen managed to do her skirt up, although she didn't hold out much hope that the button would remain attached to the waistband for the next seven and a half hours. She went downstairs, had a glass of orange juice but decided to forego breakfast as she did not want to place any extra strain on the already burdened button. As she went out of the door she shouted goodbye to whoever was listening and headed off towards Yvonne's house.

Yvonne lived on the other side of the park which sat in the middle of town, their very own Central Park, although this park was nowhere near as glamorous as its New York namesake: it had the usual play area with swings and slide, a large roundabout called the witches hat and a see-saw that had seen better days. There were two fields, one had some battered goalposts on it and the other was just patchy grass. There was a remembrance garden that had very few flowers in it but was home to a rather green pond. Karen walked through the park to get to Yvonne's house and together they walked to school.

"Do you know what today is?" Yvonne asked Karen as they approached the school.

"No," said Karen.

"It's a special day," continued Yvonne through mouthfuls of a toffee crisp. Yvonne was always eating chocolate, yet she had the clearest skin and was a skinny thing, so unfair thought Karen.

"Come on," pressed Yvonne.

"What?"

"What day is it?"

"I don't know."

"Guess."

"I don't know," said Karen much louder this time. She was a bit irritated with Yvonne's guessing game as she was rather pre-occupied with trying to keep her hair in place so as to conceal the spot which was like a red beacon in the centre of her forehead.

"Well," said Yvonne. "Today is our anniversary."

"What are you talking about?" asked Karen.

"It's a year since we met and became best friends," and with that Yvonne threw her arms around Karen and gave her a big hug. Karen felt her face colour, she could see people looking at them and pointing. Yvonne sensed her embarrassment and let go.

"You know you really must stop worrying about what others think of you. If they don't like you, screw them. They aren't worth it."

That's easy for you thought Karen. Yvonne never seemed to worry about anyone or anything, she did and said exactly as she pleased. But there again she could, everybody liked Yvonne.

"Promise me you'll try this year," continued Yvonne. "Lots of people like you, you're very funny."

Hilarious, thought Karen; I know they think I'm funny, funny weird. God, doesn't she realise that being called funny isn't actually a compliment.

"Yes, I'll try."

Their conversation was interrupted by the school bell. They quickly ran into school, up the stairs and into their tutor room. Mr. Harper, their tutor took the register then handed out timetables to everyone. Karen and Yvonne were disappointed when they realised that they weren't in as many lessons together this year. Karen's first two lessons were Science and French while Yvonne had English and Art. The bell rang again signalling the end of tutor time.

"Oh well," said Yvonne. "I'll meet you in the cloakrooms at

break-time."

"Okay," said Karen and she headed off towards the science block.

She opened the classroom door and was greeted by chaos. There were pupils laying across the tables, others were throwing a bag around like a rugby ball, Trevor Gardener was writing obscenities on the blackboard and two others were trying to melt their biros with a bunsen burner. Karen went in and sat down at the end of a table that did not have a horizontal body on it. By sitting at the end of a table she only had to worry about one person sitting next to her rather than two. Just then in walked Mr. Murray, the science teacher. He closed the door, removed the white lab coat that was hanging on a hook on the back of the door and put it on. The coat wasn't actually white anymore; it was a more greyish hue with several unattractive stains all over it. Karen thought it had most likely been hanging on the back of the door all summer, in fact she was convinced it had never been washed.

"Right settle down now," said Mr. Murray. "Find a seat, quickly please." Everyone found a seat except Paul Adams.

"There's nowhere to sit Sir," he said.

"Yes, there is," said Mr. Murray pointing at the seat next to Karen.

"I'm not sitting next to crater-face," said Paul to the amusement of the class. Oh no, thought Karen, they had noticed. She lowered her head, pulling her hair across her forehead. Mr. Murray was about to respond when in walked Mrs. Bell from the office, closely followed by a girl. The girl was very tall - well she appeared tall standing alongside the diminutive Mrs. Bell. She had long blonde hair that cascaded down her back in waves. Karen thought she looked like one of the models in her Mum's catalogue, but she was wearing a school uniform. All the boys were looking at her, even

Paul Adams had shut up. Mrs. Bell went and spoke to Mr. Murray and then left, leaving the tall, blonde girl standing there.

"Right," said Mr. Murray. "We have a newcomer. This is Sandra Davids." He directed Sandra to the seat next to Karen. Karen shifted along a little to allow Sandra room to sit next to her. Everyone was watching her, the new girl, as she slowly and deliberately took out of her bag what she needed for the lesson. Karen felt incredibly embarrassed for her. It must be horrible to start a new school and have all eyes on you. However, as she too watched her, discreetly of course, Karen sensed that Sandra seemed to be enjoying the attention, for she was taking rather longer than necessary sorting out what she needed.

The two of them didn't say much initially, they both studiously sat listening to Mr. Murray drone on about PH levels or something else equally boring, then about fifteen minutes into the lesson Sandra turned and asked Karen her name. Karen told her and then began gushing.

"Oh, my God, I love your accent. Is it Australian? My uncle had an Australian girlfriend and you sound just like her. Why would you leave Australia?" Karen rambled on, something she has a tendency to do when nervous.

"I'm from South Africa not Australia," Sandra said.

"Oh wow," said Karen stupidly.

Sandra looked at Karen in bewilderment. She wasn't quite sure what to make of her. The inane questions were annoying, she wittered on without saying anything interesting, she looked like she'd slept in her clothes and had she never heard of make-up. Yet, that said, there was something about her that Sandra liked. She sensed a kindred spirit, someone who like herself, was an outsider. Not quite accepted by most, of course clearly not for the same reasons. For her, she knew it was because she was beautiful and intelligent. Even now, at only thirteen, she knew that those qualities intimidated people. Her Dad told her, 'there are people who are lovely to look at and there are people who are incredibly clever, but there are very few people who are both. You kid are unique because you have both, beauty and brains; because of that people will admire and resent you in equal measure.'

During the lesson, Karen and Sandra compared their timetables. Karen had French next, while Sandra had Art.

"Can you tell me how to get to my next lesson?"

"I'll show you, the art corridor is above the language rooms."

The bell sounded and the girls headed off together. Paul Adams and his cronies were following them, they were firing questions at Sandra, barely giving her time to answer. Karen raised her voice slightly go get Sandra's attention but all she got was a 'shut up crater-face' from Neil Baker, Paul's sidekick. The boys left them when they reached the humanities classroom. Karen was relieved she wouldn't have to put up with them next lesson. As they reached the stairs that took them up to the art rooms Karen spotted Yvonne. She called her over and introduced her to Sandra. Yvonne also had art next so Sandra went with her and the three arranged to meet at break-time.

Bill Davids slammed down the telephone receiver and pushed himself back in his black leather chair. He breathed deeply, then leant forward and extracted a glass and bottle from the bottom drawer of his desk. He poured himself two fingers of whiskey and in a well-practised manoeuvre poured the contents of the glass down his throat. He returned the bottle and the glass to the drawer and leant back in his chair once more. He was flabbergasted by the incompetence of some people. He was not a particularly patient man and what tested his patience above all else was stupidity. Of course, over the years he'd come across many stupid people, people he deemed not worthy of his time or business; so, he'd built a network of associates he could work with, although not totally rely on, for he relied on nobody but himself. It was his self-reliance and steely resolve that he believed made him a success.

His business was hard to define, it could not be pigeonholed; he didn't buy anything, he didn't sell anything, he didn't make anything, apart from money. And with that money he then bought property, although that wasn't actually his business. What he did was bring people together; he arranged deals, he was a go-between, a broker, of sorts. People came to him if they had something to sell or buy or if they wished to acquire specialist services and he connected them with relevant trading partners; for this he got a commission or fee. He made no judgement on what they were trading in, as long as he had his percentage, that was fine, and he was very adept at keeping himself above the law. Mostly.

Small arms deals were commonplace on the African continent. The Angolan Bush War had been raging since 1966 and this had led to the Grensoorlog - Border War - which now involved not only Angola, but Namibia and South Africa too. South Africa also had its own internal struggle. The South African Defence Force representing the white minority government were not only fighting in the Border War, they were also battling the African National Congress in their liberation struggle. The South African Defence Force claimed to be shielding its citizens from roll/swart gevaar - red/black danger - the dual threat from Communism and African Nationalism.

Bill Davids viewed this unrest differently to others. It didn't scare or worry him. He didn't fret over the future of his country.

He very much lived in the present and to him the situation presented opportunities; deals waiting to be done, money waiting to be made. Black, white, even red, he didn't care, the only colour that interested him was the colour of money. After all, one man's terrorist is another man's freedom fighter.

That said, he did have one concern, his daughter. Which was why they had moved to England. The last deal he had been involved with had led to some interest from the authorities. He needed to distance himself from it, because if anything happened to him, Sandra had no-one.

July 1975

As they neared the end of term Karen felt a level of excitement about the approaching summer holidays that she hadn't felt before. Yvonne, Sandra and herself had become a very tight gang of three since the autumn and together they had been busy making plans on how they would spend the summer. Yvonne was spending the first week at her Grandmother's caravan in Weymouth and Sandra was going to Switzerland with her dad. She had hoped they might go back to South Africa for some of the holidays but her Dad said that wasn't possible at the moment. Sandra kept going on about how disappointed she was until Karen had pointed out to her that she wasn't going anywhere and in fact had not been on holiday for a long time; the last holiday she'd had was a wet weekend camping in the Brecon Beacons. This year though Karen was not bothered that she wouldn't be going away as she knew when the three of them were together they would have a great summer. There was only one thing Karen was not looking forward to and that was the 'End of Term' disco. Sandra and Yvonne both wanted to go, so reluctantly she had agreed to it.

On the last day of term the school was very noisy. It had taken on an almost carnival like atmosphere. The fifth- year pupils had returned to the school to say their final goodbyes. Some were even wearing fancy dress, one group of girls were wearing their school uniform St. Trinian's style with their skirts rolled very high and ties around their foreheads, their final act of rebellion. Some were collecting signatures on their old school shirts, while others were decorating the sports hall ready for the disco that evening. The day passed by quite quickly and when the final bell rang at 3.30 an enormous cheer went up, it was so loud that its echo seemed to hang in the air for ages afterwards. The three girls left the school together as they were going to get ready at Sandra's house and her Dad was going to take them back later.

To reach Sandra's house they had to walk back across the park. She lived on a new cul-de-sac that had been fashioned out of a dusty dirt track that didn't really lead anywhere. There were only six houses and they were huge. Sandra's house backed onto the park. Karen wasn't sure what she was more jealous of, the size of the house or the fact that it was new and nobody had lived in it before Sandra and her Dad. Karen lived in an old house, the sort that people say has character, (well that's what her Mum said), but Karen just thought it dark, dingy and dated. She was convinced someone must have died in it at some point as it was so old, though that was something she never sought to have confirmed. Sandra's room was lovely. Everything was white. Along one wall there were floor to ceiling wardrobes, on the opposite side was her bed, a double bed that Karen was sure was even bigger than her mums. She also had a sofa in her room that opened to become a bed. But the best feature of all, as far as Karen was concerned, was a huge box window that was so large the three of them could sit in it, which was great as it afforded them a perfect view of the park and everyone in it. Karen decided it was definitely the size of the house that she was more envious of. She had to share a room with her younger sister, her annoying younger sister and with so many people living in her house it was impossible to find a corner to yourself, let alone a whole room. It really wasn't fair, seven people shared Karen's house now that Grandad had come to live with them and it was less than half the size of this one that had only two people living in it.

Sandra's mum had died when Sandra was born. Karen had asked her if she missed her, but Sandra very matter-of-factly replied that as she has no memory of her it was impossible to miss her. Karen thought it a bit odd that Sandra didn't even have a photograph of her mother, it seemed she knew very little about her. When Karen and Yvonne had asked about other family Sandra said it was just her and her Dad and that was all she needed. Karen couldn't imagine not having any family at all, however she did understand when Sandra said her Dad was all she needed. Karen liked Bill, he was very friendly, funny and never embarrassing, he wasn't really like a dad at all. He always made an effort to talk to Karen and Yvonne whenever he saw them and Karen in particular enjoyed the attention.

Yvonne put on a record that she had borrowed from her brother Dean. It was called 'Disco Explosion' and she thought it would get them in the mood for tonight. She started dancing, urging Karen and Sandra to join in. Soon the three of them were dancing around the room, Pan's People they weren't, but they were having fun. When the song finished, they fell into a heap on the bed, dissolving in fits of giggles.

"Come on, we should start getting ready," said Sandra standing up.

"What are you wearing?" Yvonne asked her.

Sandra opened her wardrobe and took out a bright, red dress that was incredibly sparkly. Yvonne opened her bag to reveal a pair of dark trousers and an equally sparkly top. Karen looked at them both.

"I'm not going," she declared.

"Don't start that again," said Yvonne.

"I mean it, I'm not going. Look at my dress," she said as she pulled out a very creased, crumpled and rather plain looking dress from the bottom of her school bag.

"That's fine," Yvonne lied. "Anyway, no-one will pay attention to what you're wearing."

"They will with you two twinkling away next to me."

"You can borrow something of mine," said Sandra and she began rummaging through her cupboard. "Here try this," she said handing Karen a black dress, that was decorated with sequins "It's actually too big for me but I'm sure it will fit you," she added carelessly.

Karen's eyes smarted, but she didn't let Sandra see. She took the dress from her and tried it on.

"Hmmm. Bit tight, but I can probably fix that."

Karen knew Sandra was good with a sewing machine but she wasn't convinced she could do anything with this dress. After all she was talking about making it bigger. Sandra took the dress from her and turned it inside out.

"That's good. I can let it out from the back seam." She went downstairs and fifteen minutes later returned with the dress. "Try it on now," she said, throwing the dress to Karen. Karen did and was amazed when it fitted.

"Right now you absolutely have to come," said Yvonne whose patience was beginning to wear thin. She went to the record player, flipped over the record, turned up the volume and began gyrating again.

The disco started at seven o clock and despite the impromptu dress-making session they arrived not much after seven. Karen still didn't feel entirely comfortable, but then she never did at these sort of events, she always felt conspicuous and out of place. She was convinced everyone was looking at her, for all the wrong reasons. But as Sandra had gone to so much trouble for her, she knew she had to make an effort and at least look like she was enjoying herself.

The sports hall had taken on a whole new life. Coloured lights danced up the walls and across the ceiling. The music was so loud that the floor was vibrating. Some of the teachers were strategically standing around the hall trying to blend in while maintaining an authoritative presence. The girls decided to have a drink first. Sandra bought three cokes and they found a place to stand, just at the edge of the make-shift dance floor. They'd just finished their drinks when the first bars of Bye Bye Baby filled the hall. Nobody ever admitted to liking the Bay City Rollers, except maybe the first years, yet suddenly everyone was dancing. The girls joined in too and spent the next twenty minutes on the dance floor. The hall was packed with people and it was extremely hot so when they had finished dancing they decided to go outside for some fresh air. They sat on the wall alongside Stacey King and her friends. Stacey was two years above them but they knew who she was as she lived next door to Yvonne.

"Love your dress," said Stacey looking straight at Karen. Although Karen was surprised to receive a compliment, that didn't stop a huge grin spreading across her face.

"Yes, it looks good, doesn't it?" chipped in Sandra. "It's an old one of mine, I had to let it out a bit, but it turned out okay."

Karen couldn't believe she had said that, she turned on her heels and headed back inside.

"Nice one," Yvonne shouted at Sandra.

"What?" Said Sandra oblivious to the hurt she had caused. Yvonne didn't answer; she went back into the sports hall to look for Karen. She finally found her in the girls changing room and it was clear she had been crying.

"Oh, come on," said Yvonne. "Don't let this spoil your evening. I know you've been enjoying yourself up until now and Sandra didn't mean to upset you, she just doesn't think before she speaks. She's just – well – Sandra."

"I know, but…" before Karen could finish Sandra burst into the changing rooms.

"Quick, it's a slow dance and Paul Adams is looking for me," she shouted before running out again.

Karen and Yvonne exchanged a look, shrugged their shoulders simultaneously, stood up and followed her. I'm not in Love by 10cc was playing and the dance floor was slowly filling with pubescent couples all keen to get a decent spot. They reached the hall just in time to see Sandra being led onto the dance floor by Paul so they decided to go and get another drink. On their way, Neil Baker tapped Yvonne on the shoulder and asked her if she would like to dance. She looked at Karen apologetically then went with him.

August 1976

The three girls lay beneath a huge tree at the edge of the playing field in the park. It was so hot and the tree offered them some welcome shade.

"What's the time?" Asked Yvonne.

"Almost one," replied Sandra. "Paul will be here soon."

Sandra and Paul had been going out for about a year now and this afternoon they were going to the cinema.

"Okay, when you go, so will we. It's too hot to stay outside."

They continued to lay silently under the tree. It really was hot, too hot to even speak. The heat was heavy and its unseen mass made it an effort to do anything. Paul arrived to meet Sandra and they walked in the direction of the bus stop. Yvonne and Karen did not have the energy to move but they did not want to stay outside any longer so they forced themselves up and walked across the field towards Yvonne's house. Once there they sprawled out on the lounge floor listening to records that belonged to Yvonne's brother. He was eighteen and went to Art College, at the weekends he worked in The Crown on the High Street. Karen thought he was very cool. He always had the latest music, the latest fashions, he could drive and he was incredibly good looking. Actually, she didn't just think he was cool; she had the biggest crush on him.

He didn't have a girlfriend, as far as she knew, despite the fact that all the girls loved him. Mostly, you would find him with Graham Baker, Neil's elder brother. When Karen was alone it was Dean she often thought of. In her head, she would weave wild fantasies that led to the two of them being together. Why not? He was always so nice to her. He had even given her a lift home once.

The record they were listening to ended, Yvonne turned onto her side, propping herself up on her elbow. "What shall we do now? Do you want to go out again?"

"No, it's too hot." Although that wasn't the real reason. Karen was actually hoping that Dean might come home while she was there.

"Okay," said Yvonne "I've got this week's Jackie upstairs." They stood up and went up to Yvonne's room. They sat on the bed leafing through the magazine stopping at the 'Cathy and Clare' problem page. Yvonne started reading some of the letters out loud. There were the usual: I hate the way I look, I have terrible period pains and how do I get rid of spots? The next letter she read said;

Dear Cathy and Clare
I'm feeling very lonely at the moment. My best friend has a boyfriend and is spending all her time with him. She never has time for me anymore and I don't know how to tell her how upset I am without her thinking I'm jealous.

"That's because you are jealous," said Yvonne derisively.

"That's not fair," said Karen. "I feel a bit sorry for her. I remember how I felt when you and Sandra were going out with Neil and Paul last summer."

"How did you feel?"

"Forgotten, left out."

"But we didn't leave you out. You came out with us loads of times."

"Great, you four and me. That actually made me feel worse."

"I didn't realise you felt like that. Sorry," said Yvonne putting her arms around Karen and pulling her towards her.

"Its fine," replied Karen shrugging her off. "Read the next letter."

"Oh, the rest are boring."

They flicked through the rest of the magazine; reading an interview with Flintlock and gazing longingly at posters of David Cassidy and David Essex. They began discussing which David was the best, but their debate was interrupted by the doorbell. Yvonne went to answer it and was surprised to see her Dad standing there.

"What are you doing home and where is your key?" she asked him, sounding a lot like her mother.

"I don't feel well love," he answered as he came in. "I left my keys with Frank so he can drop my car home later. I'm going to lie down, keep the noise down for me please."

Yvonne went back upstairs and told Karen about her Dad. "I think we should go out, or go to yours."

"Let's go down the shops then," suggested Karen, who really did not want to go back to her house. She had stormed out this morning after another row with her Mum and she really wasn't ready to face her just yet. On the way down to the shops they passed Dean and Graham heading to Yvonne's house. Karen was disappointed that she and Yvonne weren't still there.

"Damn," shouted Yvonne.

"What?"

"I forgot to tell Dean that Dad's at home."

"Shall we go back then?" Karen asked hopefully.

"No, I'm not walking all the way back again."

At the shops, they each bought a drink and some sweets then

sat on the bench by the bus stop. They had only been there about ten minutes when Yvonne decided she was going to go home after all.

"It's too hot to stay out," she complained, "and I want to make sure Dad is okay. It's not like him to come home early."

"I'll come with you if you like?"

"No, it's alright. I'll see you tomorrow."

◉

"Karen, telephone."

"Who is it?"

"Yvonne. And don't be long. Dinner is almost ready," said her Mum as she handed her the receiver.

"Karen, can you come and meet me?"

"Why, what's the matter?"

"Something terrible has happened," said Yvonne between sobs. "I'm at the phone box at the top of the road."

"Okay, see you in a minute."

"Mum, put my dinner in the oven. I've got to go and see Yvonne."

Before her mum could stop her Karen charged out of the house. She ran to the top of the road as fast as she could. Although she didn't know what was wrong, she had a dreadful feeling that it was something to do with Yvonne's Dad. When she reached the phone box, Yvonne was still standing inside it. When she came out her eyes were red and puffy, her cheeks glistened, revealing the tear tracks that lined them. Fresh tears began to form as she looked at Karen.

"What is it?" Karen asked her.

"It's Dad. You remember he came home early as he wasn't well."

"Oh my God, he's dead."

"What? No," shouted Yvonne. "What made you say that?"

"I knew he wasn't feeling well and I just thought…"

"Just shut up and listen."

"Sorry."

"It's all my fault," Yvonne spluttered. "I should have told Dean he was home."

"What's your fault?"

"Dad caught him."

"Caught who?"

"Dean."

"Ohhh. Caught him doing what?"

Yvonne stared at Karen.

"What do you think?"

"I don't know. You're not making much sense at the moment."

"Dad caught Dean and Graham, you know, kissing and… stuff."

"Who were they kissing?"

"What?"

"Who – were – they - kissing?" said Karen very slowly. She was starting to get a little impatient with Yvonne now.

"Karen, are you really this thick?" The two girls just stared at each other for a moment, Karen was unsure what she had done but Yvonne's tears had abated and given way to an anger that seemed to be directed at her.

"They – were – kissing – each – other," said Yvonne, equally as slow as Karen had spoken. "Dad heard noise coming from Dean's room and when he went to check he found Dean and Graham in bed, together!"

Karen's jaw fell open as she finally grasped what Yvonne was telling her. She felt as though she had been slapped across the face. This can't be right. It was bad enough to think of Dean kissing a girl, but this, no, not Dean, not her Dean.

"Are you saying, they're, well, you know?"

"Yes, gay!" Shouted Yvonne. "Obviously. Dad threw them both out, it was horrible. He was hitting and kicking them and shouting. He was calling them dirty perverts. I've never seen my Dad so angry. Mum came back and Dad said he never wants Dean in the house again and he started throwing all his stuff out in the street and the neighbours were watching and now mum keeps crying."

"Where has he gone?"

"I don't know. Why are you crying?" asked Yvonne, as she spotted Karen wiping her eyes.

"I'm upset because you're upset, it must have been awful. I know how much you love Dean."

"I do," said Yvonne.

Yes, and so do I thought Karen, so do I.

Bill dropped Sandra off at Paul's and decided to pick up fish and chips on the way home. He parked by the bus stop and got out of the car. There were two girls sitting on the bench; as he got closer he realised it was Karen and Yvonne, Sandra's friends.

"Hey girls, alright?" he asked.

"Hi Bill," they replied together.

Bill went to get his dinner, as he returned to his car he called out to the girls asking them if they needed a lift.

"I only live down there," laughed Karen pointing down the road.

"I know that," said Bill. "I just thought you might be going somewhere, you are at a bus stop after all."

"I wouldn't mind a lift, I should be getting home," said Yvonne.

"Okay, jump in." He spotted the disappointed look on Karen's face and said, "Why don't you come along for the ride and I'll drop you back after." Karen smiled at him and got in the back as Yvonne had already claimed the front seat. Bill knew the girls liked his car, a jaguar XJS, and who could blame them, it was a great car. It only took a few minutes to get to Yvonne's house, when she got out Karen clambered out of the back and got into the front.

"Clunk-click," said Bill. She smiled at him and pulled the seat belt, it locked, she tried again and again but still it locked without giving her enough belt to go over her.

"It's stuck."

"Pull it slowly."

She pulled it slower but still it locked. Bill leaned across her and pulled the belt, very slowly. He didn't take his eyes off of her until he had fastened the seat belt.

"There, all secure," he said patting her leg, before accelerating and pulling away. The smell of fish and chips filled the car and Karen's stomach began to make noises.

"Hungry?"

"A bit, I haven't had my dinner yet."

"Me neither. Do you fancy sharing fish and chips? I always get too much."

"I think Mum might wonder where I am."

"Well you can call from mine if you like, you decide."

"Okay," said Karen. She'd rather go to Bill's than go home. She was probably already in trouble so a little bit longer wouldn't make any difference and besides those fish and chips did smell lovely.

They ate in the kitchen, when they had finished Bill picked up their drinks and they went into the lounge. Karen sat on the sofa, it was huge and incredibly soft and enveloped her in a huge embrace.

"So, what were you two up to tonight?" He asked.

Without hesitating Karen told him what had occurred at Yvonne's and before long she found herself crying again, not just a few tears but great gulping sobs that she was unable to stop. Bill put down his drink and came and sat beside her. He took her in his arms and began gently rocking her.

Karen continued talking, she told him that she liked Dean because he wasn't like the boys at school who constantly taunted and teased her. She explained how nice he was to her, he would say nice things about her and because of that she thought he liked her too. But he didn't, well not in the way that she hoped.

"Perhaps, we get on because we don't fit in. I always feel like I'm in the wrong place, even when I'm at home and I'm sure he must have felt odd about being, well, you know."

Bill gently turned her face towards his. He spoke softly, looking directly into her eyes.

"Karen, you are such a sweet girl and you must not waste time worrying over boys, because that is the problem, they are just boys and you clearly need more." As he spoke he pushed the hair from her face with his fingertips. He leant closer towards her and lightly kissed her forehead, the bridge of her nose and then her mouth. Karen leant back slightly and looked at him, puzzled. He smiled and placed his hand behind her neck gently pulling her closer and then he kissed her again. His kisses became harder and longer. Karen responded by opening her mouth allowing his tongue to probe it. As he was kissing her, he allowed his other hand to feel its way inside her blouse, cupping her right breast and gently stroking her nipple with his finger. Karen was beginning to feel a little strange, although not altogether unpleasant, the feeling was unnerving. She was unsure what he expected of her so she pulled back from him so she could ask him.

"Don't speak," he said.

She did as she was told and didn't speak. She watched him as he silently and quickly removed her blouse followed by her bra.

He pulled her further down into the sofa so they were laying side by side, then he leant towards her chest and began kissing her breasts, caressing her nipples with his tongue. She was beginning to feel a little apprehensive as she was unsure where this was heading. Bill moved his hand down lower and undid the button on her jeans then pulled the zip open. He tried to place his hands inside her jeans but they were too tight. He sat up and moved down the sofa, he took hold of the waistband of her jeans and peeled them down. He did not remove them completely but left them awkwardly around her knees. He then lay down next to her and kissed her again, at the same time he placed his hand between her legs and pushed his finger inside her. Karen had never even kissed anyone before let alone anything else, she had no idea about stuff like this, but she liked Bill. He was always nice to her and she trusted him. This must be okay, she thought to herself. After a few minutes, Bill removed his hand and just lay next to her. Karen was afraid now for she was sure he was waiting for her to do something. She lifted herself up and reached for the belt on his trousers.

"No, I need to take you home now." As he spoke he stood up and handed Karen her clothes.

Karen was confused. Had she done something wrong? She got up, rather inelegantly as her jeans were still around her knees, she pulled them up then put the rest of her clothes back on. She couldn't look at Bill as she was blinking back the tears. When she had finished dressing, Bill took her hands and explained that as much as he wanted to do more, it would be wrong.

"I cannot lead you into this, even though I want to. It must be your decision to take this any further and you must be sure."

"I am sure," Karen pleaded. "Let me stay, please."

"No, I'm taking you home. You really need to think about this."

Karen nodded without looking at him. "Then if you want to come back, if you're really sure, let me know."

"How will I get hold of you? I can't tell Sandra."

"No, you can't. And not just Sandra. You cannot tell a soul, not everyone will understand. This has to be just between us."

"So, how do I get hold of you?" she repeated.

"Next time Sandra goes to see Paul I'll pick you up at the bus stop, like today."

"But how will I know if she's going to Paul's?"

"She goes every week, anyway I'm sure she will tell you, if not ask."

"What do I tell my Mum?"

"The truth, just say you're going to Sandra's house. Come on, I need to get you home now."

They didn't speak on the way back to Karen's and the ten-minute drive seemed like an eternity. At her house, she thanked him for the lift as she always did then ran inside. He watched her go in then drove off. Would she be back next week, he wondered? Of course she would, they always came back.

2010

The waiter returned and took their order. As he left an awkward silence hung over the table. Karen searched her brain for something to say, something witty or insightful, instead settling for a safe question.

"So how long are you staying?"

"Not too long, I hope," replied Sandra. I have some meetings, things I need to deal with, papers to sign. You know the sort of thing. I haven't booked my return flight yet but hopefully I'll only be here a few days."

Karen nodded and again an uneasy pause fell between them. This time it was Sandra who spoke first.

"So, what have you been up to? Are you still living in the same place? Any more children? How are your family? Do you work? Fill me in on your exciting life." As she finished firing her questions she took several large sips of wine, all the time looking at Karen across the rim of her glass. Karen was beginning to feel a little intimidated by Sandra's rather brusque manner. She looked at her, smiled and began answering the questions thus bringing Sandra up to date on her life.

"We live just off The Ridgeway, not far from where you used to live. They developed that whole area a couple of years ago, and we bought one of the new houses. It's closer to the factory than where we used to live."

"Ah, Andrew's business. What is it he does?"

"Welded and laminated products for banks and businesses. You know the kind of thing; binders, card holders, etc. with their company logo on it."

"And how is business? Cash flow good? Or is an injection of funds needed?"

What an odd question, thought Karen. I suppose she is a businesswoman herself, but still, odd.

"Things are going well thanks. He recently got a contract from some government department."

"And you. Do you work?"

"I go in to the office if Andrew needs me to. But that's not that often anymore."

"A lady of leisure."

"Not exactly. I volunteer at the hospice shop and…"

"Ah, a do-gooder are we," said Sandra with a large dose of sarcasm. "Saint Karen."

Karen deliberately ignored her comments and instead began asking Sandra some questions. The one thing she recalled with clarity about Sandra was that she loved talking about herself.

"So, how are things in South Africa? Business good? Anyone special around?"

"God, after all these years, still as nosey."

Karen was taken aback and thought the comment a little hypocritical considering what Sandra had just asked her, but didn't voice this thought.

"Only joking," continued Sandra spotting the wounded look on Karen's face. "Work is good. The business has expanded quite a lot over the last few years which is why it's been increasingly difficult to get over here as much as I would have liked."

"I suppose with new technologies that are around now it's been easy for you and your Dad to run the business despite being on different continents," interjected Karen.

"What?"

"Well, you know with the internet and everything."

"My business is my business. I run it. I own it. Lock, stock and barrel. It does not belong to Dad, it's mine. It belongs to me and no-one but me. I'm not some spoilt, little rich girl running Daddy's business, for fucks sake."

"I'm sorry," said Karen. "I just thought…"

"Well don't think," spat Sandra. "You were never very good at it." She refilled her glass and took a large gulp of wine.

"I think I should go," said Karen.

Before she could stand up Sandra reached across the table and gripped her hand.

"Please don't," she said. "I'm sorry, but you know for years people have always assumed that everything I have has been handed to me on a plate. No credit has ever been assigned to me, I'm just a blonde- airhead who lives off Daddy."

"I've never thought that," said Karen softly.

"Then stay."

Karen really didn't wish to stay anymore but she was sure Sandra would make an even bigger scene if she left now and she could already sense people watching them.

"Let's get another bottle," said Sandra signalling to the waiter.

"No, no more for me. I have to drive."

"Get a taxi, you can collect your car tomorrow." Sandra's suggestion sounded more like an order.

Karen knew it was pointless arguing, so she allowed the waiter to fill her glass and settled back for what she knew, was going to be a bumpy ride.

September 1976

K aren always hated the first day of term. It never got any better for her and today was no exception. In fact, today was worse than any of the previous first days she had endured. The last couple of weeks of the summer holiday she had gone to great lengths to avoid Sandra and Yvonne, well primarily Sandra, but today there was nowhere to hide; no pretend illness or last minute babysitting. Today she would have to see Sandra. Karen was convinced that she would give herself away, or that maybe Sandra already knew what had happened between her and Bill. Karen had never felt so confused and worried. This whole situation was a bit scary; on the one hand she desperately wanted to see Bill again, but on the other she was feeling guilty and a bit frightened. In the end, it was the fear that came out on top, so she decided not to see him again. However, this also meant not seeing Sandra. She really wasn't sure how she would achieve this. Out of school, it was easy, she would just continue with the excuses until Sandra got bored inviting her over, but at school, well that was an entirely different matter. She shared a number of classes with her, and she knew Yvonne would want to see Sandra. Karen didn't want to lose both her friends, what a mess.

The day passed by slowly and was uneventful. Just as Karen

suspected it was very difficult to avoid Sandra completely so she had to try and behave as normal as possible. At lunchtime, no reference was made to the fact that they hadn't seen each other for a while and Sandra said nothing about Bill so maybe everything would be okay. The main topic of conversation was Sandra and Paul's relationship. Sandra was bored with him and wanted to know the best way to finish with him. She wanted to do this as soon as possible as her birthday was approaching and her Dad had said she could have a party and Paul was definitely not going to make the guest list.

"I don't think I'll invite any of the boys from our year. They are all so immature."

"You're right," added Yvonne. "We need older guys at the party. Don't we Karen?"

"What?" Asked Karen rather absently on hearing her name.

"Older guys, that's the way to go."

The colour drained from Karen's face and she stared at Sandra and Yvonne. What were they saying? Did they know? They were staring back at her and it seemed an age before anyone spoke.

"What is wrong with you?" asked Yvonne. "You're on another planet today."

"I, I'm fine. I just didn't hear you, that's all."

"We're talking about Sandra's party."

"Oh okay. What party?"

"God, you really aren't with it at all," said Sandra. "Never mind, just get your head together and come up with some ideas for the weekend. We'll have a sleepover at mine and we can make plans."

"Sleepover, I think I may have to…"

"Don't start making excuses like babysitting or whatever," piped up Yvonne. "We'll start to think that you're trying to avoid us."

"I wasn't going to say that; I need to check first, that's all," replied

Karen defensively.

"Okay," chimed in Sandra. "If you can't stay, you could always come round for a little while, Dad won't mind running you home."

"No," shouted Karen.

"What is wrong now?"

"Nothing, no. I mean I'm sure it's fine. I don't want to be a bother."

"Ok then, Saturday at mine."

Bill unlocked the boot of his car and started loading his shopping into it. As he lifted the bags from his trolley one of them split; crisps, sweets and chocolate bars dotted the ground around his feet. A lemonade bottle rolled along the ground, stopping by the tyre of the car parked alongside his.

He muttered obscenities to himself as he bent down to retrieve the items. All this crap for just three people, he thought. Sandra had given him a list this morning of things she wanted for her sleepover. Bill hadn't asked but he knew Karen would be one of those staying. He hadn't seen her since that evening, which had surprised him. He was sure she would've been back by now. Maybe he was losing his touch? Don't be daft, he said to himself. This one may be a little different though, he may have to take his time. But that's ok, it all added to the game. A game he always won.

Karen packed her bag slowly. She so did not want to go to Sandra's today, but she had rather run out of excuses. Then there had been that phone call. Karen had popped out to the shops for her Mum to get a loaf of bread when Yvonne had telephoned. When she got back her Mum told her that Yvonne's Dad would take the pair of them over to Sandra's house.

"Oh, I wasn't actually sure that I was going to go, I feel a bit unwell again. Like I did before."

"Don't be daft," said her Mum. "You've been fine all week, and I don't think you was that ill in the first place. Have you had a falling out with the girls?"

"No, what made you say that?"

"Well, you haven't seen them much lately."

"Sandra has a boyfriend and I was ill and then you made me babysit."

"As I recall you offered to babysit. Look, just go and have a nice time."

Karen was surprised at her Mums uncharacteristic behaviour. She was not a big fan of sleepovers and here she was actively encouraging her to go on one. Oh well, she'd have to go now she thought to herself, she just hoped that Bill wasn't there or if he was, she hoped he would be easy to avoid.

Yvonne and Karen arrived at Sandra's a little after 2.30.

"How comes your Dad dropped you over here? Sandra asked Yvonne. "He doesn't usually give you lifts anywhere."

"That's all changed now," said Yvonne dismally. "Since Dean went he watches everything I do. He quizzes me endlessly about where I've been, who I've seen and who I've spoken to. It's so bloody claustrophobic. Dean's lucky he's out of it."

"Why is he being like that?" asked Karen.

"I think he wants to make sure that I'm not seeing Dean."

"Are you?"

"I've seen him once and I know Mum has seen him too. He's staying at the pub where he works until he can find somewhere.

He's looking for a flat. I think he had hoped that once Dad had calmed down he might have been able to come back home, but there's no chance of that happening."

"Not ever?" asked Karen.

"Who wants a drink?" Sandra interrupted, as she was getting a little bored with the conversation. They both did, so they followed Sandra into the kitchen and she poured each of them a glass of lemonade.

"Let's go and sit in the lounge. Dads playing golf this afternoon so we've got the whole house to ourselves."

As they walked into the room Karen recalled the last time she had been in here, she avoided sitting on the sofa, instead opting to sit on one of the oversized armchairs.

"So, party plans," said Sandra lifting a pen and pad from the coffee table.

The afternoon passed by very quickly, they discussed guest lists, planned the decorations, wrote menus (which were basically a list of which flavour crisps they wanted) and even decided what songs would and wouldn't be played. The only thing they didn't decide upon was what they were going to wear but they did agree to go shopping the following week. Their discussions were interrupted by the telephone ringing. Sandra went into the hallway to answer it.

"Hey Dad. Yeah, we're good. I'll ask." Sandra covered the mouthpiece and called out to the girls. "Fish and chips, Chinese or Indian?"

"Indian," shouted Yvonne. "We never have curry or anything exotic like that at home."

"That okay for you Karen."

Karen shrugged, "I don't mind what we have." The only takeaway food Karen ever had was fish and chips so Indian would make a change, although she wasn't actually sure she would like it.

"Indian," repeated Sandra into the telephone. "Okay, see you shortly."

Karen's stomach was performing somersaults, and it wasn't due to the impending curry. Bill was on his way back, there was no escape. She would have to see him. About twenty minutes later he was home, as he walked through the door he spoke in what was an awful imitation of an Indian accent telling Sandra to get the plates out as dinner had arrived. He put the food on trays in the middle of the kitchen table and the four of them sat down together.

"Dig in, he said to them all. "I got an assortment of curries and a variety of side dishes, as I wasn't sure what you like. None of them are too hot, except that one," he said pointing to one foil dish he'd left on the side. "That's mine."

Bill was behaving just as he always did; cracking silly jokes, asking about school and their families. He was being perfectly normal, Karen was surprised, for she was finding it quite difficult to keep calm and act normally. She was still convinced that Yvonne and Sandra knew what had happened and any minute now one of them would say something regarding it. Bill finished his food and stood up.

"I've some work to do, then I'm going to watch the football. I'll watch it in the den so you girls can stay in the lounge if you want."

The three of them sat at the kitchen table a little longer, chatting and polishing off the remains of the takeaway. When they'd finished they cleared away their plates and the rubbish then went back into the lounge. They sat watching television for a little while but there wasn't really much on that appealed to them.

"Let's go upstairs, I'll give you both a makeover," said Sandra.

The other two exchanged nervous glances but got up and followed her. Once upstairs the girls decided to put their nightclothes on. They then spent the next couple of hours doing each other's hair and making their faces up as brightly and outrageously as possible. When they got bored with that, they cleaned off the make-up and got into bed. Despite the fact that she had a huge bed Sandra never allowed either of the girls to share it with her. They had to share the sofa bed which, although perfectly comfortable, was nowhere near as big as Sandra's bed. They lay there, talking for a while until one by one they fell asleep.

Karen woke and for a moment forgot where she was. She sat up blinking as she tried to accustom her eyes to the blackness. Once she got her bearings, remembering that she was in Sandra's bedroom, she got out of bed. Her mouth felt incredibly dry, she needed some water. A glimmer of light was visible under the door and Karen used the faint glow to help her manoeuvre across the room without bumping into anything or waking either Sandra or Yvonne. She tiptoed across the landing to the bathroom, there wasn't a glass in there or anything else she could drink from so she went downstairs to the kitchen. She found a glass and filled it with water. She stood by the sink with her back to the door, sipping the water; she didn't hear him come in and she didn't see him until he was standing next to her.

"Can't sleep?" He enquired.

"No, I mean yes, no, I…"

"Well, what is it, yes or no?"

"I'm just thirsty," she replied nervously.

"That'll be the curry."

Karen nodded and turned to leave, he took hold of her arm.

"How are you now? Feeling better?" he asked. She stared at him blankly. "Sandra said you've been unwell."

"Oh, yes. I'm fine now thank you." She paused and then added, "I'm sorry I wasn't able to see you."

"Its fine, you can't help being ill. There again, maybe you didn't actually want to see me anyway."

Karen wasn't sure if that last comment was a question or statement so she just ignored it. She looked at him and smiled. As she did Bill lowered his face to hers and kissed her. It was the gentlest of kisses, yet enough to make Karen put down her glass and put her arms around his waist. He held her face in his hands and kissed her some more, he then reached behind him and prised her arms from him taking her hand and leading her out of the kitchen. He took her into the den, closing the door behind them.

Karen had never been in here before, it was clearly Bill's space. It was a terribly masculine room; very dark, the only light coming from a small lamp on the desk. Karen didn't think daylight would do much to brighten the room as the decor and furniture were all equally as dark. As well as the desk, there was a cabinet under the window which housed Bill's golfing trophies and a large sofa that was pushed against a wall. Another wall was completely lined with shelves that were filled with books, rows and rows of books, except the uppermost shelf that had some storage boxes on it each with a large number on it.

As he closed the door Bill gently pushed Karen against it and began kissing her again, he allowed one hand to travel inside her pyjamas, first fondling her breasts then swiftly moving down to her groin, his hand moved between her thighs, his finger searching for her softness. He began kissing her entire face finally reaching her ear into which he groaned as his finger finally found what he was looking for, she was so ready and he was relishing the fact that he was the only man ever to have touched this place. But he knew he had to take it slow, so, quite suddenly he pulled his hand away.

"What's wrong?" she asked, suddenly fearing that perhaps Yvonne or worse, Sandra, had woken up.

"We must stop," he said. "This isn't right; the girls are upstairs and besides I don't really think you want this."

"No, you're wrong," said Karen. "I do want this, really."

Bill leant against her, his palms pressed against the door and his head resting gently on hers. She could feel his firmness, she moved her hands to touch him there but he jumped back.

"You need to go back to bed now."

"No, I do want this," she said and again she tried to touch him.

"Go to bed, now." He stepped back and pulled the door open, forcing Karen to move. She did as she was told, her eyes were smarting as she walked up the stairs. Quietly she opened the door to Sandra's bedroom and got back into bed.

"Where have you been?" asked Yvonne suddenly.

"Bathroom."

"I've just come from the bathroom and you weren't in there."

"I went to get a glass of water."

"Where is it?"

"Where is what?"

"The water."

"What?"

"You said you were getting a glass of water; so, where is it?"

"I drank it."

"Great, I could've done with some, I'm really thirsty."

"Shut up and go to sleep Yvonne."

👁

Bill got out of the shower and climbed into bed. This is going to be fun he thought as he lay there. He could have had her already, but this was so much better. Before long she would be asking him to take her, begging him and it would be all the sweeter when he did.

The Party

Despite being the end of September and officially autumn it was still quite hot; temperatures had begun to fall but they were still way above what they should be for this time of year. Therefore, it wasn't surprising that the party spilled out of the house and into the garden. Just as Sandra and Yvonne had hoped, the male contingent of the party were all older. Not only were they not the same year as them; they were not even from the same school as the girls. Karen was convinced that Sandra didn't know them at all and that they were, in fact, gate-crashers! She voiced this thought to Sandra, who was rather nonplussed by the idea.

"If we don't know them, perhaps we should put that right," she said, linking arms with Karen and Yvonne. "Come on, let's mingle."

The three of them walked down the garden to where a large group of boys were standing in a circle. At the centre of the circle was a box and several carrier bags piled up in a statuesque fashion. They were filled with cans of beer and bottles of cider. Sandra unhooked her arms from the girls and pushed her way between two of the guys, herself becoming part of the circumference of this human circle. She instantly began chatting to them, helping herself to a bottle of cider in the process. Karen recognised the guy on Sandra's left as the captain of the local football team.

Sometimes on a Saturday morning the three girls would sit in the park watching them train. Yvonne followed Sandra's example and she too pushed her way into the circle, although she didn't stand at the edge, she sat on the grass at the centre, next to the 'statue' of beer cans. Before long, she was holding court; entertaining and regaling the group with jokes and stories. Karen stood and watched as between them, Sandra and Yvonne captivated their audience. Some were clearly entranced by Sandra as she flirted and toyed with them; one minute shyly giggling and twirling her hair with her fingers and the next belly-laughing and tossing her head back confidently. The rest of them were enjoying in equal measure Yvonne's laddish humour and ebullience. Karen remained on the periphery, laughing and smiling, trying to look as if she was part of this gathering. After what seemed an age, Sandra walked back up to the house closely pursued by the two males who had flanked her a moment ago. Several moments passed, then Yvonne stood up and she too walked up to the house accompanied by someone who's ability to walk in a straight line was considerably impaired. Karen's eyes followed them until they went inside, she turned back to the group who had now reformed their circle around the icon of beer. Once again, she was a wallflower.

Bill watched the party from the window of his bedroom, he had agreed to keep his distance but he would not be going out as Sandra had hoped. He thought he'd been quite reasonable about the party, the only rules he'd stipulated were that nobody was allowed either upstairs or in his den and no spirits were allowed. He was sure the last rule had been broken several times over so he was keeping an eye on a number of suspects. Every now and then he would stroll through the house or do a circuit of the garden, just so his presence was noted. As he looked through the open window he noticed Sandra and Yvonne both going back into the house. Karen didn't appear to be with them. He scanned the garden, spotting her standing alone with her arms folded across her chest. Bill thought now would be a good idea to check that everything was still in order. He went downstairs, running his eyes across a group of kids sitting in the hallway. He wondered what the collective noun for such a group would be: a troop, a flock, a herd. He actually thought a lamentation was quite an appropriate term for them as they looked like they had forgotten they were at a party.

He briefly checked the rooms downstairs then decided to go outside. He went out of the front door and walked down the side of the house. A winding, crazy-paved path meandered around the perimeter of the garden. Bill followed the path rather than walking through the guests that were standing, sitting and even laying on the lawn, it was less intrusive and it gave him a better vantage point anyway.

Karen looked around and realised that the girls hadn't come back outside, she had no idea how long she'd been standing there - alone - but now that she was aware that she was in fact standing there - alone - she decided to go and look for them. As she went to step forward she caught sight of someone stepping out of the shadows behind her.

"Hey, enjoying the party?" Bill asked her.

"It's okay," she lied.

"I was just going back inside to find the others."

"I'll walk with you, I could do with a drink."

They walked back up to the house without speaking. Bill went into the kitchen and Karen automatically followed him. She had spotted Sandra in the hallway on the way through, but she was a little busy with the football captain at the moment. She didn't see Yvonne but figured that wherever she was, she too was probably preoccupied.

Bill opened the fridge and took out a bottle of beer, as he closed the door he realised Karen was still standing behind him.

"Want one?" he asked, waving the bottle at her.

"No thanks."

"Did you find them?"

"What, who, oh yes. Well they're out there." Karen said nodding towards the hallway.

"Look, I'm going to watch television in the den, you're welcome to join me," said Bill ever so casually as he walked past her. Again, she followed him. In the den Bill signalled for her to sit on the sofa, he locked the door, switched on the TV and then sat down next to her.

"You really don't seem to be enjoying this party much," he said.

"I don't really know anyone, other than the girls," she replied feebly.

"Parties are a good place to get to know people, make new friends. Sandra and Yvonne seem to manage. You should try."

"I do, but people don't give me a second look."

"By people, I assume you mean boys?"

Karen didn't answer. Bill put his beer bottle on the coffee table and turned towards her.

"I think I'm invisible," she mumbled.

"I've told you before," said Bill. "You are different, too grown up. You probably intimidate them."

Karen started laughing.

"It's true," pressed Bill. "They don't see the pretty, bright, exciting girl that I see." As he spoke Bill put his hand on Karen's leg and ran it up the inside of her dress. He moved closer towards her and kissed her. She responded instantly, kissing him back and parting her legs slightly to ease his path. He deftly found his way into her underwear and began massaging her sex. As he did this Karen leant across and lowered the zip on his jeans, this time he didn't stop her. She put her hand inside the fly of his jeans, fumbling, trying to get hold of him. Bill took his hand from her groin and sat back on the sofa, for a moment Karen thought he was going to stop again but instead he removed his belt and undid the button, he lowered the top of his trousers and pants exposing himself as he did. Karen stifled a small gasp, she really hadn't known what to expect; the only time she had ever seen one was when she accidentally walked in the bathroom while her youngest brother was having a shower, but this was way bigger than that. Bill took her hand and clasped it around his manhood, he kept his hand on top of hers and began slowly moving it up and down his length. Once Karen understood what he wanted her to do, he removed his hand.

Bill's climax was overshadowed by a scream, then a loud bang like a door slamming, shouts and more screaming followed. Bill jumped up, cleaned himself as best he could, refastened his trousers and shot out of the room. Karen did the same and went out of the room behind him. In the hallway, Sandra and Yvonne were shouting at each other, the front door was wide open. Leaning on the open door was one of the boys from the group in the garden. He was holding Yvonne's hand and laughing.

"What the hell is going on?" bellowed Bill.

His deep voice had a South African lilt and as he spoke each word seemed to reverberate against the walls. A momentary silence fell before Sandra and Yvonne began shouting again, but this time at Bill, each determined that their story was the one he would hear.

They both stopped shouting, for Bill's fury was plain for all to see.

"Right, Sandra, what is going on?" he asked

"He," said Sandra, pointing at the boy leaning on the door, "has been taking drugs and he gave some to Yvonne."

"No, he…" cut in Yvonne, but before she could finish Bill lunged at the boy, throwing him through the open doorway. He turned back and spoke in measured tones.

"This party is over, you have one minute to get your things and leave."

Silently everyone began filing out. Some offered mumbled thanks as they passed Sandra and Bill. Yvonne went to leave too.

"Not you," said Bill, blocking her way. After the last person had gone he shut the door and stared at Yvonne. "You silly girl," he started. "What have you taken?"

"I just had some weed," she replied, smoothing her hair from her face as she spoke.

"Liar," spat Sandra. "I saw the bag with the blue pills in it."

"I didn't take any though."

"Are you sure?" Asked Bill.

"Yes," said Yvonne. "Truly, I just smoked some weed. I'm sorry," she said through tears. "I'd better go."

"You can go if you like," Bill told her. "However, if you do I'll be obliged to tell your parents why you've come home instead of staying here as planned. Or, you can stay, help us clean up, and we can forget this happened."

Yvonne looked at Sandra who in turn looked at Bill who gave a conciliatory nod.

"Ok, let's get tidied up then," said Sandra.

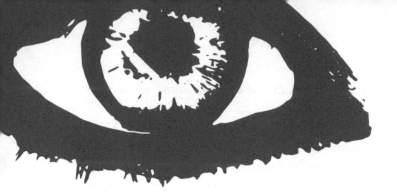

2010

The waiter approached the table holding two food laden dinner plates.

"At last, dinner is served," observed Sandra.

"Thank goodness," added Karen. "I think I'm rather in need of something to soak up all this wine."

"Yes, you always were a lightweight."

"Was I?"

"God, yes, you never could drink," reiterated Sandra.

Karen shrugged. She didn't see the point in arguing with Sandra who seemed very certain of this fact.

"I remember at a party I had," continued Sandra. "Yvonne and I hardly saw you all evening and when I asked you where you'd been you said you hadn't felt well."

"I don't remember that," said Karen vaguely.

"Yes, you were quite drunk." Sandra added before cutting into her steak and having a mouthful of it. Karen listened politely but continued eating. "In fact, you were so drunk Dad had to look after you."

Karen looked up from her dinner, Sandra was staring at her, jaw set, waiting for a response.

"The only thing I recall about your party is that was the night Yvonne met Jason."

"Oh God, it was," said Sandra, shaking her head as she spoke.

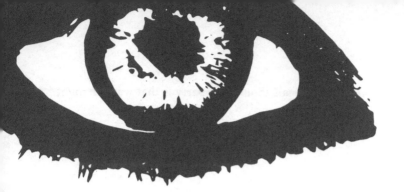

November 1976

"Are you sure you're okay about tonight?" Yvonne asked Karen for the umpteenth time as they sat on the bench at the bus stop, munching their way through a bag of jelly babies.

"It's fine."

"Really?"

"Yes, really."

It hadn't been fine. Every year Yvonne's Dad's boss held a huge firework party in the grounds of his home. Everyone who worked for him got an invite, for themselves and their family. Karen had listened in awe whenever Yvonne had told her about the amazing display, huge bonfire and fabulous food on offer. There were toffee apples and candy floss, one year there had even been an ice cream van serving free ice cream to the kids all evening. This year Yvonne was allowed to take a friend as her brother wouldn't be going with them. She had decided to take Sandra as she still felt awkward over what had happened at the party. Although Karen understood why she had asked Sandra instead of her, she still felt slighted by her choice.

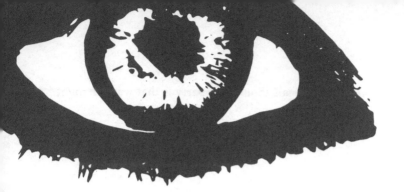

It had been a week previous that Yvonne had called Karen asking her to come to the phone box at the top of the road, saying she had something to tell her. Karen had raced up there, fearing some upset had occurred at Yvonne's house again. Perhaps her brother had come home, secretly Karen was hoping that might be the case. When Yvonne told her that she had asked Sandra to come to the firework party with her, Karen had hidden her disappointment well. She even lied to make her friend feel better.

"Its fine, I wouldn't have been able to come anyway as I promised Mum I'd babysit Debbie so she can take the boys to the display at the school."

"Well that's alright then," said a relieved Yvonne.

"I don't like fireworks much anyway," added Karen, to fully convince her friend that she was okay with her decision.

After Yvonne had left, Karen had sat at the bus stop for a while, thinking. She was in a world of her own when the car pulled up beside her.

"Hello," called Bill. "Penny for them."

"Huh."

"Everything ok?" he asked.

Realising it was Bill talking to her, Karen stood up and went over to the car, poking her head through the open window.

"I'm good."

"You sure, you look a little preoccupied."

"No, I'm okay really."

"Jump in. I'll take you for a spin."

"I need to get back," said Karen.

"Come on, once around the block and then I'll drop you back."

"Alright then," she said opening the door.

As they drove around the block, Karen told him about the firework party. Bill already knew, obviously. When they arrived back at the bus-stop, he turned and spoke.

"Why don't you come and see me? I can pick you up here, you can have dinner with me and then I'll drop you home when I go and collect Sandra from Yvonne's house."

Karen hesitated before replying.

"I'm not sure, maybe."

"Look, I'm dropping Sandra off at six so I'll be here just after. If you're not here I'll get fish and chips for one and head home alone," he said pulling a sad face.

"Alright," said Karen laughing as she opened the door and got out of the car.

"Okay, see you next week then," he said confidently, before he sped off.

◉

"So, you're really okay with me?" pressed Yvonne.

"For goodness sake, yes," said Karen staring off into the distance.

"Good, it's just you seem a bit…"

"What?" Snapped Karen.

"I dunno… kind of… odd."

"Do I?" Asked Karen turning to look at her friend.

"Yes, a bit, distant. Like there's something bothering you."

"No, there's nothing wrong," she lied. "I'd better get home."

"Yes, me too. See you Monday."

Karen slowly walked back to her house; of course, there was something bothering her, but she could hardly tell Yvonne, she couldn't tell anyone. Karen knew if she met Bill 'it' would happen, and she was terrified, but she wanted to see him. She wanted to see him and she wanted to please him no matter how scared she was.

Bill dropped Sandra at Yvonne's just before six. As he drove off, he began thinking of Karen, he knew she would be waiting for him and he felt himself harden as he thought of her. As he turned the corner he could see the bus-stop ahead, there was only one person sitting there. Bill allowed himself a smug grim as he thought of the evening ahead.

"Good evening," he said as she got into the car. "Hungry?"

"Starving," she replied.

"Good, I always cook too much."

"You've cooked?"

"I have."

Karen smiled to herself, nobody had ever cooked for her before, apart from her Mum that is, and that didn't really count as it was her job.

It took just a few short minutes to drive to Bill's house, when they got there they went straight through to the kitchen.

"Sit down," he said, nodding towards the table.

"Smells good. What are we having?"

"Wait and see."

Bill took two glasses from a cupboard and a bottle of wine from the fridge. He filled one glass and half-filled another, handing the smaller of the two to Karen.

"I'm sure a little is alright," he said smiling at her.

She took a sip and watched Bill as he lay the table. When he'd finished placing the cutlery, he put a large cork mat in the centre of the table. He opened the oven and took out a huge earthenware pot.

"Voila," he said as he put the dish onto the mat. "Bobotie*."

*(Pronounced ba-boor-tea)

"What?" Enquired Karen.

"Bobotie. It's a South African dish; a speciality of mine."

"But what is it?" Asked Karen again. It looked lovely, it smelt lovely, but Karen really needed to know what it was before she would see if it tasted lovely too.

"It's a bit like a moussaka."

"Mou, who?" She said revealing her culinary ignorance.

"Moussaka, it's Greek." He looked at Karen who was staring at him blankly, clearly still none the wiser.

"I suppose it's a bit like Shepherd's Pie; yes, that's it. It's a South African Shepherd's Pie, except the meat is curried and the top isn't potato."

"What is the top?"

"It's like a custard."

"Custard!" exclaimed Karen, whose joy at having someone cook for her was fading fast. I'd rather have fish and chips she thought to herself.

"It's a savoury custard," explained Bill. "Look, just try it, I'm sure you'll like it," he added, trying hard to hide his irritation. He dished up two platefuls, sat down and began to eat. Karen tentatively lifted the fork to her lips. The spicy aroma filled her nostrils, steam swirled in front of her. She put the fork into her mouth and was pleasantly surprised.

"It's lovely," she said.

"Well I'm glad you like it. The alternative would have been beans-on-toast."

They ate the rest of their dinner without saying much, when they'd finished Bill cleared the plates and swapped the earthenware pot for a large glass dish containing dessert.

"Mulva Pudding. Another South African dish I'm afraid."

He dished up two bowlfuls, placing one in front of Karen.

"Thank you," she said politely.

"No questions this time?" he asked.

"No," laughed Karen. "I think I've had this here before."

"Most likely," said Bill. "It's Sandra's favourite."

The mention of Sandra gave Karen a jolt; she had almost forgotten that Bill was in fact her friend's Dad.

2010

The two women ate their dinner without saying very much. The mention of Yvonne's name and more significantly Jason had cast a cloud across the table. They both missed Yvonne immensely. In life she had been the one who balanced their trio, the link between them and the cornerstone of their friendship. In death she had been the force that had held their fragile friendship; a friendship that without her memory to bind them would have naturally ended, many years before it finally did.

By recalling that evening; the evening on which Jason and Yvonne had met, Karen and Sandra had unwittingly opened the box that held the memories of that time. Neither wanted to address this subject, yet both knew they would, they had to. Neither wanted to be the first to speak of it. Eventually it was Sandra who ended the silence.

"I do think of her, often actually."

"Me too," responded Karen. "And I still feel, well a bit responsible."

"Why?" asked Sandra in astonishment.

"I just think we should have done more, tried harder to stop her."

"Yvonne made her own choices, so I don't see what we could

BEWARE THE CUCKOO

have done to change things."

"Perhaps if we'd told someone," said Karen. "We knew what was going on and we knew what Jason was like. Maybe we couldn't have stopped her but someone else might have been able to."

"We this, we that. Stop trying to take me on this guilt trip with you. She made her choices. She chose Jason and she chose to take drugs and yes, she paid the ultimate price for those choices. But that's life, everything has a consequence. I learnt that a long time ago." Sandra looked up, she could tell her tirade had shocked Karen. "That said," she continued, "doesn't mean I didn't care or that I don't still miss her, because I do. But I do not feel responsible and neither should you." Her rant over, she topped up her wine glass and took a huge swig.

To all who met her Sandra came across as strident, disciplined and unemotional. A view that Sandra herself would not have been unhappy with. In fact, it was an image she had actively set out to create, but behind the facade was someone who did care and cared deeply about many things. She hated revealing this side of her character. To her, it was a weakness that had no place in her life.

Karen looked at Sandra, she was sure it was genuine sadness she saw in her eyes despite her attempts to hide it. She too refilled her wine glass and held it aloft.

"To Yvonne."

November 7th 1976

Karen lay on her bed staring at the ceiling. She had not expected it to hurt. It was meant to be a wonderful thing, amazing even. But it wasn't, it was uncomfortable, and not just uncomfortable, painful. As she recalled the previous evening she began to weep, ever so quietly, gentle tears rolled down her cheeks dampening the pillow.

She had asked Bill to stop at one point, but he hadn't heard her. Her requests were silenced by his kisses and his weight on top of her had prevented her from moving. When he was spent, he had rolled off of her and reached for his cigarettes on the bedside table. It was then that she had moved and noticed the blood. Almost immediately Bill noticed too, he put down the cigarette packet and before panic seized her he put his arms around her and told her it was perfectly normal. In fact, it was proof that what they had done was right, for she was ready. He said he was so very happy with her, proud of her. She couldn't tell him that she hadn't actually enjoyed it, she had wanted to please him and clearly she had done that. There was no point saying anything and spoiling his mood.

Yet, this morning she felt very confused. Bill kept saying she was different, more mature than her peers, special, a woman, but right at this moment that was not how she felt. No: lost, hurt, alone, that was how she felt. She felt like a little girl, a lost child longing for her mother. In fact, at that moment she would give anything for her mum to open the bedroom door and come in and give her a hug; the kind of hug she used to give her when Karen had fallen in the playground and grazed her knees or when kids had been teasing her or if she'd been left out of some game. The all-encompassing big embrace only a mother can offer. Magic hugs they used to call them and they were magic because instantly Karen's woes would fade, her fear was diminished and the tears would subside. Well magic hugs and chocolate biscuits that was her Mum's special formula.

Karen decided to take a bath, she sat up, swinging her legs off of the bed. As she did she felt an ache at the top of her legs, she touched herself, again recalling the discomfort.

When her bath was ready she lowered herself into the warm bubbles, as she did, she thought maybe next time would be better. She would just have to try harder, she wanted to get it right. She wanted to keep pleasing Bill for he had noticed her when she was invisible.

2010

The dinner plates were removed and deftly replaced with dessert menus. Karen gave the menu in front of her a cursory glance but she already knew she didn't want anything more.

"I'm going to pass," she said to Sandra who was still reading her menu. "In fact, I think the only thing I should order is a taxi, it's rather late," she continued.

The waiter approached the table, pad in hand. "Any desserts ladies?"

"I think I'll give the cheesecake a go," said Sandra to him, completely ignoring Karen.

"And for you?" he asked looking directly at Karen.

"Oh, I erm, just coffee for me, thank you." she replied handing back the menu.

"Cappuccino, Americano, latte, espre...?"

"Regular coffee," said Karen a little sharply, interrupting the waiter reciting his well-rehearsed list. God she hated all the endless choices on offer these days. Especially when what she really wanted was to go home, but she knew she couldn't do that yet; good manners required her to wait until they'd both finished before she left. "Just, regular coffee, thank you." she added, sensing the waiter's irritation.

"One Americano," he said as he walked away.

"Here, let's finish this," said Sandra sharing the remainder of the wine between them.

Karen knew protests were futile so she smiled and polished off the glass rather quickly. Sandra's cheesecake arrived, shortly followed by Karen's coffee.

"Can I have a coffee please?" asked Sandra. "Cappuccino."

"Certainly Madam," said the waiter with a friendly smile. He clearly preferred Sandra to Karen.

"I really must order a taxi," said Karen.

"For goodness sake, we haven't seen each other in years. What's the rush?"

"It's late," snapped Karen. "And it's a school night."

"God, how old are you? Twelve? School night, what nonsense. Surely one late night won't upset things?" Karen went to protest but Sandra talked right over her. "Before you go I have some things I need to show you, they're up in my room. You can order a taxi from there."

Karen conceded defeat. "Fine, but I'd better just phone Andrew. I'm not normally out this late."

"Oh yes, better check in," mumbled Sandra sarcastically.

If Karen heard her she didn't let on. She continued fumbling in her handbag looking for her mobile phone.

"Ahh, there you are," she said when she located it, as if it were a child hiding from her rather than an inanimate object that had just disappeared into the depths of her bag. "Oh, no signal."

"There you are then, come upstairs, we can order a taxi and you can call Anthony." said Sandra triumphantly.

"Andrew." said Karen, a little too loudly.

"Sorry."

"Andrew, not Anthony."

"Whatever. You know what I'm like with names." Sandra said smirking.

The waiter brought over Sandra's coffee. As he set it down Sandra asked him for the bill.

"So what is it you have to show me?" Karen asked her.

"Some photos and I have a couple of papers I need a witness signature on."

"Okay. What sort of papers?"

Just then the waiter returned with the bill, he placed it between the two women. Karen reached for it but before she could pick it up, Sandra placed her hand on top of it.

"This is on me." she said.

"Don't be daft, we'll split it."

"No, you're my guest. I'll get it. Besides, I can put it through the business."

"Well, if you insist. Thank you." said Karen.

Sandra signed the bill and told the waiter her room number. She stood up, draining the last of her coffee as she did. "Come on then," she said to Karen who was also standing and she began striding out of the restaurant. Karen followed her, across the lobby past the now empty lounge bar and into the lifts.

New Year's Eve 1976

Sandra had been going out with Ryan Haywood, since her party; he was the captain of the local football team. They were clearly besotted with each other and spent most of their spare time together so it came as no surprise that they wanted to spend New Year's Eve together. His parents were having a party and they were both going to it. Yvonne was equally besotted with her new boyfriend, Jason Roberts. They had also met at Sandra's party but they had only just started going out together. She had yet to share this information with Karen and Sandra on account of what had happened at the party. She knew they'd give her a hard time over it, especially Sandra and their disapproval, she could do without. Yvonne and Jason were spending their New Year's Eve at one of his friends' houses but she had told the girls that she was going to a family party with her parents. Karen had resigned herself to the prospect of babysitting on New Year's Eve until Bill had convinced her to spend the evening with him, well not just the evening, the entire night! She told her Mum she was staying at Sandra's, so at least she wasn't lying to her, she just omitted to say that Sandra wouldn't be there.

Karen was excited and apprehensive at the same time. She had met Bill twice since 'that night' and although 'it' wasn't so uncomfortable, it still didn't feel right. She was still waiting for the amazing experience that she believed it should be. She liked it when Bill touched her, kissed her and spoke to her. His touch was gentle, his kisses light and words almost poetic. But as things progressed, he became rougher, heavier and his language was a little shocking. Karen accepted this though, because he still made her feel special; he noticed her and spoilt her.

Bill picked her up from the bus stop just before six, after he'd dropped Sandra at Ryan's.

"Hey." she said as she got into his car.

He smiled at her before accelerating away. He had ordered a Chinese so they took a detour to collect it. As they drove along the High Street, Karen spotted Dean, Yvonne's brother, walking on the opposite side. Instinctively she leant to her right and started waving enthusiastically. The car swerved a little and Bill pushed her out of his sightline, shouting at the same time.

"What are you doing? Are you trying to get us killed? Stupid poepol."

Karen slumped back in her seat, mortified. She had no idea what a poepol was, but she knew by Bill's tone that it wasn't a compliment. She had heard him shout before, on the telephone and at the party, but that wasn't aimed at her. His wrath hung above her like a rain-filled cloud waiting to spill its load and his insult was resounding in her head, 'stupid poepol'.

The car slowed down and Karen looked out of the window as they pulled into the layby in front of the Chinese. Bill got out of the car without speaking. It was only a couple of minutes before he came out of the Chinese clutching two small brown paper bags. He pulled his seat forward and put the bags on the floor behind it. He got back into the car accelerating before he'd even fastened his seat belt, the journey continued with an uneasy silence between them. When they reached the house, Karen got out of the car and followed Bill inside. She watched as he began taking the foil cartons out of the brown paper carrier bags, placing them on a tray. When he'd finished, he scrunched up the bags and put them into the bin, it was then he finally spoke.

"What were you thinking?" he asked.

"Sorry?" said Karen absently. "Thinking about what?"

"Earlier, back then. Waving and jumping around in the car; getting excitable. What was that for?"

"Oh, that was Yvonne's brother, Dean. I didn't mean to get in your way, it's just… I haven't seen him in ages."

"It's not that you were in my way." replied Bill.

"Oh?" Karen was a little confused, she wasn't quite sure what she'd done wrong and then the penny dropped, Bill was jealous. After all he was well aware of how she used to feel about Dean. How could she be so stupid? "I was just pleased to see him, he doesn't mean anything to me anymore." She placed her hand on Bill's as she spoke. "You are the one I…"

"No, you are missing the point." He removed her hand from his and pulled out a chair from under the table gesturing for her to sit.

"What is it then?" she asked, defiantly standing.

"You should not draw attention to yourself like that."

"Like what? I was waving to a friend, that's all."

"Okay, what I mean is you shouldn't draw attention to us like that." Karen stared at him as he continued. "I've told you before, not everyone would understand about us. Therefore we have to be discreet."

"Oh, I see. I didn't think."

"Clearly."

"But people know I'm friends with Sandra, so it's fine really. They'll think that's the reason why I'm in your car," said Karen innocently.

"For goodness sake," said Bill, raising his voice again. "Where is Sandra? Is she here? Was she in the car with us?"

"Stop shouting at me, I just meant that…"

"You don't seem to understand that some people would think that you and I being together is wrong. They would say things about you and I don't want that."

"What things?"

"Unpleasant things. People would think you were a… look we must be careful, discreet. Nobody can know about us. Nobody."

"Okay."

"Let's eat before this gets cold."

Karen sat down and Bill served up the Chinese, kissing the top of Karen's head as he put the plate down in front of her. She smiled at him, relieved that he'd stopped talking. He poured them both a glass of wine remembering to top Karen's up with lemonade to make it more palatable for her.

"What's a poepol?" She asked while trying to manoeuvre egg fried rice from her plate to her mouth using chopsticks. Bill looked at her, he paused before replying.

"I suppose the closest English word to it is idiot. I am sorry, but you, well, you startled me."

"It's fine," she replied smiling. She was sure it meant something much worse than idiot but she didn't want to push it. She was just rather pleased that he had apologised to her.

When they finished eating, they cleared up together and took their glasses and the rest of the wine bottle into the lounge. Karen sat down on the sofa thinking Bill would sit next to her. But he didn't. He sat in the armchair opposite her.

"I have something for you," he said, reaching an arm behind the chair as he spoke. He handed her a small parcel wrapped in red paper that was printed with pictures of holly and Christmas trees.

"Thank you," said Karen slightly embarrassed. "I'm afraid I haven't got you anything."

"That's fine, this is actually a present we can both enjoy." Karen looked at him, at the same time squeezing the present, trying to work out what it might be. "Open it," he said a little impatiently. Karen tore off the paper to reveal what she thought was a silky top but as she held it up she realised it was a very, very short and rather see through nightdress with matching knickers. The fabric was delicate, translucent. Diaphanous fabric so sheer that she could see straight through it at Bill's grinning face. She dropped it into her lap and leant forward to kiss him and as she did, something else dropped to the floor. She bent down and picked it up. It was a pocket-sized diary with flowers on the front of it; similar to the one she had bought her Grandma for Christmas. She looked at it, a little puzzled as to why he'd bought it for her.

"It's for your dates," said Bill, sensing her confusion.

"Dates?"

"Yes."

"Our dates? When we meet?"

"No, yours."

"I don't follow."

"I need to know your dates; when you bleed." Karen's cheeks felt warm and she knew she was blushing. Bill smiled at her, he was rather enjoying her embarrassment.

"Why?" Asked Karen naively.

"I'm being prudent," he replied. "Let's finish this wine and then you can try on your present." Bill drunk his wine very quickly, Karen sensing the urgency swiftly poured the rest of her glass down her throat dribbling a little as she did. Bill stood up, took her hand and led her upstairs. When they reached his bedroom, he pointed towards the en-suite and told her to go in there to get changed. It took her a while as she was a little unsteady on her feet, the wine was beginning to take effect. Once she had the lingerie on she wanted to look at herself in a mirror before she showed Bill. The only mirror available was a small one on the cabinet above the sink so she was only able to see the top half. She thought about standing on the edge of the bath to get a better view but wisely decided against it, standing on the floor was hard enough without attempting to balance on a porcelain surface that was only four inches wide. She stood on tip-toes and looked at her reflection, she was a little shocked. The material hid nothing and she could see her breasts through it, not just the contours, but everything, as clear as if she were standing there naked. She knew the bottom half would be the same, so was actually grateful that a full-length mirror wasn't available to her. She suddenly felt incredibly self-conscious. Why? She didn't know, after all Bill had seen her undressed several times now.

"Are you ever coming out?" she heard him call.

She didn't reply, she composed herself, opened the door and went through to the bedroom. Bill was laying on his back with his hands behind his head. He was still fully clothed. Karen went to sit on the bed.

"No. Stay there." he said. "And turn around."

She did as he asked and as she turned around she heard him move. He shuffled along and sat on the edge of the bed pulling Karen towards him, still with her back facing him. He began caressing her through the fabric, very gently. He then turned her around so she was looking at him. He ran his hands up and down her sides, stopping at her breasts, pressing her nipples with his thumbs. His hands travelled down her back pulling her closer still. He began kissing her through the fabric, he kissed her breasts, her sides, her stomach. His kisses moved lower still until he was kissing her there. Karen froze, momentarily, as his tongue slipped behind the satin briefs. He stopped and began removing his clothes; Karen moved away from him, she needed to sit down, the hastily drunk wine was making the room spin. Bill took hold of her wrist and pulled her onto the bed.

"Come here my poes," he mumbled in her ear. "Come here."

2010

Karen should not have been surprised by the size of Sandra's hotel room; of course, she would have the biggest or best possible. However, she was still astonished, even the family rooms that she occupied with Andrew and the boys were only a fraction of the size of this room. Well it wasn't a room, it was rooms, a suite. Bedroom, bathroom and lounge. The lounge had a work station in the corner, a large sofa, coffee table and television. The desk was littered with papers as was the smoked glass coffee table. There were clothes draped over one of the sofas which Sandra swooped upon very quickly and moved into the bedroom. She was clearly using all the space but Karen thought it was still a little over the top for a couple of days.

"Sit down," said Sandra nodding at the sofa as she walked back into the lounge from the bedroom. "I'll get us a drink."

"I think I'll pass," said Karen.

"Oh come on, have a nightcap. What's your poison?" Sandra bent down and opened the door of a cupboard beneath the television, which housed the mini bar. Karen sighed, conceding defeat again.

"Whatever you're having is fine."

Sandra removed two miniature bottles of whiskey from the

cabinet and poured one into each of the two glasses she had placed by the television. She had her back to Karen so Karen did not see when she added a few drops of something into one of the glasses. Sandra swilled the whiskey around a little to ensure the drops were well mixed in before handing the glass to Karen.

"Thank you." Karen took a large gulp, the back of her throat burned and she coughed and spluttered. "Good God, that's strong. What is it?"

"Whiskey."

"I'm not really one for spirits."

"Well you did say you would have whatever I was having."

"It's fine. It just took me by surprise that's all."

Sandra smiled at her, raising her own glass to her lips. Karen did the same, but this time taking a sip rather than a gulp. She scoured the coffee table looking for somewhere to set the glass down, there were papers covering it, a big blur of papers that appeared to be sliding and moving across the table. Sandra noticed Karen's hand with the glass in it hovering above the table so she took it from her before the remainder of her whiskey ended up all over the documents. She placed the glass on a lamp table to the right of the sofa.

"Are you okay?" She enquired of Karen.

"I think that whiskey was a drink too far," she answered in slightly slurred tones. "Anyway, where are these photos you wanted to show me?" she asked and began leafing through the papers in front of her.

"I'll get them in a minute, just let me sort these first," she said taking the papers from Karen's shaky reach. "Actually, this is the document I need witnessing," she said with feigned surprise. "Let's do that first." She went over to the desk and got a pen, then sat next to Karen on the sofa. "I need to sign here," Sandra said while expertly and swiftly signing her name at the bottom of the page. "And you need to sign there," she said to Karen indicating a rectangular box on the left-hand side of the paper. She handed her the pen as Karen tried to pick up the paper. "Just here," persisted Sandra holding down the document.

"You know you should never sign anything without reading it first," said Karen, while still trying to pick up the piece of paper. Her speech was slow, drawn out and barely coherent and Sandra knew she only had a few moments left in which to get her to sign it.

"Can you lean forward and read it then?" Sandra asked. "Only these documents are all in order ready for me to deal with." Karen shifted forward and leant across the coffee table. Sandra was glad, she just hoped that Karen didn't notice that she was actually holding a document across the top of the one she wanted her to sign.

"Oh God. I can't see this. Where are my glasses?" she bemoaned. She flung herself across the sofa to reach her handbag and began rifling around in it. The room had started to spin and looking through her bag was requiring a monumental effort. She so wanted her bed right now.

"Shall I read it to you?" snapped Sandra impatiently. She was starting to worry that the melatonin would take affect before she had got her signature.

"Yes," said Karen laying back on the sofa. Sandra began 'reading' the document to her. Sandra's entire working life had been spent with documents and contracts, so it wasn't difficult for her to make what she was saying sound plausible. She spoke quickly, adding the odd legal term to give it authenticity. When she had finished, she helped Karen sit up as by now she was barely conscious.

"Here," said Sandra, stabbing the document with a perfectly

manicured finger. Karen leant forward and signed the paper. Sandra's relief was palpable. As Karen collapsed into the welcoming softness of the sofa, she muttered.

"I always thought the witness signed on the right side of the page. Is it the other way round because it's a South African document?"

"Yes, that's it," Sandra snorted in disdain. "You stupid fuck," she added, knowing full well that Karen was now asleep.

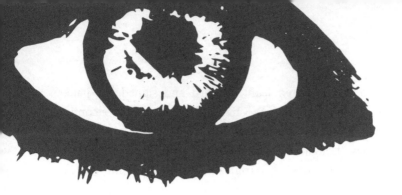

January 1977

"We've been waiting ages. Did you forget you were supposed to meet us?" Sandra asked Yvonne as she came out of the school gates. "We were going to give you two more minutes and then we would have gone without you," she continued.

"Bloody Baldwin kept me back again - she hates me you know."

"What have you done this time?" asked Karen.

"Nothing."

"You must have done something."

"It wasn't me."

"It never is," chipped in Sandra.

Yvonne glared at her before continuing. "I was just passing this note on and I got caught; it wasn't for me and it wasn't from me."

"Who wrote it then?"

"That's what she asked me."

"Who?"

"Baldwin."

"What did you say?"

"I told her I didn't know."

"And she kept you back for that?"

"Yep, over the top or what."

"You didn't say anything else?" Karen pressed.

"Well I may have told her to shut up and then she was shouting and saying don't use that language in here."

"So you probably said a little more than shut up."

"I don't know, maybe. I don't think I did."

Karen and Sandra exchanged a look and at the same time both said:

"You did."

Yvonne looked at them both and started laughing.

"Silly cow has put me on report again."

"Yvonne, you've only been back at school for a week and already you're on report again," said Karen.

"God, you sound like my mother!"

"Come on, let's go. It's freezing today," said Sandra. The three linked arms and crossed the road, heading towards the park. It had snowed the day before and overnight the temperatures had plummeted so the roads and footpaths were treacherous to walk on. The snow on the pavements had been rubbed smooth and to a high sheen by the many feet that had walked across them so the girls had to watch their step. It was like walking on wet glass. They reached the entrance to the park safely and Karen for one was relieved to see that a layer of grit had been tossed across the footpaths inside the park. It meant the paths were slushy and the slush was a horrible orangey muddy colour but at least they weren't slippery.

Yvonne unhooked her arm from Karen's and began rummaging around in her bag, finally pulling out a packet of Embassy No.10 and a box of matches.

"You have not started smoking," shouted Sandra. "Are you mad?"

"There's nothing wrong with smoking," Yvonne said defensively. "Your Dad smokes," she added.

"He's a man."

"So what."

"Men smoke."

"So do women."

"Well they shouldn't. Dad says…"

"Oh here we go," said Yvonne. "Dad says this and Dad says that. Don't you have an opinion of your own Sandra?"

Before Sandra could reply Karen intervened.

"Will you two shut up?" Sandra and Yvonne looked at Karen, then at each other. "Just stop arguing and let's go home. It's cold."

"Well I still want a smoke," said Yvonne. "Let's go over there behind the kiosk."

"But someone might see."

"No they won't. It only opens in the summer so there won't be anyone over there." Yvonne and Karen started walking across the field towards the kiosk, Sandra reluctantly followed them.

"Do you know what a poepol is?" Karen asked Sandra.

Sandra stared at her, not speaking. "Do you?" pressed Karen.

"Yes, it's an Afrikaans word. Why are you asking?"

"I heard it on this television programme I was watching and I wondered what it meant."

"Well it's not nice, Dad says it when he's really angry. It's an insult."

"In English. What does it mean in English?"

"Arsehole."

"Oh. What about poes? What does that mean?"

"What?" said Sandra astonished at what her friend had just said.

"Poes." Karen repeated. "What does poes mean?"

"I heard you. I just can't believe you said it. What kind of television programme were you watching?"

"Why? What is it?"

"It's the worst word you can say."

"What word?"

"I'm not saying it," said Sandra.

"Don't be daft. Tell me."

"It's, you know. That word."

"No, I don't know."

"She means the 'C' word," said a rather bored Yvonne.

Karen stared at Sandra, open-mouthed.

"It can't be."

"Well it is."

Karen couldn't believe that Bill would say that word to her. Maybe I misheard him, she thought, knowing full well she hadn't.

"I can see you're shocked," said Sandra. "So am I. I can't believe they'd put it on television. Wait until Dad hears."

"No, don't tell him," said Karen. Sandra looked at her quizzically. "It may not have been on the telly after all. I might have just overheard it somewhere. I'm not sure now."

"Well, wherever you heard it, it's really not nice."

"As interesting as this conversation is," piped up Yvonne, who had now finished her cigarette. "It's really cold and I'd like to get home sometime soon."

"God, we were only waiting for you anyway," said Sandra.

2010

Sandra picked up the papers from the coffee table. She put some into a folder and placed them on the desk, the important document, the one with Karen's signature she put into an A4 Manila envelope. She sealed it and tucked it into her briefcase which she then locked. She picked up her mobile phone and tapped out the briefest of messages; 'It's done'. As she hit the send button she heard music, faintly coming from somewhere inside the room. Unsure where the sound was actually coming from she began to look around trying to locate it. Her eyes fell on Karen's handbag, as she opened it she realised that the sound wasn't music exactly, but a ring-tone. Karen's phone was ringing. Sandra took hold of it and looked at the display: Andrew

"Hello."

"Any chance I may see you some time tonight?" Sandra instantly recognised the voice despite its angry tone.

"I'll oblige if you want darling," said Sandra seductively, "but I think you'd rather it was your wife who came home to you." His silence was deafening, Sandra stifled a laugh. "Andrew darling, it's Sandra."

"Sandra, of course. How are you? So sorry to hear about your Dad."

"Thank you darling. I'm fine, considering. I'm afraid Karen's not so fine. Too much vino I'm afraid. She never could hold her drink as I recall," she added provocatively.

His pause was brief, but telling.

"Could I speak to Karen please?"

"Okay, I'll try and wake her. Karen, Karen. Wake up Karen, Andrew wants to speak to you. He's a little anxious, come on." Karen stirred slightly, but not enough to hold the phone let alone a conversation. "I can't seem to rouse her I'm afraid. I'll keep trying and get her to call you back if you like."

"I suppose that's all you can do," sniffed Andrew. "How exactly is she planning to get home? She clearly can't drive and I can't come for her as the boys are in bed. They have school in the morning so I can't wake them."

God, you're so boring, thought Sandra. And to think once upon a time… ughhh.

"She was planning to order a taxi but fell asleep before she could. Look, she's in my suite, there's plenty of room. She may as well stay and come home in the morning."

"She's in your suite?"

"Yes. You know how it is. We were reminiscing about Yvonne and came up here to look at some photos that I have and time just slips away."

"Okay, fine. It probably is best she stays with you now, but if she wakes please get her to call me."

"I will sweetie. I promise," said Sandra in a sickly-sweet voice. She replaced the phone in Karen's bag and then went into the bedroom, she took a blanket and pillow from the top shelf of the wardrobe. She lay the blanket over Karen and put the pillow beside her. She picked up Karen's glass from the lamp table and poured the contents into the bathroom sink, she rinsed the glass and put it back on the silver salver by the television. She took a final look around the lounge before turning off the lights and going to bed.

Easter 1977

K aren declined the offer of a lift from her mum and decided to walk across the park to Sandra's house. She needed to clear her head and ready herself for Sandra and Yvonne. She was feeling a little apprehensive about this evening; after all it was the first sleepover since 'the party'. Well the first with the girls, she had stayed over at Sandra's house a couple of times with Bill when Sandra had not been there, but obviously that was different. Karen picked up the faded canvas rucksack that held her overnight things and slung it over one shoulder, with the other hand she picked up the Woolworths carrier bag that held the sweets and magazines, obligatory kit for a sleepover.

As she walked across the playing field in the park, Karen wished she'd let her mum drop her after all. The wind was quite strong and it was raining, well drizzling but the wind was coming straight at her making the fine raindrops feel like tiny needles as they stung her face. She glanced up and was grateful that she could just about make out Sandra's house. Thank God, nearly there, she thought. She pulled her jacket tighter around her and tried to walk quicker, it was then she heard something, it was someone calling her name.

"Karen, Karen."

She looked up at the window of Sandra's bedroom, she was

still too far away to see if anyone was at the window and certainly too far to ascertain if anyone was calling her from the house. She figured it must have been the wind.

"Karen, oy, Karen. Wait up."

That was definitely someone calling me, she thought. Karen looked up again and then turned around. She could make out a figure running towards her, clad in black, frantically waving their arms at her. Karen stopped, focused and realised the figure adorned in black was Yvonne. She raised her hand in acknowledgement and started walking back towards her. Yvonne stopped waving her arms in the air like a deranged air-traffic controller and slowed her pace to a walk.

"Hey." They both said simultaneously when they met.

"I thought you were going to Sandra's earlier," said Karen.

"I was meant to, but I had to stop off at Jason's to drop something off and I kind of lost track of time. Walk over this way a bit," Yvonne said pulling Karen sideways.

"But the gates over there," pointed Karen.

"I know. I want a quick smoke and I don't want to be seen. Want one?"

"No."

"You sure?" asked Yvonne.

"I'm sure. Bill would hate it."

"What's it got to do with Bill?"

Karen faltered as she realised what she'd said. "I erm, I just mean it's not fair going in his house smelling of cigarettes when we know how much he dislikes it."

"But he smokes."

"Yes, I know. But Sandra doesn't and she doesn't like it either."

"Sandra just agrees with Daddy all the time. I'm sure none of her thoughts are her own, you know."

"Maybe."

"I think he's an MCP."

"MCP?"

"Male Chauvinist PIG," said Yvonne, emphasising the word pig.

"I don't think he is," said Karen.

"Oh he is. All this 'women should do this and not do that' crap. Unless it's my precious Sandra of course. She can do whatever she likes."

"That's not true. She's not allowed to smoke."

"She probably could if she wanted to, but she likes to agree with daddy. I think it's all a bit odd."

"What's odd?"

"The way they are and that it's just the two of them."

"That's because her mum died. You know that."

"I know, but that was years ago. You'd think he'd have married again by now. I don't even think he has a girlfriend."

"Maybe he has." said Karen hoping her friend wouldn't notice her blushes.

"No. He's just, I don't know. He gives me the creeps, that's all."

"That's not fair. He's always nice to us," protested Karen.

"Why are you defending him?" asked Yvonne.

"I'm not. I think you're off with him because of what happened at the party."

"Yeah and why not. That was a bit over the top."

"Not really. You were taking drugs in his house!"

"I wasn't actually," said Yvonne as she extinguished the cigarette with the heel of her boot.

"Come on," said Karen. "Or we'll both be late."

When they reached Sandra's house she was standing by the front door, waiting for them.

"You took your time," she said moving aside so they could go into the house.

"Hello to you too," said Yvonne sarcastically.

"And what are you wearing?" Sandra asked looking straight at Yvonne.

"You like it?" Yvonne said as she twirled in front of Sandra.

"You look like you've come from a funeral and you do realise those are men's boots that you have on."

"So, look at what you're wearing."

"What's wrong with it?" Sandra asked holding the hem of her top.

"What's right with it?" Retorted Yvonne.

"Not again. You're always arguing these days." shouted Karen.

"No we're not," they said together.

Karen rolled her eyes at them.

"Leave your bags there," said Sandra. "And come outside, I've got something to show you." Karen and Yvonne did as they were told and dropped their bags at the bottom of the stairs. They followed Sandra through the house and out into the garden, once through the patio doors Sandra stopped. "Ta dah," she said pointing down the garden. "What do you think?"

"Of what?" Asked Yvonne.

"That," said Sandra waving her outstretched hand.

"It's a shed."

"No it's not."

"Yeah it is."

"Sheds are smaller."

"Okay, it's a big shed then."

"No, it's a summerhouse."

"But it's not summer," laughed Yvonne, who really was enjoying baiting Sandra. Sandra ignored her and turned to Karen instead.

"What do you think of it?" She asked her.

"It's lovely."

"Well don't be too enthusiastic," said a disappointed Sandra.

"No it is really lovely. But I have already seen it."

"No you haven't."

"Yes I have," she argued. Sandra looked at her quizzically.

"When?"

"I, actually no. You're right I haven't," backtracked Karen as she realised her mistake.

�◉

She had seen it and it had seen her! Karen recalled the intimate evening she had spent in the summerhouse with Bill. It was a week earlier. He had dropped Sandra at Manor House Rec on the other side of town so she could watch Ryan play football and he'd picked Karen up at the bus stop on the way back. He made them both a drink and they went outside to the newly erected summerhouse. It really was lovely; apparently a mini version of the colonial style homes of South Africa. It had electricity and a small sink with running water, only cold water mind. It was furnished with a couple of sofa beds, a small table, portable television and a fridge. Two fan heaters kept it warm and a couple of wall lights illuminated it. It looked very pretty with lots of feminine touches which were obviously Sandra's influence rather than Bill's.

"Sit down," said Bill. Karen did as she was told. As she sat down Bill handed her one of the drinks. He sat down next to her and took a large mouthful of his drink before placing it on the table. He turned to Karen, took the glass from her hand and placed it next to his. She went to protest as she hadn't even had a sip yet but Bills lips were on hers before she could speak. He kissed her lips, he kissed her face, her ears and then her neck. He stopped and looked at her for a moment, smiling at her. Then he got up, locked the door and lowered the blinds over the windows. Karen knew why he'd done this and it was not because it was dark. He turned around and started loosening the belt on his trousers. Karen leant forward and picked up her glass, she knocked back her drink. Instantly she felt better, she always preferred to have a drink before… Bill removed his trousers and underpants and sat down next to her once more. He kept his shirt on and made no attempt to remove her clothes. He was just looking at her and Karen was a little unsure what to do. She began unbuttoning her blouse but Bill stopped her.

"Kiss me." She moved towards him and lifted her face to his and went to kiss him.

"Not there," he said, gently touching her face and lowering it towards his groin.

"Kiss me here."

It took a couple of seconds for his request to register. She looked at him, wide-eyed and slightly afraid. She didn't want to do this. He smiled and gently guided her face down onto him. She kissed it, hoping that would be enough.

"Open your mouth." She did as he asked; he raised his hips slightly, pushing himself into her mouth, still holding her head. Karen tried to sit up but Bill held her head firm. She couldn't do this; it was uncomfortable and she wanted to stop. She pushed him away and sat up without speaking or looking at him for she knew he would be angry. He stood up and put his trousers back on. He picked up his glass and finished his drink before he finally spoke.

"That's something we'll have to work on my darling."

◉

"I thought I'd seen it, but no, you're right, I haven't. I just remember you telling me about it," said Karen.

"Really?" Sandra asked. "I was sure I hadn't told anybody."

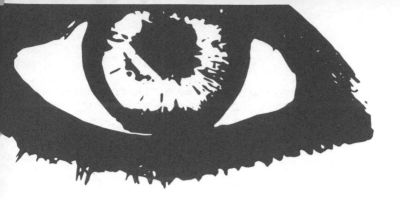

2010

She slowly opened her eyes, the emerging shapes and shadows were unfamiliar to her. She lifted her head slightly, it hurt, so she lowered it again. Her mouth was dry, rasping; dry to the point of soreness. The room was half lit and as she again looked around she had a faint recollection of the previous evening. Dinner with Sandra, yes, she remembered that. But that still didn't explain where she was now. And what is that tapping sound? She lifted her head again at the same time swinging her legs round in one fluid movement, discarding the heavy beige blanket that lay across her.

"Good morning," said a familiar voice. "I hope I didn't wake you. I need to get these emails off ASAP."

Karen turned toward the voice that was addressing her, Sandra was sitting at the desk, typing on a laptop.

"Morning," she replied. "I'm at a bit of a loss. I'm not sure what I'm doing here."

"Aah, well," said Sandra turning to face her. "You passed out last night. It appears your capacity for alcohol has not improved with age."

"Oh God. I don't remember. Andrew, he'll be worried sick."

"He's fine. I spoke to him last night," said Sandra rising from the work station. "Tea or coffee?"

"You spoke to him? How?"

"He called, on your mobile. I answered it and explained the situation. I said you could stay here and you'd call once you woke up."

"You should have woken me."

"I did try, but you were out cold. Tea or coffee? You didn't say."

"Coffee, thank you. Was he angry?"

"Who?"

"Andrew."

"I don't know. Not especially. It's hard to tell on the phone though."

"Well he ought to be angry."

"Sugar?"

"No, thank you."

"Why should he be angry?"

"He expected me home. He has every right to be cross?"

"Every right! For God's sake, he's your husband not your father."

"I'd better call him. What is the time?"

"Just gone half past eight."

"No. Oh, he would've had to do the school run. Shit!" Karen said jumping up. "I think I'll leave the coffee and just go."

"I rather think you need a little adjustment before you leave darling."

"Adjustment?"

"You're a little bit dishevelled. I'd go and freshen up before you go. Text him and tell him you'll be home in an hour. That'll give you time to repair and prepare," said Sandra with a smile.

"Okay." Karen hated to agree with Sandra, but what she said did make sense.

❧

Andrew dropped the boys at school then headed to work. He had been briefly tempted to drive to the hotel but thought better of it. His mood was foul and he knew he'd say something he would later regret and besides he had no wish to see Sandra. Even speaking to her last night had so stirred and agitated him that sleep became a longed-for luxury that eluded him all night. He was surprised Karen hadn't called yet. As this thought crossed his mind, his phone pinged notifying him that he had received a message. He knew it was Karen, typical, just a text. *Stay out all flaming night and all I get is a bloody text.* He pulled into his parking space in the car park and picked up the phone.

Sorry darling. B with u shortly. XX

He didn't bother to reply.

◉

Karen looked at her reflection in the mirror, took a deep breath and exhaled slowly. *You'll have to do* she said to herself before adding a final touch of lipstick. As she came out of the bathroom she spotted Sandra in the bedroom, an open suitcase on the bed.

"Are you going home?" Karen asked her.

"In a couple of days. I'm just checking out of here. I still have a few more things to deal with before I return home."

"Where are you going to stay?"

"With a friend."

"Anyone I know?" enquired Karen.

"No."

Karen realised that Sandra was not going to offer any more information.

"Right, I'm off now. Do I look presentable?"

"Not bad," replied Sandra, shutting the suitcase.

"Well it's been lovely seeing you." said Karen. "Despite the circumstances, of course."

Sandra smiled but didn't say anything.

"Okay then." As she spoke Karen took a step towards Sandra and put her arms around her. "Take care and have a safe trip home."

"Thank you, I will," said Sandra, as she freed herself from the awkward embrace.

"Keep in touch," added Karen as Sandra opened the door for her. Again, Sandra's response was a smile.

"Bye then," called Karen as she walked up the hotel corridor. Sandra closed the door, as she did she began unkindly mimicking Karen.

"Keep in touch." Not bloody likely she thought. She picked up her phone, scrolled through her contacts, when she found the number she was looking for she hit the call button.

"She's gone, I'll be with you in about forty minutes."

June 1977

No matter how hard she tried Karen was unable to get back to sleep. Reluctantly she decided to get up. She knew there was lots to do but did they really have to start so early. It felt like the middle of the night. For the past few months the main topic of conversation among everybody had been the Jubilee and the impending celebrations. Karen did not share most people's enthusiasm for it. A view that was hardened now by the banging, clattering and shouting going on outside as people readied the street for this afternoon's party. She pulled back her bedroom curtains and was greeted by a sea of red, white and blue. Flags were hanging in almost every window and the Union Jack bunting was dancing fiercely between the lamp-posts. Two perfectly straight lines of trestle tables filled the streets and at the end of the road stood a huge pile of folding chairs waiting to be put out alongside the tables. This vision did not change her mind, in fact it reinforced her view that the whole thing was a complete waste of time and money. Yvonne agreed with Karen, well Yvonne actually thought that most things were a waste of time and money. She was anti everything. If there was a March or protest going on, Yvonne would be there, when she was able to escape her parents reach, that is. Half the time she didn't know what she was actually protesting about, but that didn't stop her. Trouble with Yvonne was that she was permanently angry these days. She dressed from head to toe in black, the only colour she wore was on her head. Her hair colour changed every week; blue, green, even jet black to compliment the rest of her attire. Last time Karen had seen her it was a very shocking pink... such a contrast to her normal look. Yvonne's natural hair colour was a kind of mousy, dirty blonde. She wasn't tall, but somehow the different hair shades not only made her stand out but also stand tall. It changed people's view of her, not always in a good way. But that never bothered Yvonne, she never cared what people thought of her. Sandra was convinced the change occurred when she met Jason, but Karen thought it had more to do with things at home. She knew it had been tough for Yvonne since Dean had gone. It was most likely a combination of both, either way Yvonne's look and attitude had altered dramatically of late.

Sandra was the polar opposite to Yvonne and as you'd expect she loved the whole Jubilee circus. The idea of street parties, celebrations and communal fun thrilled Sandra. Probably because it gave her the opportunity for shining before a larger audience. Wherever Sandra went, somehow she would always manage to bewitch and beguile someone and normally more than just one someone. These polarising views meant the three girls were quite divided on what they would like to do today. In the end, Sandra got her way, well almost. Between them they found a compromise; they would go to the Jubilee Fair being held in the park. This compromise suited Karen, the alternative suggestions being attending one or more of the many street parties taking place in the neighbourhood or camping out in Bluebell woods. The latter probably would've meant putting up with Yvonne singing God Save the Queen, (the Sex Pistol's version) over and over again and listening to her and some of her weirder friends extolling the virtues of Johnny Rotten as a potential Prime-minister.

The girls weren't meeting until midday and Karen knew if she didn't make herself scarce she'd get roped in to help by her Mum. She decided to get up and take a walk down the High Road and look in the shops. The centre of town was dead, the reason soon became apparent; everything was closed, just for a minute she wondered why but then remembered that today was a bank holiday. That's why she wasn't at school. She looked at her watch, it wasn't quite 10 o clock. Two hours to kill. She headed back in the direction of the park. She'd been walking for a few minutes when she noticed someone walking almost beside her. As she glanced up he spoke.

"Hey, alright."

Karen smiled at him. He looked vaguely familiar. He spoke again.

"You're Sandra's mate, aren't you?" he asked. "Think I've seen you with her," he added. "I'm Ryan's mate, well team-mate. We play for the same football team. What's your name?"

"Karen," she replied, surprised that he'd actually allowed her to speak. He talked incredibly fast, without daring to take a breath in between sentences.

"Where you heading? The Park? I'm going that way. Meeting some of the lads for a kick about before all this Jubilee nonsense starts. You can walk with me if you like."

"Thanks," said Karen with a bemused look, as she'd actually been under the impression that he was walking with her.

The park was busier than the town, mainly on account of the fair. The big field was covered with rides and side-shows: a waltzer, dodgems, ferris wheel, swing boats and a helter skelter at the centre, a coconut shy, shooting range, hoop-la, hook-a-duck and fortune tellers around the edge all encircled by a railway track on which a miniature train travelled. The smaller field was home to the caravans that belonged to those who worked at the fair. Karen thought the idea of travelling from town to town, working on the fair sounded quite exciting, liberating even. Offering anonymity and freedom she suspected, how marvellous. Her thoughts were interrupted by someone speaking.

"Well?" said the voice.

"Sorry," said Karen.

"Boring you am I? Ha-ha. I asked if you'd been yet. To the fair? A few of us went after the match on Saturday, it's not bad. Rides are a bit tame. Don't bother with the side shows, you won't win anything. They're all a bit of a con."

"Oh okay. I'm going this afternoon with Sandra and Yvonne."

"Is Yvonne the one who goes out with Jay, Jay Roberts?"

"Do you mean Jason?" asked Karen.

"Yeah, we all know him as Jay though. He used to play in our team."

"Oh right, yes she does."

"She's a weird one."

"I think it's him who's the weird one," said Karen jumping to her friend's defence. The pair walked on in silence for a few minutes. They reached the playground and both sat down on the swings. "What time are you meeting your friends?"

"Any second now, that's them over there," he said nodding towards a group of boys. Karen looked up, she spotted the group, recognising Ryan straight away. They were walking slowly, kicking a ball between them as they did.

"I'd better head off now," she said.

"You don't have to go, you can hang out with us if you like."

"No, it's fine." She jumped off the swing. "See you."

"Maybe later," he shouted after her.

Karen decided to call for Yvonne, it was almost 11.30 and she felt sure she would be up by now. She knocked on the door, thankfully it was Yvonne who answered. Karen always felt a bit awkward talking to Yvonne's parents, especially her Dad. As the door opened Karen was greeted by Yvonne sporting a shock of green hair, not a light hint but a bright in your face emerald green.

"Am I glad to see you," said Yvonne pulling on her boots. "Get me out of this MADHOUSE," she shouted, clearly for the benefit of whoever was in the house.

"What's up now?" asked Karen as they walked up the road.

"Usual; what I wear, what I say, how I say it, my hair colour."

"It is rather... green," interjected Karen.

"Well spotted Sherlock."

The fair was much quieter than the girls expected. Presumably most people were attending the street parties. The lack of crowds meant they did not have to waste time queueing for the rides. Sandra spent a stupid amount of money trying to win an oversized teddy bear, despite Karen repeatedly telling her it was a con. The hoop she had to throw was clearly smaller than the wooden block it had to hook over. When they'd spent most of their money and been on all of the rides that they wanted to go on they each bought a stick of candy-floss and went over to the playground to sit and eat them. They hadn't been there long when Ryan and his friends came over. Yvonne wasn't impressed with their arrival and kept scowling at Sandra, convinced that she had pre-arranged the meeting with Ryan. Eventually she decided to leave, she was getting a bit cold just sitting there.

"I'm off," she said to whoever was listening.

"I thought we were spending the day together," protested Sandra.

"That's what I thought," replied Yvonne.

"So why are you going?" sked Sandra.

Here we go again, thought Karen, another row.

"I don't want to just sit here, it's boring and I'm cold."

"Let's go back to mine then," said Sandra.

"Won't your Dad mind?" Ryan asked, hoping the invitation included him too.

"No, it'll be fine. Besides we can go out to the summerhouse so we don't disturb him. That's why we got it."

Yvonne wasn't keen, but the alternatives were either going home or going to Bluebell Wood. Both options she knew would leave her feeling cold; one emotionally, the other physically.

"Okay then," said Yvonne. "Let's go."

When they got to Sandra's. They didn't go through the house, instead she unlocked the gate and they filed down the garden to the summerhouse.

"Who wants a drink?" asked Sandra opening the fridge. A collective sound followed implying that everyone wanted one. There wasn't enough in the fridge so Sandra went up to the house for some more, Karen went with her. "I think you have an admirer," said Sandra as they walked up the garden.

"What?"

"I think you have an admirer," repeated Sandra.

"I heard you the first time, I just don't think… who?"

Sandra slid open the patio doors and the pair walked through to the kitchen. Bill was sitting at the kitchen table reading the newspaper.

"We're just getting some drinks to take down to the summerhouse," Sandra said to him.

Bill nodded acknowledgement, he looked up briefly, spotting Karen.

"Hello Karen. How are you?"

"Fine thank you," she answered a little too politely.

"Karen has an admirer Dad," laughed Sandra. Bill looked up again, his interest piqued.

"Really, who might that be?"

"One of Ryan's friends from the football team," shouted Sandra from inside the larder.

"And is that who you're entertaining in the summerhouse?" His question was directed at Sandra but his gaze was fixed on Karen. Sandra emerged from the cupboard holding a large bag of crisps in one hand and dragging a box full of fizzy drinks with the other.

"Give us a hand," she said to Karen.

"I'll bring it down for you," said Bill standing up and removing his reading glasses.

"Thanks Dad."

Bill effortlessly picked up the box and followed the girls back outside. His offer of help was not an act of chivalry. No, he wanted to see the punk who had designs on Karen. He walked into the summerhouse behind Karen and placed the box on the floor by the fridge. He had expected to find just Ryan and 'his friend' in there, but in all there were another six people. Yvonne, with very green hair, Ryan he knew and four other boys he did not. They all acknowledged him as he studied each of them in turn. So which one is it? He thought to himself.

"Thanks Dad," said Sandra, clearly wanting him to go.

"Do you need anything else?" he asked, while still looking around, hopeful that whoever it was would give himself away. Hah, there it was, the lad on the sofa by the window just stood up to let Karen sit down. What a gentleman. Bill clocked the way he smiled at her, he knew what this one was thinking.

"We're fine thanks... Dad?"

"Sorry, what?" Said Bill looking at Sandra.

"You can go now."

"Yes sure." He walked out of the door but now before pausing momentarily, turning back and looking at Karen. Karen saw him look at her, his eyes dark and menacing. That brooding look that both repelled and attracted. One thing she was sure of, he was not happy.

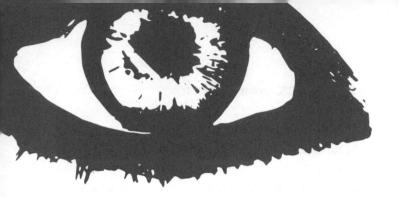

2010

Karen decided to head home, she knew Andrew would have gone straight to work after taking the boys to school and a confrontation there didn't seem like a good idea; besides, her head was banging and she really didn't look her best, despite the restoration she had attempted in Sandra's hotel room. Shower, siesta and Andrews favourite meal as a conciliatory gesture was more appropriate. She pulled onto the driveway of their house, as she got out of the car she spotted Sheila, her next-door neighbour putting rubbish in the dustbin. Karen waved her arm towards her but avoided making eye contact. The last thing she needed this morning was an update on the toing's and froing's of Walker Drive. Sheila was the 'street spy', she knew what was going on with everybody. In fact, she was probably well aware that Karen had not been home all night. Her 'spying' was legendary, all done under the guise of the neighbourhood watch, of course. Whenever she was challenged about her nosiness and interference, her defence was always the same.

'Well I am the Neighbourhood Watch Co-ordinator you know, therefore it is my business to keep a close eye on what occurs in our midst. I'm sorry if that offends you, but I'm sure you don't want your house broken into or your car stolen and since becoming co-

BEWARE THE CUCKOO

ordinator not a single incident has occurred on our road.'

She always conveniently forgot to mention that prior to her becoming co-ordinator there hadn't been an incident on Walker Drive, unless you counted the exchange between Barry and Phyllis when she reversed over his prized irises. The police were called but neither of them were arrested. It was a domestic matter said the police officer dealing with it and as it was their first disagreement in sixty-two years of marriage he didn't think it warranted further police time. Although he did politely suggest that perhaps Phyllis should refrain from driving.

Karen made it into the house without having to have a conversation with Sheila, no mean feat. She closed the door firmly behind her and went into the kitchen, planning to get a couple of pain-killers and a glass of water before jumping in the shower. But what greeted her stopped her in her tracks. The kitchen resembled a war-zone. The work top was strewn with foil cartons, some still containing food – remnants of a Chinese takeaway - the table was home to dirty breakfast bowls encrusted with a variety of cereals, a rice krispie trail ran across the table and down onto the floor, the dishwasher was open and Karen could see that someone had forced a couple of plates into the full dishwasher. Full of clean crockery – well it had been clean - until someone had laid dirty plates across the cups on the top rack. Karen sat down at the table and put her head in her hands. She had a thumping headache and could do without this. She knew there was an impending row with Andrew on the horizon too. And for what? She couldn't even remember if she'd had a nice time with Sandra. In fact, she was fairly certain she hadn't. She stood up and got the tablets she needed from the cabinet, she took them, looked around and thought, shower first.

Across town Sandra was searching for a parking place, she had to drive around the block a couple of times before she found somewhere. It was a little way down the street from the house but was the closest she could find. Why had she allowed herself to be talked into renting a house; a horrible little house at that. She was quite happy at the hotel. Yes, it was expensive, but once everything was finalised with Dad's estate she could easily afford it. Instead she had to make do with a tiny mid-terraced ex-council house in the middle of a rundown estate. As she walked towards the house she passed a group of boys sitting on the kerb; well she assumed they were boys, you couldn't actually tell on account of the over-sized hoodies they were wearing. Did I lock the car? She asked herself, her suspicion kicking in as a result of stereo-typing. Don't be silly, they're just kids. She was sure she had locked it, anyway there was nothing of particular value in it. Apart from her suitcase, which she had left in the boot, she wasn't wheeling that all the way along the road. She did have her briefcase though, which contained the envelope. She smiled to herself as she thought about the contents of the envelope. It had been much easier than she had anticipated, although it had still been a long and tedious night, but thankfully over. As she pushed open the gate it squeaked, loudly. An annoying sound, but useful as it alerted Nikolaas that she was back and he opened the front door for her. He smiled as she walked past him into the house.

"Where is it then?" he asked, closing the door as he did. Sandra waved the briefcase at him, he reached for it but she playfully put it behind her back.

"Don't I at least deserve a kiss first?" Nikolaas stepped towards her, put one arm around her and kissed her, briefly. Then he grabbed the briefcase from her with his other hand. "Hey, that's not fair," protested Sandra.

Nikolaas laughed. "Since when have you played fair?"

"It's locked anyway." It was Sandra's turn to laugh.

"Then give me the key and pour me a drink will you."

"A little early, isn't it?" she questioned as she threw him the key.

"Don't start. We're meant to be celebrating."

Sandra sighed and reluctantly got up to fix him a drink. She poured him a whiskey from the decanter on the sideboard. She turned to hand it to him but something caught her across the face sending her sprawling to the floor, the glass hit the fireplace exploding into several pieces. She looked up just in time to see Nikolaas' foot coming towards her. She rolled out of the way and his foot missed her, he lunged at her, pulling her to her feet and screaming at her in Afrikaans.

"Jy bleddie fool, dom, dom vrou."

(You bloody fool, stupid, stupid woman)

"What's the matter? What have I done?" she asked bringing herself back to her feet.

"This," he said waving the document at Sandra. "This is bloody useless." He lunged at her again, but she put her hands up and pushed him away.

"What do you mean? You drew up the contract." It was her turn to get angry now. "I've had to endure a long night with a simpering bitch just to get back what is rightfully mine. If you've screwed up…"

"I have not screwed up," he paused before continuing. "Tell me Sandra, how many deals have you done that involve contracts?"

"What kind of question is that?"

"How many?"

"I don't know, lots. I still don't see…"

"How many of those contracts required a witness signature?" he asked interrupting her.

"Most of them. Nikolaas what is your point?"

"The witness has to be independent, right? They cannot be the buyer, seller or BENEFICIARY!"

Sandra stared at him, the penny had dropped; she had signed the contract as witness to Karen's signature.

"All for nothing," said Nikolaas. "I said this wouldn't work. This elaborate charade has cost a small fortune. Fake funerals, flights, this house and not to mention your hotel bill. You should've listened to me, my way would've been so much cheaper and we wouldn't have even had to leave Cape Town."

"Blackmail was not the answer."

"Okay, what now?" Asked Nikolaas.

"Can't we do something with my signature?"

"Like what?"

"Change it, or can't we just draw up a new contract and forge Karen's signature. We must know someone who can do that."

"Maybe at home, but not here and we really do not have the time. Besides the less people involved with this the better."

"Can't we persuade Benjamin to file this document and release the money? We could increase his cut," pleaded Sandra, who was desperate for all her effort not to have been in vain.

"No, his reputation is paramount to him, you know that. Despite being your father's lawyer for years he always managed to keep himself on the right side of the law. He is happy to help us, but legally. Which is why all you had to do was get this damn form signed and then he could have released the money without Karen ever knowing about her inheritance."

"Okay, I know I messed up, but there has to be some way to salvage this. If I don't get the money I'm finished, we're both finished."

Nikolaas stared at her, for she was right. The business was in dire straits and some of the people they owed money to were not the most patient of people.

"My original plan is the only option," he said. "Although unfortunately we'll probably have to get our hands dirty."

"What do you mean?" asked Sandra.

"I mean, we will have to do the blackmailing ourselves. I don't know anyone here who I trust enough with this. You do still have the photographs?"

"I do."

Sandra sat down on the threadbare sofa, her head in her hands. She did not want to be involved with anything as seedy as blackmail. That was Nikolaas' world, not hers. And besides, she really did not want to see Karen again…

July 1977

"You can stay at mine on Saturday," Sandra said to Karen, somehow making it sound more like an order than an offer.

"I'll have to check with Mum first," Karen replied hesitantly. "We may be going out early Sunday so she might want me to be at home," she added.

"Just tell her to pick you up on the way out, if you stay at mine the boys can walk us back."

"What's happening Saturday?" enquired Yvonne.

"It's the end of season party at the football club."

"So why haven't I been invited?"

"Jason was thrown out of the football club."

"Actually he left. You still could've asked me though," Yvonne persisted.

"You hate football."

"Yeah, so. I like parties."

"It's not that kind of party."

"Still would've have been nice to have been asked," said Yvonne, clearly sulking.

"Do you want to come?" asked Sandra.

"No."

BEWARE THE CUCKOO

"So stop moaning then."

"Shut up," shouted Karen who was becoming seriously bored with both of them.

"I'm going to meet Jason now, see you later."

They watched Yvonne go, stomping off in a petulant manner.

"There's something wrong with her." said Sandra to Karen.

"She's alright, she never has liked being left out. You know that."

"No it's more than that. Look at her. She looks a mess, she's always miserable and she argues with everybody these days."

As much as she didn't want to, Karen had to agree with Sandra's assessment of Yvonne. She knew Yvonne missed having Dean at home but it was more than that, there was something wrong but Karen didn't know what it was. When she had asked Yvonne if everything was ok. Yvonne had just blamed her parents. 'You should try living with them,' Yvonne had said when Karen had tried to defend them. 'They just don't get me; Dad's always shouting and Mum's new best friend is Jesus. It's like living in a fuckin' asylum.' Karen hadn't pressed her anymore, she did think Yvonne's parents were a little odd, but thought it was probably due to the fact they were quite old as parents go.

"So, what shall we do now?" asked Sandra.

"We could go over the park for a bit, see who's around."

"Or we could go back to mine, I've got some new tapes we could listen to." Again, Sandra made this sound like an order.

"I should probably go home I have stuff to do," said Karen feebly.

"Like what?"

"Well... I..."

"Just shut up and come on. Dad's in London today so we have the place to ourselves, we can have the music as loud as we like. Get in the mood for Saturday, we can also sort out what to wear."

Karen knew she was beat so she did as she was told. She was

relieved to hear that Bill wasn't at home. He was the reason she was reluctant to go. She hadn't seen him since the summerhouse incident and she didn't want to. He was making her do things she didn't want to and his manner had become more menacing of late. The unease and anxiety he caused her wasn't worth it, but she didn't know how to say no to him. She didn't want to see him anymore, yet she missed him. She didn't want him, yet she thought she loved him. She was a mass of contradictory feelings that she could not control. His very presence was persuasion. That's why she had decided the best course of action was to avoid him altogether, but it wasn't easy.

"Cheese or ham?"

"Sorry?"

"In your sandwich, cheese or ham?" repeated Sandra.

"Whatever you're having."

"Make a decision Karen."

"Cheese then."

The girls were eating their lunch when they heard a car pull up outside. The engine sound was very distinctive and they both instantly knew it was Bill's car. Karen's heart sunk, but raced at the same time. She tried to compose herself, she didn't want Sandra to notice the change in her demeanour although she felt sure it was obvious. Sandra herself seemed quite excited that her Dad was home; not surprised at all that he was supposedly early. They heard the front door open and Sandra got up from the table and went out into the hallway.

"Did you get it?" she asked him.

"Don't I even get a hello?" he asked, half-jokingly.

"Hello Dad. Did you get it?"

"Yes, it's in the car." Sandra pushed past him and went outside, Bill stood looking at Karen for a few seconds before he spoke.

"Hello Karen."

"Hello Bill."

"Where have you been hiding?" Before Karen could answer Sandra came running into the kitchen clutching a huge carrier bag.

"Thank you Daddy. You're the best. I'm going to try it on."

"I'll come with you," said Karen standing.

"No, stay there. I'll come down and show you both when I've got it on." Karen reluctantly sat down.

"Are you trying to avoid me?" asked Bill.

"No, I just thought she might need a hand."

"I'm sure she's fine," said Bill, moving closer to Karen as he spoke. "So, how's the boyfriend?" he asked staring at her.

"I don't have a boyfriend."

"Really, what about this boy from the football club?"

"He's just a friend."

"So he doesn't do this then?" he asked as he pulled her to him, trying to kiss her.

Karen extricated herself from him before answering.

"No. He doesn't."

"Good, because that wouldn't be right. Would it?" said Bill seemingly ignoring her rebuff. He went to say something more but was halted by the sound of Sandra coming down the stairs.

"What do you think?" She said, as she swept into the kitchen in a stunning dress, twirling in front of them for good measure.

"Pragtige," said Bill. "Beautiful," he repeated in English.

"Wow," said Karen, who was almost lost for words. The dress was beautiful but made Sandra look so much older than she actually was. Karen's mother would never let her wear a dress like that. Although there was no danger of her ever being able to afford one in the first place. "Are you going to wear it on Saturday?" Karen asked.

"No, Daddy is taking me to a new restaurant in Mayfair. I shall wear it then. This is far too good for the football club."

"Right, I need to do some work," said Bill. "I'll see you girls later."

"Okay," said Sandra. "Oh, Karen is staying over on Saturday."

"I'll see you on Saturday then," said Bill to Karen with a wry smile.

◉

The football club party was a long, tedious evening and both Sandra and Karen were bored very quickly. Sandra tried to persuade Ryan to leave half way through but he wasn't going to go before the presentations had been made. This was because it was patently obvious that he would win the lion's share of the awards: he was the leading goal scorer again, club captain and he hadn't missed a match or training session. The more cynical among the team believed it had more to do with the fact that his Dad supplied the kit than his footballing ability. Either way the girls had to prepare for a long evening. When the final award had been handed out Sandra stood up and looked at Ryan, her expression clearly saying let's go now. She walked towards the door, the others followed barely having time to say goodbye to anyone.

The clubhouse was on the opposite side of the park to Sandra's house so they decided to walk across the park. Karen hoped that nobody she knew saw her as she was not allowed to walk across the park at night. Sandra and Ryan walked ahead, they stopped when they reached a small clump of trees and sat down at the foot of an old sycamore. Karen and her 'friend' went to sit there too.

"Hey mate, find your own tree," said Ryan, winking.

They walked along a little further, there were no more trees so they settled on the first bench that they found. They had been sitting there, in silence for about ten minutes before he made his move; very subtly stretching then lowering his arm behind Karen's back, as he did this she turned towards him, he leant across her to kiss her, clumsily missing her mouth. He tried again, this time he reached his target, it was still clumsy and awkward but Karen found herself responding regardless. He did not try anything else, they sat talking for a while before they were interrupted by Sandra and Ryan.

"We'd better get back," said Sandra to Karen. The four walked across the playing field to Sandra's house, they said a long, lingering goodnight at the back gate before the girls went into the house. When Bill heard them close the door he straightened the curtains in Sandra's room then tiptoed across the landing into his own room.

Karen woke up to a whirring sound, she looked up and saw Sandra sitting at her dressing table blow-drying her hair. She raised herself up on her elbows, as she did Sandra saw her reflection in the mirror.

"Morning sleepyhead," she said turning off the hairdryer. "What time is your Mum coming?"

"What?"

"Your Mum, what time is she picking you up?"

"She's not," said a bemused Karen.

Sandra turned round to face her instead of conducting a conversation through the mirror.

"You said you were going out, that's why you weren't sure if you could stay."

"Oh yes." Karen had completely forgotten the story she had told Sandra when she was trying to come up with reasons not to stay. "I'm not going with them now."

"I wish you had said. I've arranged to meet Ryan, in about twenty minutes," she said looking at her watch.

"That's fine. I'll get up now and walk home." As Karen got out of bed there was a knock on the bedroom door.

"Come in Dad."

"Morning girls," said Bill handing each of them a cup of tea. "What's your plan today?"

"Well, I'm meeting Ryan. Karen's going home."

"I can drop you both off."

"I'm meeting Ryan in the park."

"And I'm happy to walk," said Karen quickly.

"Nonsense, I'll drop you home, I have to drop into the office anyway. You don't need to rush though," he said noting that Karen wasn't even dressed yet. "Just come downstairs when you're ready."

Karen didn't argue, it wasn't worth wasting her breath. He always got his way. She got ready quickly and went downstairs with Sandra who said her goodbyes and went to meet Ryan.

"I'll get my shoes," said Karen to Bill. He took hold of her arm and pulled her towards him.

"I said there's no rush. Anyway, I want to hear all about your evening."

"It was fun," said Karen, offering no more than that.

"Fun! How so?"

Karen stared at Bill, he didn't seem happy.

"I saw you," he continued when Karen didn't answer him. "With him, sitting on the bench. You get a good view of the park from

Sandra's room."

"We weren't doing anything."

"I think you were, but let's be clear. It won't happen again. I'll drop you home now." Karen was relieved that he was taking her home. She thought he would want her to stay and she didn't want to, certainly not when he was in one of his moods. She put on her shoes and picked up her overnight bag from the bottom of the stairs. They got into the car and Bill accelerated off the drive, he turned left instead of right. Karen looked at him.

"I have to pick something up from the office," he said, answering her unspoken question. "I thought you might like to come for the ride." Karen smiled nervously, she really just wanted to go home but it seemed there wasn't a choice.

Bill's office was actually a flat above a shop in town, he owned the shop too but leased that out. The flat had a kitchen, bathroom and three other rooms. The largest of the rooms was his office; it had a huge oak desk by the window with a large black leather chair. There were three telephones on the desk, she wondered why he needed three. Along one wall was a row of grey metal filing cabinets, above them were four clocks, all set at different times. Along the opposite wall was a large chesterfield sofa. Pinned on the wall above the sofa was a map of the world which almost covered the entire wall. The room next to the office had a further three sofas in it, they sat around a very large coffee table. Karen was unable to see what was in the third room as the door was closed.

Bill walked into the office and sat at the desk, he motioned for Karen to sit on the sofa. He rummaged through a few papers then swung the chair round to look at Karen.

"What shall we do now?" he asked her.

"You're going to take me home," said Karen, surprised at her assertiveness.

"What's the hurry?" he said, lowering himself from the chair until he was kneeling at Karen's feet. He began running his hands along her legs, smiling at her.

"I can't be late back," she said.

Bill ignored her and pulled at her trousers. Karen wished she had put her jeans on instead of her joggers, this was far too easy for him.

"I don't think we have time," protested Karen.

He didn't speak. When it was over he got up and left the room. Karen touched her cheeks, they were wet, she hadn't realised she was crying. Bill came back into the room, he sat down on the sofa and pulled Karen close to him.

"I'm sorry," he whispered. "I'm truly sorry, I didn't mean for it to be like that. I didn't mean to upset you." He gently kissed her face. "The thought of someone else touching you makes me a little crazy, you are so very special to me."

They sat silently side by side for a moment. "Are you okay?" he asked. She nodded. "I have something for you." He stood up and went to the desk. He opened the bottom drawer and took out a small box, handing it to Karen. She opened it, inside were a pair of earrings, gold with a pale blue stone or was it violet, the colour seemed to change in the light. "That's tanzanite," said Bill.

"They're beautiful."

"Like you."

"Thank you."

"Come on, I'll take you home now."

2010

S he gave the work surface another wipe down then stood back to admire her handiwork. The kitchen was gleaming; bright as a new pin, that's what her Nan would've said. Cleaning had been quite therapeutic and it seemed to have lessened the effects of her hangover, or maybe the tablets had kicked in. Either way she felt more human and was ready to face Andrew. As she thought of Andrew she realised she had better let him know she was able to pick up the boys from school. She picked up the phone, but then thought better of it. I'll text, she thought to herself. She replaced the hand-set in its cradle and took her mobile out of her handbag. His reply was almost instant;

'Leaving work early. I'll pick up boys. Coming home for overnight bags then dropping them at Mum and Dads X'

"Shit," said Karen out loud.

She clearly was in trouble, the only time Andrew arranged for the boys to stay with his parents was their anniversary when he hoped for an 'intimate' evening or when he had something serious to discuss with her. She rubbed her head, the headache was returning. Although she wasn't looking forward to this evening she was quite glad she didn't have to do the school run or think about feeding the boys. She'd stick to her original plan; cook

Andrew's favourite meal and hope it lessened his anger. But first she needed to sleep.

"So how do we go about this? I've never actually blackmailed anyone before," asked Sandra.

Nikolaas raised his eyebrows at her.

"Well not personally."

"First things first. You need to call her and arrange to meet again."

"I know that. But what do I actually say. Meet me, because if you don't I've got some interesting photos to show your friends and family."

"You don't mention anything about the photos or money until you see her, face to face. She mustn't have time to think or time to tell anybody else. You'll have to come up with a plausible reason as to why you want to meet."

"Like what? We really did say everything we had to say last night."

"Think, you're an intelligent woman and a devious one at that. I'm sure you can come up with something."

Sandra slumped back in the armchair. She had hoped that after last night she would not have to look at Karen's face ever again.

"I suppose I could say I have some photos to show her, give her even. Photos of us with Yvonne; I did mention photos last night. I could say I forgot to give them to her."

"Okay, good. You must be friendly towards her, get her to meet you somewhere public, lunch tomorrow."

"Then what?"

"Then you show her the photos."

"Of Yvonne?"

"For goodness sake. No." Nikolaas held his head in his hands despairingly; but then lifted his head smiling.

"Actually yes."

"What?" Asked a confused Sandra.

"Show her the photos of Yvonne and in amongst them put the other photos. When she sees them she'll be horrified."

"Obviously."

"And that is your moment. You explain you need her to meet you next week and sign a contract relinquishing any monies bequeathed to her by your Dad. Tell her when she's done that you will give her the photos."

"If she refuses."

"Then you tell her you'll send them to friends and family," said Nikolaas. "And to her husband's clients. He may only make folders and the likes, but he deals with some big companies who would balk at any embarrassing scandal being linked to them, no matter how tenuous."

"My, you have done your homework," Sandra muttered with a hint of sarcasm.

"One of us had to."

She glared at him.

"Why can't she sign tomorrow?" she asked.

"Because we don't have a contract yet. I'll need to get Benjamin to find someone here we can trust and get them to draw up a new document. Okay?"

"Okay."

"Phone her."

"Now?"

"No time like the present."

"I'll do it later."

"Do it now. We only have a few days left to complete this, so let's not waste any more time."

"And what are you going to do?"

"I'm going to contact Benjamin. Thank goodness they're only an hour ahead at home. I don't think he'd appreciate being woken in the small hours for this.

As he left the room Sandra scowled at him. Sometimes he forgets who's in charge here, she thought to herself. She picked up her mobile and searched her contacts. How fortunate it was that Andrew called last night, it had given Sandra the opportunity to obtain his and Karen's phone numbers. She pressed the call button. It rang several times before going to voicemail, she hung up without leaving a message and immediately tried again.

Karen turned over in her bed, she wasn't asleep, yet not fully awake either. She was in that blissful moment where if she closed her eyes and nestled down into the duvet she would succumb to sleep once more. She had set her alarm so as to give her time to get ready for Andrew and the boys, but it hadn't gone off yet so she could allow sleep to win. As her eyes closed and she pulled the duvet over her shoulders once more she heard a sound. It took a few seconds for it to register that it was her phone, she stretched an arm out from under the covers and reached over to the bedside cabinet where she had left it. As she picked it up it stopped ringing; missed call, unknown number. She put it down, almost instantly it rang again, same thing, caller display said unknown number. Probably some marketing call she thought. Karen muted the phone and placed it back on the cabinet. She lay there for a minute but the moment had passed, she was awake, properly awake. The possibility of an additional few minutes sleep had been denied so she got up.

Sandra hung up a second time, slightly miffed that Karen hadn't answered. Little early for the school run, she thought looking at her watch for confirmation. She'd try again in a little while, for now she'd see how Nikolaas was getting on. The door of the other room was closed, she could hear him talking, in Afrikaans. She chuckled to herself, she had convinced him that her knowledge of this language had disappeared along with her childhood. She stood outside, straining to hear the one-sided conversation.

"So hoeveel… Vyftien duisend… dit is 'n baie… Ja, ek weet dit is kort kennisgewing… ok dit stelso."

(How much… Fifteen thousand… that's a lot… I know its short notice… Okay set it up)

Sandra opened the door just as Nikolaas ended the call.

"All good?" she asked.

"Yes, Benjamin knows someone who can help. He will fax a template through to him and he'll draw up the paperwork. He also has an office we can use."

"That's good."

"It doesn't come cheap though."

"How much?"

"£25,000"

"What?"

"I know."

"Twenty-five grand for a piece of paper."

"And use of his office and an independent witness. He is taking a risk and it has to be done quickly."

"I suppose we have to go with it then," said Sandra.

"We do babe. Have you arranged to meet Karen?"

"No answer."

"Then why are you in here? Keep trying," shouted Nikolaas.

Sandra hated how his mood would turn at the drop of a hat, but she nodded and left the room. She still ached from his earlier wrath. She picked up her phone and tried Karen's number again, while it was ringing she pondered something, who would get the additional £10,000? Voicemail again, this time Sandra left a message.

"Karen darling, it's Sandra. You know I've just realised I never got to show you the photographs that I have. In fact I'd like you to have some of them. How about lunch tomorrow? 1 o'clock at The Melrose. I believe that's still there. Ciao."

Karen's phone rang again, she picked it up, caller unknown. God they're persistent she thought. She was about to put the phone back down when it pinged, alerting her to the fact that a message had been left. She was about to listen to it when the back door flew open and in walked Andrew and the boys.

"Mummy," screeched Seb, who was always pleased to see her. "Did you go on the big truck with the flashing lights?"

"Sorry?" she said looking at Seb quizzically.

"He's talking about the car. I told them about your puncture. They wondered where you were this morning," said Andrew.

"Oh the puncture, yes. Well no I didn't go on a truck.They just came and changed the wheel for me this morning."

"Oh," said Seb, clearly disappointed.

"Right, get changed and get the bits together that you want to take to Grandmas."

"I need a snack first," said Seb, his head already inside the cupboard.

"I don't want to go," said Charlie. "Grandma's house sucks."

"Just get your stuff and don't speak like that," snapped Andrew.

Charlie, please don't argue with your Dad, thought Karen. Not now. I don't need his mood worsened by one of your tantrums.

"Come on," said Karen. "You know you'll have a nice time."

"Yeah great. No Xbox, no sky and rubbish food," mumbled Charlie as he went upstairs.

When both boys had gone upstairs to get their bags, Karen walked over to Andrew and wound her arms around his waist.

"I'm sorry."

"I know," he replied, peeling her arms from him. "But we still need to talk."

"Okay. How long will you be dropping the boys?"

"Well I can't just dump them and run, especially the mood Charlie's in."

"Oh your Mum can handle Charlie."

"I'll probably be a couple of hours."

"Text when you're on the way back and I'll get dinner on."

"I fancy a curry tonight."

"I'll make curry then."

"No I'll pick one up."

"You can't have a takeaway again," said Karen.

"Why not?" Asked Andrew looking incredulously at her.

"No that's fine, absolutely fine."

"Right I'll see you later then. Come on now you two," he shouted up the stairs.

September 1977

"Can you believe it?" said Sandra as she walked up the road to school with Karen and Yvonne "It's our final year. We're fifth years now."

"Thank God," said Yvonne. "The sooner I leave this dump the better."

"It's not that bad," replied Sandra. "Is it Karen?"

"I'm with Yvonne on this one. I will not be sorry to see the back of this place."

"Wow, you're agreeing with me over Sandra," said Yvonne sarcastically. "Wonders will never cease."

"What do you mean by that?" Karen asked.

"Well, you do rather do whatever Sandra wants most of the time."

"I do not."

"You do."

"She does not. Stop being stupid Yvonne," shouted Sandra. "Can't we start this year without you being grouchy all the time?"

"I am not grouchy."

"You are. You have been all summer."

"That's rich, I've hardly seen either of you all summer. The pair of you have been too busy, spending all your time with Ryan and his pal."

"Actually, Ryan's pal, as you call him, is no longer his pal. He changed football teams over the summer and doesn't hang around with him anymore. I don't think Karen has seen him either."

Yvonne looked at Karen.

"Sorry."

"It's no big deal," said Karen shrugging her shoulders.

"Why didn't you call me?" asked Yvonne.

"Because you're always with Jason."

"Well I haven't been. Jason chucked me."

"So why didn't you call me?" asked Karen.

Yvonne and Karen looked at each other laughing and shaking their heads.

"You both could've called me," said Sandra.

"Why has Ryan chucked you too?"

"Don't be ridiculous."

This made Karen and Yvonne laugh even harder.

They made it into school just as the bell rang.

"See you at break-time," said Sandra whose tutor room was in the opposite direction to Karen and Yvonne's.

"So, what have you been doing all summer?" Yvonne asked Karen.

"Not a lot."

Karen could hardly tell her what she had been doing. Every Friday evening she met Bill at his office in town. This was the new arrangement; it was harder to snatch time together and more often than not Sandra was at home or entertaining in the summerhouse, so Bill decided they should have a place to meet at a regular time on a regular day. He said his office was the perfect place as Sandra never went there. When he had suggested this to her Karen was not very impressed by the idea as she didn't think it the most romantic of settings in which to meet, but he was adamant it was the only place they could spend time together. The first time she met him there she was pleasantly surprised; the third room in the flat was in fact a bedroom, a large bedroom, tastefully decorated. It reminded her of a posh hotel room, not that she'd ever stayed in a posh hotel, or any hotel for that matter, but this was how Karen imagined a posh hotel room would look. It was subtly lit and he had put flowers in the room. That first evening was lovely, Bill was a gentleman. Not only had he bought flowers, but wine and chocolates too. They had a takeaway and went to bed; he was gentle and undemanding. For the first time, Karen truly felt like his girlfriend, for surely that was what she was now. Not that he had actually said that, of course. But that was what she thought. The subsequent Fridays weren't always like the first, sometimes he was clearly not in such a romantic mood, he just needed the relief that Karen offered. She looked forward to and dreaded Fridays in equal measure. Her relationship with Bill still confused her; but she loved him and was sure that he loved her too, despite how he treated her on some occasions.

The girls met up at break-time. They were bemoaning the fact that they were in hardly any lessons together this year. This was because it was their final year and the focus was on exams; they hadn't actually chosen many of the same subjects and the subjects that they were all studying like English, Maths and Science were streamed. Sandra as always was in the top set, Karen one below and Yvonne in the bottom. This had more to do with Yvonne's attitude and attendance than her ability.

"We're never going to see each other," moaned Yvonne.

"We need to pick a regular day to get together and stick to it," said Sandra.

"Okay, When?"

"How about Fridays. We can go to mine straight from school and spend the evening. My Dad goes out every Friday to some meeting so we'll have the place to ourselves."

"What about Ryan? He might not like that," said a cynical Yvonne.

"Football training."

"I can't do Fridays," said Karen.

"Fridays it is then."

"I can't do Fridays," repeated Karen a little louder this time.

"Of course you can," said Sandra.

"No I can't."

"Why not?"

"I have to babysit."

"Every Friday?"

"Yep."

"Why?"

"Mum goes out every Friday."

"Where?"

"Evening classes," said Karen surprised at how easy the lies were coming.

"Can't your step-dad babysit?"

"He does shift work, so he's not always there."

"Well Friday is the only day we can do."

"We could pick another day," said Yvonne.

"No Friday is the day," insisted Sandra.

"I can't do Fridays, so if there isn't another day you'll have to count me out," said Karen hoping to call Sandra's bluff.

"Fine," said Sandra.

"Why don't we make it Fridays but when Karen has to babysit we go to hers and when her step-dad is home we can come to yours," Yvonne said to Sandra, desperately trying to find a compromise.

"That won't be much fun. There's no room for a start and if she's babysitting we'll have to put up with her brothers who are so irritating and Debbie."

This remark rankled Karen, despite the fact that it was true; it was one thing for her to criticise her family but she didn't actually like it when somebody else did it, especially when that somebody else was Sandra. If she was completely honest she didn't want the girls to come to hers anyway, but she wanted to be the one who said it.

"Just do it at yours and I'll come when I can," said Karen giving into Sandra.

"Great," said Sandra with a triumphant grin on her face. "Let's start this Friday."

2010

"I got you a Chicken Balti," Andrew said as he removed the foil cartons from the bag.

"Thank you." Karen reached up and took a couple of plates from the cupboard. "I'll dish up. You open some wine."

"You want wine? Didn't you have enough last night?"

Here we go, thought Karen. She ignored him and continued dishing up. They ate in the kitchen instead of the dining room. She watched as forkfuls of curry disappeared from Andrews's plate very quickly. It was almost as if he didn't want his mouth to be empty therefore allowing him an opportunity to speak. Karen sensed this so she spoke first.

"I am sorry." He nodded but continued eating. "I don't know what else to say."

Andrew put his fork down and pushed his plate away.

"You didn't even phone, I was worried. But you were clearly having such a great time that you couldn't even be bothered to phone."

"It wasn't like that. I must have passed out."

"Christ. How much did you drink?"

"Too much to drive I know, but I don't know why I passed out. It must have been the whiskey."

"You don't like whiskey."

"I know, but Sandra wanted me to go to her room and look at something and I was going to call a taxi and she said have a nightcap before you go and I did and then…"

"What? Then what?"

"That's when I must've passed out."

"And that's it, that's all that happened?" Andrew shouted.

"Yes, that's all that happened. Look I'm sorry. I didn't plan it, I've never done it before and I won't do it again. Now stop shouting at me."

"Why didn't you call before you went up to her room?"

"I was going to but I had no signal in the restaurant, then … well the rest you know. I'm not going to keep repeating myself."

"I was worried, okay, I spent half the night awake worrying about you."

"I don't know why. Sandra said she spoke to you, so you knew I was safe."

"I knew you weren't lying in a ditch somewhere, I knew you hadn't crashed the car, I did not know you were safe."

"What?"

"You were with her."

"Is that it? After all these years she still intimidates you."

"She's a nasty, vindictive bitch."

"Well yesterday she was a grieving daughter and she needed a friend and that's what we were, once. Friends."

"And are you friends again?"

"No, not really."

"So you have no plans to see her again."

"No."

"Good."

"Anyway she'll be returning to South Africa in a few days so I'm sure I won't ever see her again."

"Just promise me you won't."

"Don't be daft."

"Please, every time she turns up she brings trouble with her."

"Andrew you have to move on you know."

"Promise me."

"Fine. I promise."

Karen began clearing away the dinner plates and loading the dishwasher.

"Leave that," said Andrew, topping up their wine glasses. "Let's watch a film or do you fancy an early night?"

Karen grinned at him.

"Let me clear up and I'll be with you. I'd really rather not come down to this in the morning," she said.

"Okay, don't be long."

She continued tidying up, set the dishwasher and wiped over the worktops. She picked up her mobile phone to put it on charge overnight and noticed she had a voicemail. That's right she remembered, that came through as the boys arrived home, she decided to listen to it before she went to bed.

"Damn," she whispered to herself after listening to Sandra's message. She couldn't meet her, not after promising Andrew and besides she had photos of Yvonne. She didn't look at them anymore, but she had them. Karen wasn't sure whether to ignore the message or call her back. She didn't really want to speak to her, she decided to text her. Sandra replied instantly:

'So sorry you're unable to make lunch. But I think it's vital you see the photos I have. I'll bring them to you. I don't mind waiting. The Ridgeway, isn't it? What number? Sandra X'

Karen looked at the text, horrified. Sandra was coming here, no that couldn't happen. Bloody hell! What is so 'vital' about these photos? Although Sandra didn't have her exact address Karen knew it wouldn't take much for her to find it. She had no choice, she would have to meet her, despite her promise to Andrew. There was no way she could allow her to come to her home. Karen texted back:

'I can meet you after all, a little later though. 2 pm. Karen X'

Sandra's reply was brief:

'Perfect X'

Karen put her phone on charge, turned off the light and went up to bed. As she walked into the bedroom she could hear the faint rumblings that was Andrew snoring. Thank God for small mercies she said to herself.

December 1977

Autumn gave way to winter very quickly; the days were dark and damp, sometimes it was hard to tell if the night had ever left. For Karen, the miserable outlook reflected her own feelings. Life at home was difficult, whatever she did or said was wrong. Her Mum was constantly moaning at her and before long the moaning became full blown angry tirades. Karen argued back, she felt her Mum's criticisms of her were unfair. Her Mum responded in kind and so the arguing and shouting at each other continued on a daily basis upsetting everyone in the house. It was clear they all blamed Karen for the discord in their home and before long she didn't have an ally left. Her only respite was school and Friday evenings with Bill. School had never been her favourite place but she enjoyed catching up with Sandra and Yvonne, however Karen often felt side-lined by them both these days. It was plain to see that Sandra and Yvonne had become closer over the past few months due to the 'Friday club'. Karen had only been able to go to twice, when Bill had been unable to see her as he had things to attend to. She resented their friendship, especially as it was her who had brought them together in the first place and so often in the past it had been her who had to keep the peace between them. Yes, school was becoming as depressing a place as home was.

Karen often found herself in detention: usually for back chatting or not doing her homework or just being disruptive. But quite frankly, she was beginning not to care. When she felt certain teachers were picking on her she just decided to skip their classes. It became quite easy to 'bunk off', as long as you were there at tutor time when the registers were taken nobody seemed to notice if you didn't actually go to all of your lessons. The problem with skipping class was knowing what to do with yourself or where to go. She couldn't go home as there was always someone at her house and she could hardly walk around the streets, someone who knew her or worse knew her Mum was bound to spot her. So she started going to Bluebell Wood and it wasn't long before she realised she wasn't the only person hiding there.

"Well look who it isn't?" said Paul Adams. "Have you come over to the dark side?" he laughed at his use of the phrase made famous by the Star Wars movie.

"Get lost," said a belligerent Karen. She was in no mood for Paul Adams. She was fed up, cold and now it was starting to rain.

"Don't be like that. I'll keep you company if you like."

"I don't like."

"Suit yourself." He went to walk away when the heavens opened, so instead he joined Karen under the tree she was sitting beneath. The tree canopy offered little protection from the rain and before long they were soaked.

"We can't stay here," said Paul.

"Where do you suggest we go? We can hardly go back to school yet."

"I'm going to Trev's. Come if you like."

"Trev's?"

"Trevor Gardener."

"I thought he'd moved?"

"No, he just don't really bother with school anymore."

"Can't say I blame him, yes I'll come. If you're sure he won't mind."

"No, it's cool."

It only took about five minutes to walk to Trevor's house but by the time they got there they were both soaked through. Trevor opened the door. He was surprised to see Karen but happily let her in.

"Got some clothes I can borrow mate while my uniform dries?" Paul asked him.

"Yeah, sure."

"Do you want something else to put on?" Trevor said looking at Karen.

"No, I'll be fine."

"Suit yourself."

The three of them went to Trevor's room. The boys sat on his bed, Karen sat on a chair by the window. She was feeling uncomfortable as she was wet and cold, a feeling that wasn't helped when Paul decided to opened the window.

"Do you have to open that?" she asked him.

"Yeah, we're gonna have a smoke."

"Seriously, just put on a pair of my trackies until your clothes are dry," said Trevor.

Karen looked at them both.

"Okay I will."

Trevor got off the bed and got her a pair of tracksuit bottoms and jumper from his wardrobe, he threw them at her giving her directions to the bathroom at the same time.

"Or you can get changed in here," said Paul, "we don't mind."

Karen went to the bathroom, got changed and hung her clothes on the radiator. When she walked back into the bedroom the boys were rolling a cigarette, a rather large cigarette.

"What's that?" she asked.

"Come on Kaz, don't play dumb. You must smoke this stuff all the time with your junkie pal."

"I don't have a junkie pal"

This comment elicited hoots of laughter from the two boys.

"Surely you've had a smoke with Yvonne?" asked Paul.

"No, I haven't and anyway she smokes cigarettes, roll-ups sometimes, but not that stuff."

More laughter ensued.

"What's so funny?" she asked.

"Karen, Yvonne smokes this more than we do."

"Yeah and she does a lot of other stuff too," added Trevor.

"Like what?"

"All sorts, she gets in from that boyfriend of hers, Jay."

"Ex-boyfriend," corrected Karen.

"You want some?" asked Paul holding the joint out towards her.

"No," said a horrified Karen.

"God, you sound like your other mate now. The uptight one."

"You mean Sandra."

"Yeah, Sandra. I went out with her for a bit you know."

"I remember."

"She was a nightmare. Don't do this, don't do that. Talk about bossy."

Karen laughed, that did sound like Sandra.

"Come and sit down," said Paul shifting up the bed to make space for her. She did, he offered her the joint again and this time she took it. It took a few attempts before she inhaled properly, when she did she wasn't sure what the fuss was about.

"I don't feel anything," she said, a little disappointed.

"You will."

They passed the joint around a few more times, he was right, she did feel something but it wasn't nice, she actually felt a bit sick."

"I think I need to get to the bathroom," she said, trying to get up from the bed. She stood up and sat down again straight away. "I feel a bit wobbly."

"Here, I'll help you," said Paul laughing at her. He got up and escorted her to the bathroom, he shut the door behind them.

"You okay?" he asked.

"Yes," said Karen through mouthfuls of giggles.

"What's funny?"

"I dunno." She turned round, stumbling, pushing Paul against the door with her body.

"Sorry."

"It's fine."

She tried to stand up straight, but Paul held onto her. As she looked at him, he kissed her.

"Why did you do that?" she asked.

He shrugged.

"But you've never liked me."

"I like you now."

Karen looked at him, then she kissed him. He kissed her back and then slid his hands up under Trevor's over-sized jumper. She in turn put her hands into his trousers searching for him. A knock on the door made them stop.

"Oi, hurry up. I need to get in there."

Reluctantly, they opened the door and let Trevor in.

"Take your time mate," whispered Paul as they passed each other.

Back in Trevor's room, Paul and Karen picked up where they'd left off and before long they had both removed 'Trevor's clothes' and were laying on his bed. Karen was astonished when Paul admitted he'd never done it before, she said nothing. He was clumsy and awkward, unlike Bill and it was over very quickly.

◉

"Where have you been?" Yvonne asked Karen at afternoon registration.

"I went home for lunch today." Karen looked at Yvonne who was staring at her. "Sorry, I meant to tell you."

"Forget lunch, what about before? "

"Before what?"

"Lunch?"

"What?"

"We had a fire drill. You weren't here."

It was Karen's turn to stare at Yvonne. The bell went signalling the end of tutor-time. Above the sound of scraping chairs and childish chatter Karen heard Mr. Harpers voice.

"Karen Matthews, stay behind please."

◉

"So, what happened?" asked Yvonne as they walked home.

"I'm on report."

"That's not so bad."

"So where were you, earlier?"

"Bluebell Wood."

"Tell me next time I'll come with you."

"Don't encourage her," chimed in Sandra. "She got off lightly this time, next time they'll probably call her Mum."

"They did call her," chipped in Karen.

"For a first offence, that's out of order," said Yvonne.

"It's because of the fire drill. Apparently they have to locate everyone who should be in school. They thought maybe I had a dentist or doctor's appointment and hadn't told Harper."

"But it was only a drill."

"I know, but they have to act as if it's a real fire. They had to search the school for me and it made the drill longer than it should've been."

"So it's your fault we had to stand outside in the rain," said Sandra.

"I wasn't the only one."

"Really, who else?" asked Yvonne.

"I don't know," she lied. "Harper said I wasn't the only person missing. I'd better get home, get this over with."

"Good luck."

◉

"Do you have any idea how embarrassing it is to get a phone call like that?"

"So you were embarrassed not worried," shouted Karen back at her Mum.

"I'm talking about the second call. When they first called, of course I was worried. But when they phoned to say they had found you and you'd been playing hooky… "

"Hooky. Is that even a word?" Said Karen laughing at her Mum.

"Don't get smart with me. You are in a whole heap of trouble young lady. So where have you been?"

"School."

"You're trying my patience."

"Just walking around. Can I go now?"

"No, we are going to get to the bottom of this."

"Bottom of what?"

"This, you, your attitude."

"I bunked off, got caught, end of story."

"Karen, what is going on with you lately? You're moody all the time, you're argumentative. Even the school said they're concerned about you. This isn't like you, is there something wrong?"

"Give it a rest Mum. I hadn't done my homework so I decided not to go to that lesson. Just my luck they had a fire drill." Karen walked out of the room, slamming the door behind her. She stomped upstairs to her bedroom, slamming that door too. She threw herself down on her bed. What a day! She lay on her bed looking around her room, she hated her room. It was tiny, just enough space for her bed and a dressing table. A small recess had been turned into a wardrobe; well it had a rail between the two walls, no door, just a bright red curtain across it. The walls were lined with woodchip wallpaper; around her bed it was ripped where Karen had picked out the small wooden pieces during moments of boredom. It was painted an off-white colour which just made it look dirty. White artex covered the ceiling, there was no definite pattern to it as is usual with artex; this ceiling was just covered with random swirls and incomplete circles. There were some posters on the wall, but they were faded and curling up on the corners; clearly they'd seen better days. Yes, she did hate this room and she hated this house, this street, this neighbourhood, school. She wanted to pack a bag and leave, right there and then. But where would she go? She knew she had to bide her time, but she resolved in that moment that she would leave as soon as she was able. I'm going to leave school, get a job and a flat of my own. This became her mantra.

2010

K aren woke early, she tiptoed out of the bedroom so as not to wake Andrew and went downstairs. She made a pot of coffee and then began planning how she could keep Andrew and the boys busy this afternoon while she went to meet Sandra.

◉

Sandra woke early, she tiptoed out of the bedroom so as not to wake Nikolaas and went downstairs. She made a pot of coffee as she went over in her head the plan for this afternoons meeting with Karen.

◉

Karen was lost in her thoughts when she heard the flip flap of the letter-box as the newspaper was delivered. She poured a cup of coffee for Andrew, then refilled her own cup and took them upstairs. She collected the paper on the way.

"Morning."

"Hi," said Andrew sleepily.

Karen placed the coffee cups at their respective bedsides then got back into bed. She plumped up her pillows and began reading the paper.

"Do you have to read that?" Asked Andrew placing his arm across her.

"No," answered Karen realising he had other ideas. She folded the paper and dropped it on the floor then slid back under the duvet. She wasn't really in the mood but decided it would make him more agreeable to her plan.

Afterwards she lay with her head on his chest.

"Do you have plans today? She asked.

"No. I have a free day, no work to catch up on, thank goodness. I've actually got a whole weekend off. You got anything on?"

"Not really. I do have to pop into town: return a dress and pick up some dry cleaning. Thought I might have a look around the shops while I'm there. You want to join me?"

Andrew gave her a look that clearly said, no thanks.

"Didn't think so. Why don't you take the boys to the cinema?"

"Maybe."

"Go on, I could drop you then meet you afterwards and we could go out for dinner, the four of us, we haven't done that for a while."

"Sounds like you have it all planned."

"I do," she said.

"Okay then. Why not?"

❧

Sandra finished her coffee and put the cup in the sink. Footsteps overhead told her that Nikolaas was now awake. She sighed, no doubt he would make her go over the plan yet again. They'd rehearsed it endlessly last night, going over all the possible responses they might get from Karen. Sandra was sure they had covered everything, although she was unhappy that they were having to resort to blackmail; a situation that was her fault, as Nikolaas kept reminding her. She felt sure it would go smoothly, one thing she was certain of was Karen's love for Andrew; after all she had obviously forgiven him those indiscretions that Sandra had told her about. No, she most certainly would not want Andrew to see these photos, thought Sandra.

"Morning," said Nikolaas walking into the kitchen.

"Hey," said Sandra.

"Sleep well?"

"Yes."

"Quite happy about today?"

"Happy is not the right term."

"You know what I mean," said Nikolaas, pouring himself a cup of coffee. "Are you okay about it?"

"Yes fine. I'm going to have a shower," she said.

"I thought I'd come with you this afternoon."

Sandra stopped in the doorway.

"Why?"

"In case a bit of persuasion is required."

"I think the photographs are persuasive enough on their own."

"Alright, maybe persuasion is the wrong word; intimidation."

"You're going to be intimidating?"

"Yes I am, or menacing, whatever it takes. She needs to know who she's dealing with."

"I think I can adequately convey that," said Sandra. She went to walk away when Nikolaas jumped up and grabbed her arm.

"I am coming with you."

Sandra shook her arm from his grasp.

"Fine," she said.

end of school.

"Don't blame you," said Yvonne. "Don't fancy P.E much myself, Maybe I'll join you."

"Oh, alright."

"Where you going then?"

"Just the woods."

"You gonna just sit in the woods?"

Karen shrugged. "There's nowhere else to go."

"We could go to Jay's. I was supposed to meet him after school anyway."

"You back together?" asked Karen.

"Nah, just need to see him about something. You want to come?"

"No thanks."

Karen quickly walked across the field and ducked through the hedge and crossed the road to the footpath that led to the woods. Yvonne went the opposite way towards the park. As she walked Karen heard someone call her name, she turned round to see Paul running towards her.

"You walk fast," he said.

"Sorry."

They walked along silently for a few minutes, then Karen spoke.

"Where we going?"

"Trev's, for a smoke."

"Okay."

When they reached Trevor's house they went round to the back garden and let themselves in the back door.

"Hey," called out Paul. "You here Trev?"

"Up here."

They went upstairs to Trevor's room. He had another friend with him who Karen didn't recognise. They were already smoking a huge joint which they passed to Paul first. He had a few puffs then passed it to Karen. This time she took it without hesitation. A couple of joints later and Karen and Paul both began to get very giggly and flirty, it wasn't long before they started kissing.

"Take it outside," said Trevor's friend.

Karen just laughed, but Paul stood up and took Karen's hand and led her out of the room. He pushed open a door opposite but stopped when he heard Trevor.

"Not in there mate, that's Mum's room."

They went into the bathroom. As they closed and locked the door someone shouted downstairs.

"Come up," shouted Trevor. Two people came up the stairs and into the room. "Got my stuff?" One of them threw a small plastic bag into Trevor's lap.

"Cheers."

"Can I use your loo?" asked the other one.

"Paul's in there having a shag," said Trevor.

"Don't you mean having a ..."

"No, I mean a shag. He's got a girl in there."

The bathroom door opened, Paul came out, closely followed by Karen. They walked across the landing and back into the bedroom. The bedroom was a little crowded now so they had to manoeuvre themselves around to find some space, as they did Karen was horrified when she came face to face with Yvonne.

◉

"You and Paul Adams?" Yvonne asked Karen as they walked to school the next day.

"No," said Karen defensively.

"I do know what you were doing in the bathroom."

"We weren't doing anything." Karen could feel her cheeks warm as she began blushing.

"You so were."

"We were not. Anyway, what about you and Jason?"

"We're friends."

"So are Paul and I."

"Good friends I'd say. Sandra is going to love this."

"You can't tell her."

"Why not?"

"Yvonne, please," Karen pleaded.

"Oh alright. So are you going out with him?"

"No. I told you, we're just friends."

"I've missed you my sweet," said Bill as Karen walked up the stairs to the flat. She smiled to herself. They walked through to the room that served as Bill's meeting room, he'd bought fish and chips which he'd already plated up on the coffee table. "Tuck in while they're still hot," he said.

While Karen started eating Bill went into the kitchen and got a bottle of wine from the fridge and two glasses. He came back in poured them each a glass and sat down next to her. They finished their meal and drunk a glass of wine each. Bill took the empty plates into the kitchen, when he came back he picked up the wine bottle to refill their glasses.

"No more for me," said Karen who despite her best efforts still had not developed a liking for wine. Bill ignored her and filled up her glass.

"Have another, then you can have your Christmas present."

Karen sipped the wine, it wasn't nice: dry, acidic and it left an after taste in her mouth that wasn't pleasant. She'd much rather be drinking lemonade or juice; something sweet tasting that wasn't going to make her a little woozy, but Bill clearly expected her to drink the wine, so she did. When she had finished he picked up the bottle and glasses and beckoned for her to follow him into the bedroom, she was a little disappointed as she had hoped she would get her present now. On the bed, in the centre was a beautifully gift wrapped box. It clearly wasn't jewellery, thought Karen, as it was too large. It wasn't huge, but it was larger than most of the gifts Bill had given her before, unless it was a large box with a smaller one inside. Her Mum used to do that with Karen's birthday presents to prevent her from working out what it was before she opened it; a habit that would infuriate her Mum as Karen more often than not got it right. 'You take all the fun out of it' her Mum used to say; but for Karen that was the fun.

"Aren't you going to open it?" Bill asked.

She smiled and nodded. This one had her stumped, she couldn't imagine what was in the box. She hopped onto the bed and sat cross-legged with the present in front of her. Bill put the bottle and glasses down and sat on the edge of the bed watching her. She turned the box around, so that what appeared to be the front was facing her. She took hold of the ends of the large gold bow and pulled, the ribbon delicately fell to the side. She began tearing the paper, quickly as she was excited to discover what it was. With the paper gone she was still unsure what it was. A brown cardboard sleeve had her present trapped inside it. She lifted the box and tried to slide the sleeve off, Bill laughed as he watched her struggle; eventually she removed it and her present was revealed. It was a camera, an instamatic camera. Karen didn't have a camera so she was thrilled with it until she realised she would not be able to take this gift home. The earrings and small items that Bill had bought for her were easy to conceal but this would be impossible to hide; her Mum would find this and questions would be asked.

As if hearing her thoughts Bill said, "It's probably best if you leave it here, rather than having to explain where it came from. I don't want to get you into any trouble. You can always come and take it when you want to use it." Karen wasn't sure how that would work but didn't say so. "In the meantime we can have some fun with it," said Bill. He took the box from her and began removing the plastic casing and ties that were holding the camera firmly in the box.

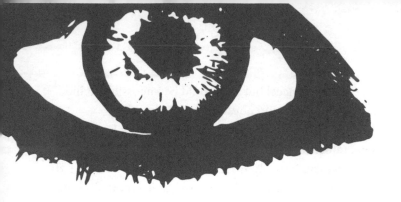

2010

Karen dropped Andrew and the boys at the cinema then headed into town. She had plenty of time before she was due to meet Sandra so she picked up her dry cleaning, changed her dress and decided to have a look around the shops. She went in and out of a number of shops, she usually always found something she liked but today nothing appealed to her; more due to her preoccupation with Sandra than the fashions that were on offer. She gave up on the shopping and headed over to The Melrose. Sandra wasn't due for another twenty minutes so Karen ordered herself a coffee and picked up one of the complimentary newspapers from a stand by the bar. She had visited The Melrose many times, but never on her own so she felt a little conspicuous. She looked around for somewhere to sit, opting for a table in the corner that allowed her to see the comings and goings but still afforded her a little privacy. She wanted to limit the risk of seeing anybody she knew, or worse who knew Andrew.

◉

Sandra and Nikolaas drove into town in relative silence; she only spoke to offer him directions as he was not familiar with The

Melrose or its location. The drive took a little longer than expected and she was already ten minutes late when they pulled into the car park. She undid her seat belt before they'd even come to a stop, once they had stopped Nikolaas took her by the arm for the second time that day.

"Right. Let's make sure we know how this goes."

"Nikolaas, I'm not going over it again. I know what to do."

Nikolaas eyed her, he thought better of pushing it further and hoped that this time she did not make a mistake. But if she did, at least he was here to rectify it.

Karen finished her coffee and folded the newspaper, she looked at her watch; it was almost a quarter past two, Maybe Sandra had forgotten, she wouldn't mind if she had, but then she may remember later and decide to come to the house. Karen began to panic, she could not have her at the house. She'd give her another five minutes, then call her. As she agreed this plan with herself the door of The Melrose opened and Sandra walked in, a man behind her was holding the door for her. Are they together? Karen wondered. He was a handsome man, broad-shouldered and tanned, maybe European, Aryan. Karen raised her arm, discreetly though, Sandra spotted her, nodding her acknowledgement of her before she turned and spoke to the man who had held the door for her. So, they are together, or maybe not. Karen was unsure as Sandra walked towards her but the handsome looking man went and sat on a stool at the end of the bar.

"Hi," said Sandra. "Sorry I'm late, traffic."

"It's fine."

"What are you drinking? Wine?"

"Coffee is fine, thanks."

"Oh come on. Don't let me drink alone," insisted Sandra. "Anyway, you may be glad of it," she mumbled.

"Just a small one," said Karen. "I'm driving."

"You were driving the other night. I'll get a couple of glasses." Sandra went up to the bar to order the drinks, she smiled at the man on the stool. Definitely together, thought Karen, or maybe would like to be. "There you go," said Sandra placing two glasses on the table.

"Thanks. Do you know him?" asked Karen indicating the man at the bar.

"Yes. He drove me here."

"He's welcome to join us," Karen continued.

"He's fine. So how are you? Recovered?"

It was obvious Sandra was not going to offer any more information on her companion, not even a name was forthcoming. But Karen's curiosity wasn't going to give up that easily.

"Fully recovered thank you. Does he have a name, your friend?"

"His name is Nikolaas, we work together. Was Andrew cross with you when you got home?"

"Not really."

Sandra raised her eyebrows at her.

"Well maybe a little," Karen added. "But he's fine now."

"Good. I'd hate to be the cause of any marital discord." Sandra said this with a visible smirk on her face. Karen didn't notice as she was rather pre-occupied with trying to discover a little more about the mystery man at the bar, who in turn was watching the two women very closely.

"Is Nikolaas just a work colleague or something more?"

"Karen," snapped Sandra clearly irritated. "I wish I'd driven myself now," she muttered.

"I'm just interested."

"Nosey, more like."

"Sorry. I won't ask any more questions."

"Good."

"Let's see these photos then."

BEWARE THE CUCKOO

165

"Good."

"Let's see these photos then."

April 1978

Karen could not believe she was being suspended from school. Her Mum would go mad. This was Paul's fault. He had told her she couldn't go round Trev's with him anymore, in fact, he didn't want her hanging round at all and if she was going to continue bunking off she had to find somewhere else to go. She had politely informed him that he did not own Bluebell Wood and if she wanted to go there she would. Which she did a few times, but it was boring on her own; almost as boring as the lessons she was avoiding. Karen didn't get it, she thought Paul was her friend, a good friend, she even let him… for God's sake. Now he wouldn't even acknowledge her, he barely even looked at her if they passed in the school corridor and because she couldn't hang out with him and Trevor she had been caught out. She had been wandering around and was bored and hungry so she had ventured into the housing estate that was on the other side of the wood so she could go to the shop and get a drink and something to eat. As she left the shop a car passed her, it stopped and reversed back, she was horrified to see her form tutor staring at her. He didn't speak, he pointedly looked at his watch, then looked back at Karen and then he drove off. Busted; there was no way Karen was going to get back to school before he did.

BEWARE THE CUCKOO

Her suspension was for a week and she was right her Mum did go mad. She added her own punishment. Not only was she not allowed at school, she wasn't allowed to go anywhere either. This meant she would not see Bill this week and she so wanted to as she hadn't seen him last week, she also had no way of letting him know. He had never given her his office phone number and he made it crystal clear that she wasn't to call him at home in case Sandra answered. She could call his home number and just pretend it was Sandra she wanted to speak to, but thought better of it. Sandra would lecture her and she didn't want to hear that at the moment and what would she say to Bill if he happened to answer? Sorry, can't see you as I've been suspended from school and Mum has stopped me going out; that sounded so juvenile and that's not how Bill saw her. He said it often enough; you're different, mature. He was right, that's why school is such a bore and why living at home is stifling and frustrating. She had outgrown them, not just school and home but her family and friends too. She had outgrown them all. Nobody gets me like he does, she said to herself, nobody.

The week really was the longest of her life. Her Mum took time off work to 'supervise' her; guard me more like, thought Karen. She had been set work by the school that she had to complete in order to try and catch up with what she had missed. Karen tried to convince her Mum that she needed to see the girls to find out how to do some of the work but her Mum was having none of it. Not only was she not allowed to see Sandra and Yvonne, she was not allowed to speak to them either. No visits, no phone calls, nothing; she was under house arrest and her mum was the jailer.

During the week Karen made plans for her future, she had already decided that once she had left school she would get a job and leave home, but now she added more details to this plan. It was having a plan that would get her through the remaining time at school. It would be virtually impossible for her to skip classes now, she had drawn far too much attention to herself. Still, there was only one term remaining, she could cope with that. The only obstacle on the horizon was Sandra, for Karen's 'plan' very much centred on Bill.

Karen's first day back at school was not great. As well as being on report she had to visit the office at the end of each lesson and at break times too. They really were going to keep an eye on her this term. She thought the girls would be pleased to see her but neither seemed too fussed over her return. Yvonne did ask a few questions about her week but Sandra wasn't interested in the slightest, In fact she was distinctly off with her. Karen recalled that Sandra had been a bit weird before the suspension. She asked Yvonne if she knew what was up with her, Yvonne had said she was just stressing out over the forthcoming exams.

"You know Sandra. The perfectionist, she has to come top in everything."

Karen did know, but she wasn't convinced that was the reason for Sandra's mood. Especially as Yvonne had looked rather embarrassed when she had asked about Sandra. Almost as if she knew what was wrong but couldn't or wouldn't say. Karen didn't ask again. She just concentrated on getting through the week, Friday was approaching which was not only the end of the school week it also meant she would see Bill. Karen was looking forward to seeing him, it had been three long weeks since the last time they had met. She left her house early as she decided to walk to Bill's office instead of getting the bus. She was determined to save as much of her money as possible from now on. It didn't take long to walk, the worst bit was walking along the alleyway that ran at the back of the shops. The bus would have dropped her on the main road and then she only had to walk down the side of the shop and up the backstairs; the alleyway was the quickest route but it was overgrown and not well lit. She quickened her pace as she walked through the alley and before long she could see the stairs that led to Bill's office. The door at the top of the stairs opened and a figure stepped out, it was a woman. Karen stopped walking and watched. The woman was tall with long, blonde hair. She was wearing a long coat, belted at the middle. She was standing having a conversation with someone in the doorway. At first Karen couldn't see who it was, but then as the person moved forward she could see it was Bill. He handed the woman something and then kissed her. Not a long passionate kiss, but a kiss nonetheless. Karen remained in the alleyway, watching and waiting for the woman to come down the stairs. As she disappeared from view, Karen breathed out, only then realising she had been holding her breath. The woman did not come along the alleyway so she must have walked around the side of the building to the main road. Before Karen reached the top step, the door opened to reveal Bill standing in the doorway she smiled at him and went inside. He shut the door behind her and when Karen looked at him closely she immediately knew he was unhappy about something.

"Where have you been?" he asked her.

"Am I late?" she replied, although she was sure she wasn't. The walk hadn't taken her as long as she had thought it would.

"Yes, by at least a week," was Bill's sarcastic reply.

"Oh." She got it now, he was alluding to her no show last week. "I had to babysit," she lied. "And I couldn't phone you, sorry."

"Ah yes, babysitting." He was staring at her as he spoke. "Sandra says you have to babysit most Fridays which is why you can't join her and Yvonne, but you and I know that when you say you're babysitting you're not, as you are actually here with me." He paused before continuing. "But not last week." Karen didn't speak, she knew that Bill knew she was not babysitting. How could she be so stupid; of course Sandra would have told him what had happened at school. "Are you going to tell me what happened?" he continued.

"I had a bit of trouble at school."

"You had a bit of trouble at school," he repeated. Karen nodded. "Tell me about this trouble at school."

"It's nothing really. I hadn't done my homework so I skipped a class and I got caught."

"A class?"

"Yes."

"And for that they suspended you?"

Why was she surprised that he knew that? Sandra would have told him about the suspension, in fact she would have left nothing out. She had probably added a few opinions and details of her own. Bill was no doubt fully aware of Karen's turbulent school-life so she decided to come clean, although she wasn't sure what the big deal was. It wasn't like he was her Dad.

"Okay. I've done it before. That's why they suspended me."

"Where did you go?"

"When?"

"When you should have been at school. Where did you go?"

"Just walked around."

"Just walked around."

Karen hated it when he repeated what she had said. It was the sort of thing her Mum would do or worse, a teacher.

"Do we have to keep talking about this? I'm sorry it happened because that's why I wasn't here last week but I'm here now."

"I think we do have to talk about it. I'd like to know what you were doing."

"I've told you," said Karen. "I was just walking around."

"Just walking around."

He was starting to irritate her now.

"Yes," she answered in a manner that she hoped told him to back off.

"On your own?"

"Yes."

"Are you always on your own?" Bill asked.

"Yes."

"Are you sure about that?"

"Yes, I a…"

Then the penny dropped; he knew she hadn't been alone. He probably knew she had been with Paul. But if he knew… how? Sandra must have told him, so she knew. That would explain her behaviour, why she had been a bit off with her. How did she know? Cheers Yvonne, thought Karen. Oh no, what exactly did Yvonne tell Sandra. Panic engulfed her, she looked at Bill.

He was watching her waiting for an answer, but her face said it all. As realisation dawned she had given herself away. She had not been alone, he did know that and now she had confirmed it. Exactly what had passed between them he wasn't sure, Sandra hadn't known either. He had his suspicions; however the situation would not occur again, he had seen to that. This was the second one he'd had to dissuade from paying Karen attention. He wouldn't tell her that, no he would just let her know how disappointed he was and she would have to make it up to him.

Karen did not know what to say, but she knew she had to say something. Her mind was racing, what to do: lie, confess, apologise or explain. She settled on explanation.

"Bill, I…"

The sound of the telephone ringing interrupted her, Bill answered it. He had quite an animated conversation with whoever was on the other end of the line, not that Karen could understand it as he was talking in Afrikaans. When he had finished he replaced the receiver on the handset and turned to look at her.

"I have to go out. I shouldn't be long, half an hour at most."

"Can't I come with you?"

"No," he snapped. "I'll be as quick as I can," he said a little more gently. "Wait for me, in there," he said nodding towards the bedroom.

Bill left and Karen went into the kitchen to get a drink, she opened the fridge, wine and milk were all that greeted her so she settled for a glass of water. She went into the office and looked out of the window, she watched as Bill drove off down the road, as he did she relaxed a little. This evening really wasn't going as she'd hoped. She wanted to talk to Bill about the decisions she had made, her plans, but so far there hadn't been an opportunity and she didn't expect that would change when he got back. Karen sat down at Bill's desk, there wasn't much on it. The three telephones sat side by side in a perfect straight line, there were some papers sitting neatly beneath a highly-polished piece of stone and a large leather blotter which didn't look as though it had ever been used as the paper was unmarked by ink although it had greyed with age. She spun herself around in the chair a couple of times. When it stopped spinning she noticed that the bottom drawer of the desk wasn't closed properly. She pulled it open and looked inside. It was a deep drawer but it wasn't full. On the top was what looked like a photo album, Karen took it out and opened it. It was a photo album but the photos weren't very interesting. They were just pictures of cars, not even nice looking cars. No sports cars or racing cars, these were jeeps, land rovers and small vans, all very dull and boring. At the back of the album were pictures of guns, lots of guns, all shapes and sizes. Strange thought Karen and then recalled that her Grandad collected pictures of trains and Mr. Pryor, the next door neighbour had a display cabinet full of model buses. Men are interested in odd things, she thought. She went to replace the album then spotted an envelope in the bottom of the drawer. It wasn't sealed so she took it out and looked inside. There were two photos inside held together by a paper clip. Karen was surprised to see that the photos were of Paul. She was confused why Bill would have photographs of him. Sandra had gone out with Paul, maybe they were hers, although these photos looked quite recent. She looked at them again, in both of them he was going into or maybe coming out of a house. She didn't think it was where Paul lived as she recognised this house and she'd never been to Paul's. She had seen this house recently, she concentrated for a moment, then realised it was Trevor's house. Karen was puzzled. Why were these photos here? Karen looked out of the window and spotted Bill driving down the road. She carefully replaced the photos in the envelope and put everything back in the drawer exactly as she had found it. She went into the bedroom and waited for him.

Bill hopped up the back stairs two at a time. Today had been a long stressful day but finally it had all come together, despite some last-minute hiccups. He was ready for a drink and Karen. He went into the flat and stuck his head around the bedroom door. She was sitting on the bed flicking through an old magazine.

"Hey," he said, causing Karen to look up. "I'll be with you in a minute, I just have to make a quick phone call. Get the camera out, we'll have some fun with it." He winked as he said this.

Karen smiled at him, but when he left she let out a huge sigh. He seemed in a better mood, which was good. But he wanted to get the camera out which was not good. 'Get the camera out and we'll have some fun with it.' It wasn't fun, not for her. It started out as fun; they'd pull silly faces, stand strangely, mimic people. But then he started making suggestions to her, they weren't too bad initially, you know, sit this way and that, put your hair up, then down. But as time went on he asked her to do other stuff that she wasn't keen on. Stuff that she felt awkward about and embarrassed and even a little disturbed. Reluctantly she took the camera out of the wardrobe; she would do as he asked, she always did. She decided to tell him her plan while he was taking the pictures, it might distract her from what she was doing.

2010

Karen gasped. Her distress was audible. Her mouth instantly dried and her hands began to shake. She felt light-headed and sick, physically sick. She prayed the feeling did not manifest itself as she was unable to move. Then her heart joined in, racing. The palpitations were loud; to her anyway. She could hear her heartbeat, it was getting louder. She was sure everyone could hear it, a rhythmic beat getting faster and faster, drumming in her ears like rain on a tin roof. It was disorientating; this must be what shock feels like. She knew Sandra was looking at her but she did not want to meet those eyes, she could not, she dare not. What could she say? They say a picture paints a thousand words. Karen put the photograph face down in her lap, as she did she saw the next one, it was worse, then the next and the next. Interspersed between photos of herself with Sandra and Yvonne were photos of her and Bill. She stopped looking at them and looked up at Sandra instead.

"Oh, you haven't reached my favourite one yet," said Sandra. "Here let me show you," she said reaching her hand across the table.

"No," said Karen. She picked up the photos and held them close so Sandra was unable to reach them. In a soft voice that was barely even a whisper she uttered an apology. "I'm so sorry."

"Sorry. You fuck my Dad and all you can say is sorry." Sandra's voice was rising; she had been devastated when she had discovered this truth but that devastation had given way to anger; an anger that had been simmering away for quite a while. She'd had to keep it in check for such a long time, but now it was ready to boil over.

"I'm really, truly…" Karen tried to continue.

"Save it for Andrew," Sandra said, for once remembering his name.

"You wouldn't?"

"Oh I would and not just Andrew. Your family and business associates too."

"Well you're not having them back," said Karen trying to quickly push the photos into her shopping bags.

"Oh silly me, I didn't think to make copies." Sandra feigned an exaggerated shocked expression.

"You have copies?" repeated Karen.

Sandra nodded.

"I do. Well that's not strictly true, in fact what you have are the copies; I have the originals."

"Who else has seen them?"

"You and I. Dad, obviously and Nikolaas," answered Sandra indicating her friend at the bar. Karen looked at Nikolaas, he raised his glass and winked at her. The nausea that had begun to abate, returned.

"The question is, not who has seen them but who will see them?"

"What do you want Sandra?"

"Money."

"Money? I don't have any money. Well not much."

"Oh but you do. It appears my Father has left you some money, my money actually and I want it."

"I don't know what you're talking about. I haven't received any money."

"No not yet, you haven't."

"Okay, then if I do I'll give it to you, that's fine. I don't want any money."

"Very generous of you," Sandra said with a note of sarcasm. "But that's not how it works."

"It's not?"

"No. What I need is for you to sign a document relinquishing this bequest."

"Fine. Give it here, I'll do it now." Karen was desperate to put an end to this. She wanted Sandra gone and she needed to destroy the photos. She had kept Bill and those times hidden away deep in some far off corner of her memory and now she could feel them slowly travelling back into her consciousness. If she wasn't careful Bill would return from the grave and disrupt her life all over again; a life that he had no business being part of anymore, a life that she loved and would do anything to preserve.

"I'm glad you understand," said Sandra. "However, it cannot be done today."

"Why?"

"One, I don't have the paperwork and two, it needs to be formally witnessed."

"So how, when do we do it?" Panic was seeping into Karen's voice again.

"Monday morning. Nine o clock. You come here," Sandra handed Karen a business card and pointed to the address on it. "You sign the papers, I give you the photographs and that's that. We never have to see each other again."

"Okay." Karen put the business card into her purse, tucking it into the folds of her driving license and stood up. Sandra also stood up, as did Nikolaas. The three of them left The Melrose together. They walked round to the car park and were surprised to find they had parked alongside each other.

"Until Monday then," said Sandra with a smile. Pleased that it had all gone to plan.

"Monday," repeated Karen faintly.

◉

Karen let Sandra and Nikolaas leave the car park first. Once they had gone she sat there for a moment, draped across the steering wheel. Tears stung her eyes, then she felt something rise in her throat, she leapt out of the car vomiting as she did. When she was done she went to the back of the car, she opened the boot and got a bottle of water from a multi pack that was in there. She took a few large swills then poured the rest of the water over her stomach contents that were leering at her from the tarmac of the car park. She looked around, thankfully there was no-one about. Glancing at her watch told her there was still a little while before she had to meet Andrew and the boys. Karen needed to get rid of the photos she had, there wasn't time to go home and she didn't just want to drop them in a bin or skip somewhere for fear they'd be found. She had to hide them until she could destroy them. She drove to the Retail Park and went to the stationers; she bought a large padded envelope, (well she bought a pack of them as this particular stationer didn't sell them individually - only bulk buys allowed) and some tape. She went back to the car and drove over to the far corner of the car park. In the safety of the car she took the photos out of her bag. She sorted through them, removing those of her, Yvonne and Sandra. The others she put into one of the envelopes. She sealed the envelope then wrapped several strands of sticky tape around it so it would be impossible to open without at the very least a pair of scissors. She got out of the car and opened the rear side door, then she lifted the back seat and taped the envelope to the underside of it. She then lowered it down and locked it back into position, being careful not to catch the seatbelt under it. The only time the rear seats were raised was if they had to transport something that wouldn't fit in the boot and they certainly wouldn't be doing that today as they had the boys with them. Karen was pleased with her hiding place, she would then be able to destroy these along with the originals that Sandra would give her on Monday. She sat in the front seat flicking through the pictures of herself with Sandra and Yvonne; three friends having fun. She sighed heavily as she recalled a simpler, more innocent time. Before sex and money complicated things. Before boyfriends, jobs, careers and children. When just passing the time with friends and having fun was all you cared about. Before Bill. From inside her handbag she heard her phone, it was a text from Andrew to say the film had finished. She put the photos in her handbag and went to meet him and the boys.

Sandra and Nikolaas decided to begin packing as soon as they got back to the house. They were on a deadline, once Karen had signed the money over they had seven days in which to get the document to Ben for him to file with the court. Then the nightmare would be over, the financial nightmare at least. Bill's legacy was not a great one, what Sandra had learnt about her father was not something she would ever reconcile herself with. It wasn't the women or girls, it wasn't even the gun-running. It was the lies and betrayals. Her whole life had been built on a series of untruths; from the fact that her mother was very much alive and kicking to the idea that Bill Davids was a legitimate businessman. The consolation to all this had been the money, so then to discover that was being taken from her too, well that was the final straw.

Sandra felt no guilt over her treatment of Karen, despite her reluctance to resort to blackmail. As far as she was concerned Karen had brought it on herself. Sandra had learnt about her Dad's weakness; a weakness fuelled and encouraged by girls like Karen. They all had ulterior motives; Dad's journals had taught her that. They all wanted something, mostly money. Some were blatant in their greed, straight out asking for money. Others were more subtle, pretending they really wanted him, a life with him. Even Karen had tried to entice Bill away, but he hadn't gone. He had seen through them all. So what changed? Why, in death did he want to give so much to Karen? What made her different? Sandra knew what she was, nothing more than a bloody cuckoo. She had always wanted what Sandra had. Her clothes, her house, her Dad and her money. Her musings were interrupted by a voice. Someone was speaking to her.

"Did you hear me?" Asked Nikolaas.

"No, sorry. I was miles away."

"I said, I've got us a flight Wednesday evening."

"Was that the earliest?"

"Yes. But, it's fine. We can go and see Benjamin straight from the airport and he can file the papers first thing Thursday. We're almost home now."

Sandra smiled at him. Yes the end was almost in sight. Debts paid and scores settled, that was all she wanted.

　　　　　　　　　　　BEWARE THE CUCKOO

Karen lost the argument. Pizza it was; her least favourite food, although truth be told she still didn't have much of an appetite following her 'episode' in The Melrose car-park.

"So how was the film?" she asked.

"Brilliant," said Seb.

"Bit boring," said Charlie.

"Special effects were good," said Andrew. "How was your day?"

"Good."

"I thought we could go to London tomorrow," said Andrew. "What do you think?"

"Maybe," said Karen. "What about you two?" she asked the boys.

"If I can get my trainers, then yes," said Charlie.

"Science museum," shouted Seb.

"We've already sorted it," said Andrew.

"So I see."

They planned Sunday's trip to London over dinner then headed home. Once home the boys went upstairs. Karen sat in the lounge.

"Wine?" Asked Andrew.

"No thanks."

"Are you alright?" He asked. "You were quiet at dinner and didn't eat a lot."

"I'm fine. Bit of headache, that's all."

Andrew poured himself a glass of wine then sat down next to Karen. He began flicking through the channels, finally opting for a film that had only been on for a few minutes. Karen tried to watch it but couldn't concentrate. It wasn't that the film required that much effort it was just that Karen's head was full of Sandra and the photos. She decided to go to bed.

She woke early Sunday morning after a fitful night's sleep. She lay there for a bit, trying to get back to sleep but eventually decided to get up and make a drink. As she sat on the edge of the bed, feet searching for her slippers Andrew woke and slipped a hand around her waist.

"Hey. How are you this morning?"

"Not bad," she answered.

"You didn't sleep well."

"I know, sorry. I didn't mean to wake you."

"It's fine. Are you sure you're up for our trip today?" he asked.

"Maybe. I'll see how I feel once I've had a drink."

"You stay here, I'll make it."

She didn't argue with him, instead she turned and slipped her feet back under the duvet. They had failed to find her slippers anyway. She awoke about half an hour later, the coffee on her bedside table was barely warm. She could hear Andrew in the shower. She didn't fancy going to London today, she didn't fancy going anyway today. The door of the en-suite opened and Andrew came into the bedroom, towel tied around his waist, he was still wet and water was dripping from him onto the carpet. Karen couldn't be bothered to moan at him.

"Why don't you stay here?" he said.

"Will you be able to cope with Charlie? You know how he gets."

"I also know he really wants those new trainers and as Regents Street is the last place on our itinerary I'm sure he will behave."

Karen smiled, it was true enough. Charlie would be fine if there was a bribe in it for him.

"Okay, I will stay here then." Karen stayed in bed until she heard them leave, then she got up and made a fresh pot of coffee. She took it into the lounge, curled up on the sofa and let the tears flow.

July 1978

Karen got up early and headed into town. She wanted to be at the job centre as soon as it opened. She was determined to show them. They'd all laughed at her when she said she was going to get a job and a flat, her Mum, Sandra, Yvonne, even Bill, especially Bill. He had laughed loudest. So, now the exams were over, she had officially finished school and she'd finally had her sixteenth birthday, it was time to prove them wrong. The job centre was a bit like the library; jobs were categorised by subject as books would be and nobody spoke as they walked around scanning the boards. After about fifteen minutes, walking from board to board and not finding anything at all a very official looking, bespectacled lady came over and asked if she needed some help.

"I'm looking for a job," said Karen.

"Yes, I thought so," said the woman amused, a slight smile played across her thin lips. "Any particular sort of job?"

"Don't mind."

"Why don't you come with me and we'll see what we can find."

Karen followed the lady to a desk in the corner of the job centre. Over an hour later, after endless form filling and phone calls Karen left the job centre. She had four interviews lined up, two that day and two more later that week. She headed back home to change, the lady at the job centre said it was best not to wear jeans to an interview even if it was only a shop job.

By the end of the week Karen had three job offers; two in a shop and one in a factory. One of the shop jobs was her clear favourite but she had to work out if it was worth it as she had to take two buses to get there. She was so pleased with herself, her Mum unfortunately did not share her joy.

"What about college?" Asked her Mum.

"I'm not going to college."

"Since when?"

"Since I decided I'm not going."

"Don't be cheeky. The plan was always for you to go to college."

"Your plan Mum. Not mine."

"Going to college will open up more opportunities for you. You could get a city job."

"I don't want a city job."

"But you're…"

"Mum, I'm not going to college. I've told you. I want a job, I want to earn some money and get a flat."

"It's not that easy."

"Well clearly it is. I have a choice of three jobs already so I'm halfway there." With that statement Karen flounced out of the house slamming the door behind her. She was going to meet Bill tonight, hopefully he would share her excitement or at least admit he was wrong. He hadn't thought Karen was employable either.

As she walked towards the park it started raining, she had neither an umbrella nor raincoat so decided to stop at the next bus stop and catch the bus. Karen had been trying to walk everywhere she went in an effort to save money but decided she would rather arrive at Bills dry. She only had to wait about five minutes for the bus, as she got on it a car she recognised went past. It was Bill, bad timing thought Karen, he could've picked me up. The bus had to stop at the next junction as the traffic lights were red, it pulled alongside Bills car. Karen looked down from her elevated position on the bus. She couldn't see all of Bill, just his arm and hand, a hand which was clearly on the leg of his passenger. Karen recognised the woman, but from where she wasn't sure. The lights turned green and Bill's car disappeared before the bus had rolled forward an inch. Karen reached Bill's office about twenty minutes later, his car was where he always parked it so he was here. Karen wondered if he was alone. She went up the stairs, the back door was open.

"Hello," she called out as she walked through the door.

"In here." His voice came from the office, Karen walked through and found Bill sitting at his desk reading a letter, he was on his own.

"How are you?" he asked without looking up.

"Fine."

"Just fine?" He asked placing the letter on the desk and turning to look at her.

"Actually, better than fine. I've got a job."

"Well done, that'll keep you busy in the holiday."

"It's not a holiday job."

"It's not?" He gave her a quizzical look.

"No, it's a full-time job, a permanent one."

"But what about college?"

"I'm not going."

"Don't be daft."

"What's daft?"

"You can't not go to college. Sandra and Yvonne are going."

"Good for them."

"What sort of job is it?"

"It's in a shop."

"A shop?"

"Yeah. It's a bit like Woolworths, you know sells everything. Well that's the one I think I'll take. I got offered three jobs but this one pays the most so I can save more and get a flat."

"A flat?"

"Yeah, I told you my plan ages ago."

"Christ. You haven't got a clue."

"Why are you being so horrible? I'm doing it for us too."

"What?" Shouted Bill. "Don't bring me into your foolhardy decisions."

"It's not foolhardy. It'll be good for us."

"How so?"

"If I have a flat you can come and see me and stay. We could tell Sandra about us too and then we can be together without it being a secret."

"NO," bellowed Bill.

"But, we… "

"No. We will not be telling Sandra anything."

"Bill, we have to eventually."

"Why? What do you think this is?"

"I don't understand," said Karen.

"You think we might live together? Get married? Is that what you think?"

"I thought, maybe, one day."

"Stop being so serious and come here." Bill pulled her towards him.

She hooked her arms around his neck and kissed him.

"Eventually though, it'll happen?"

"What will?"

"We'll get married."

Bill started laughing, a derisive laugh that angered her.

"But you love me," she shouted.

"I've never said that."

"You must love me."

"Must I?"

"Well you say I'm special. Isn't that enough?"

"Not for marriage it isn't."

"What is it enough for?" Asked Karen through angry tears.

"Nothing," spat Bill. "I'm not even sure that you're that special anymore. Not since others have been here," he said pointing at her crotch.

"That's not true," protested Karen.

"Don't lie to me."

"What about you? Who have you been with today?"

Bill stared at her.

"I saw you with her."

"What?"

"In your car."

"Have you been spying on me?"

"I saw you."

"And what exactly did you see?"

Karen couldn't really answer that question. After all, what had she seen... when she actually thought about it she didn't really know.

"Tell me," he repeated raising his voice.

"Nothing. I saw nothing."

"Go home Karen."

"Please Bill, don't send me away."

"I was wrong about you. You're just a stupid little girl, now go."

"I'm not Bill, please. Let me stay. I'm sorry." Karen was pleading with him now, at the same time holding onto him, touching him.

"Goeie god. Wat probeer jy vir my om te doen?"

(Good god. What are you trying to do to me?)

He grabbed her firmly by her forearms. "What do you want Karen?"

"You. I want you."

"I know exactly what you want," he said pulling her into the bedroom. When he was done, he looked at Karen and spoke to her with such vehemence. "Go home. You're not doing this to me anymore."

◉

Karen had been working at the shop about three weeks when she spotted the postcard. One of her duties was to remove and replace the advertisements that people put on the notice board. For a small weekly fee customers of the shop were allowed to place postcards on the board offering to buy, sell or, as in this case, let things. This was a new card so Karen knew she was the first person to see it. It read, 'Furnished flat to let – suit professional person' followed by a telephone number. The card didn't say where the flat was, but the phone number was a local one so hopefully that meant the flat was local. She wondered what constituted a professional person, she figured it just meant someone who was working. She decided to call at lunchtime so she removed the card from the board, folded it in half and slipped it into her pocket so no-one else would see it.

She arranged to view the flat on her way home from work. It was only a few streets away. I could walk to work she thought, getting ahead of herself. The flat was the first floor of an old terraced house. She rang the bell, she could hear someone coming down the stairs. The door opened to reveal a rather scruffy looking man, he wasn't very tall, with dark hair which Karen initially thought had flecks of grey in it but on closer inspection realised the grey flecks was actually white paint.

"Hi," he said.

"Hello," said Karen.

They stood looking at each other for a couple of seconds then he spoke again;

"Can I help you?"

"I've come to look at the flat."

"Have you?"

"Yes, I called earlier."

"Oh right. Are you on your own?"

"Yes."

"And you want to rent the flat?"

"Yes."

The man started laughing, it was a friendly laugh but Karen wasn't sure what he was laughing at.

"Terry sent you, right?"

"Terry who?" asked Karen.

He laughed again, then stopped abruptly.

"He didn't send you?"

"No-one sent me. I called earlier. I'm interested in the flat."

The man looked at her, scratching his head. As he did bits of emulsion floated from his scalp like fine snowflakes.

"How old are you love?"

"Sixteen."

"Sixteen," he repeated.

Why do adults always repeat what you say? Thought Karen. It had become a pet hate of hers.

"I have a job."

"That's as maybe, but I don't think this is right for you."

"Why not?"

He told her how much the rent would be and Karen had to agree, it wasn't right for her. She would need to earn at least four times what she was earning and then she wouldn't have money left for food or anything else. Her face dropped, she apologised for wasting the man's time and turned to leave.

"Hang on love," he called after her.

Karen listened as he explained that he did have other properties for rent.

"They're not like this though. They're bedsits."

"Bedsits?"

"Yeah, basically a room in a shared house. A locked room mind and quite large. Some have kitchen areas in them, others you share a kitchen and of course you share the bathroom."

Karen turned up her nose, she didn't fancy sharing a bathroom with people she didn't know.

"Thank you, but I think I'll keep looking."

"Okay love. But if you change your mind you have my number."

Karen headed home, she was incredibly disappointed, but she still felt sure she'd find a flat she could afford. However following another week of intolerable rows at home and fruitless searches in the classified columns of the local newspapers Karen decided she would have to rethink her options.

A bedsit it would have to be.

September 1978

It didn't take long to move into her new home. Karen didn't have much, just her clothes, some records and tapes and a few trinkets. It felt more like she was going on holiday than leaving home. She had butterflies, they were dancing around in her stomach, excitement or nervousness, could be either, she wasn't sure which. Her Mum's mood however was one of complete indifference. She offered no help or advice, although she did sort out some bed linen and towels for her to take and she allowed Karen's step-dad to drive her. The only hint that she even cared was the box of food that he handed to her when he dropped her off.

"This is from your Mum," he said.

After he had gone, Karen sat on the bed and looked around. It was a bit grim looking but the landlord had said she could put up pictures, change the curtains and even paint the walls if she felt so inclined. She was glad she had opted for the larger room that had its own kitchen area but was still rather nervous about sharing a bathroom. There were five other bedsits in the house, three were occupied by men, the one next door was another girl a few years older than Karen and the last one, the smallest room in the house, the other option available to her, was vacant. Karen began unpacking, the wardrobe was a huge wooden affair with plenty of room for her clothes, although for now they would have to be folded and put on the floor of the wardrobe as there were only two coat hangers and Karen hadn't thought to bring any from home. But first she decided to give it a good old scrub as a strange smell was emanating from it, a fusty odour that reminded her of the school changing rooms. As she unpacked she began making a list of the things that she would need to buy. The list was quite long, she wouldn't be able to get everything straight away, although most of what she needed she could buy at work, her staff discount would help. When she'd finished she decided to make herself a cup of tea; she had no kettle. There was a small saucepan in a cupboard in the kitchen area, probably left by a previous tenant. Karen gave it a wipe over and filled it with water. It took forever to boil, so kettle went to the top of her list.

◉

"I can't believe you've actually done it," said Yvonne. "I'm so jealous, I'd give anything to leave home."

"So when do we get to see your new abode?" Asked Sandra.

"Soon," said Karen. "Maybe next week," she added when she realised Sandra wanted her to be more specific."

"How about Friday?" Asked Sandra. "You obviously don't have to babysit anymore."

Karen didn't have to 'babysit'. She didn't do anything on Fridays anymore, not since…

"I have to be at work early on Saturday morning though. Can't you come Saturday or Sunday?"

"Sunday please," said Yvonne. "Sundays are soooo boring." She exaggerated the word so as if to prove her point.

"Sunday it is then," said Karen quickly before Sandra voiced an objection.

After she left the girls, Karen realised she had just over a week to get her room ready for guests, not just any guests either, this was Sandra she had to impress.

The days flew by very quickly, and before long it was Sunday. Karen got up early to give the room a thorough cleaning, not that it needed it but Karen wanted it to look as good as was possible when Sandra arrived. She had even bought a small bunch of flowers from work, they had to stand in an old jug she found in the cupboard as she didn't have a vase. Karen had painted the wall in the kitchen area to brighten it up and cover up some of the black marks caused by damp. It wasn't a cold day so she was able to open the window to let in some fresh air and get rid of the smell of paint. She looked around to see if there was anything else she could do, despite knowing that no matter what she did Sandra would find something to criticise.

"This is cool," said Yvonne.

"Thanks," said Karen. She looked at Sandra bracing herself for her comment. When it came it wasn't as cutting as she expected.

"I couldn't live in one room, but for you its fine. You probably have more space than you did before."

"I do," laughed Karen.

After a couple of hours Sandra suggested going for a walk. They walked down to the precinct. Everywhere was closed and there wasn't anybody around. Karen was surprised at how different it looked and felt when it was empty. It was eerie and soulless, like a ghost town.

"I'll show you where I work." She led the girls along to the top end of the precinct. "There."

"You don't have to walk far then," said Yvonne.

"No, it's perfect. I had to get two buses before."

"Is this what you intend to do forever?" asked Sandra.

"What do you mean?"

"You're a shop assistant," said Sandra with such a derisive tone.

"What's wrong with being a shop assistant?" Karen's voice was rising now as she became defensive.

"Come on you two, lighten up." Yvonne could see where this was heading and she did not want to be caught between one of their arguments.

"I don't see the point. I..."

"The point is I wanted a flat so I had to get a job," interrupted Karen.

"But you haven't even done that. I mean your room hardly qualifies as a flat."

"Sandra," shouted Yvonne. "I happen to think her room is fine, at least she has a place of her own."

"Well I think she's wasting her time and so does Dad actually."

"What's it got to do with your Dad?" asked Yvonne.

"What did he say?" asked Karen.

"It doesn't matter what he said." Yvonne was getting cross now. "So just shut up, both of you."

Surprisingly they did shut up. Yvonne looked at her watch, it was time she was getting back. She had an essay to hand in at college tomorrow and she hadn't even started it yet. Karen was lucky, she didn't have homework anymore or times to be home. She didn't have to answer to anyone, she could do as she pleased. Yvonne would give anything for that.

"I need to get back."

"Me too," said Sandra.

"I'll walk to the bus stop with you," said Karen. They walked without speaking, when they reached the bus stop they sat on the bench and Yvonne lit up a cigarette. She inhaled deeply, this had been her first cigarette for a few hours. She released the smoke slowly in rings.

"That's so unattractive," Sandra said turning up her nose.

"So, who am I trying to attract?"

Sandra didn't answer her.

"I reckon Karen will be first," said Yvonne.

"First what?"

"First one married. She'll marry a rich man and have lots of babies, then it will be irrelevant whether she went to college or not."

Sandra raised her eyebrows and Karen laughed.

Once the bus had disappeared round the corner Karen walked back home, as she did she played over what Sandra had said. Bill had voiced an opinion about her job, maybe he did still care? And what was it Yvonne had said? That Karen would be the first to marry and have lots of babies. She smiled to herself, but only for a second, for in that moment something occurred to her. Something so shocking that she ran the rest of the way home.

2010

A text came through on her phone, freeing her from a trance-like state. It was Andrew just to let her know that he and the boys had arrived in London and were on their way to the science museum. She sent a text back then reached for her coffee, it was cold. She looked at the time on her phone, she'd been laying here for over an hour. She stood up, remembering as she did the photos that she had hidden in the car. She decided to get rid of these ones today, less to deal with on Monday. She went upstairs, washed her face that was still damp from her earlier tears and pulled on an old pair of jeans and a sweatshirt. She went through the kitchen, putting the kettle on as she did and went out of the back door. She had decided it would be prudent to put the car in the garage while she retrieved the photos, free from prying eyes, particularly Sheila's prying eyes. Once she had removed the photos she cleaned the inside of the car, thoroughly, just to be sure no stray photo had slipped between the seats. When she'd finished she put the car back on the drive and went inside. She put the envelope containing the photos on the kitchen table and made herself a fresh coffee. She sat at the table, one hand wrapped around her cup the other palm down on the envelope as if she were afraid it would disappear before her eyes. Karen sat like this for a few minutes, then she put

BEWARE THE CUCKOO

down her cup and picked up the envelope. She wondered what would be the best way to dispose of the envelope and its contents. She didn't want there to be any possibility that the photos would be found. She had to destroy them completely. She figured burning them was the best option, but to burn them effectively she would have to open the envelope.

She took a pair of scissors from the drawer and began snipping through the layers of tape that she had wound around the envelope. When it was free of tape she removed the contents; she picked up a box of matches from the kitchen counter and went into the lounge. Today she was so grateful that Andrew had won the battle over whether to open up the fireplace or not. She had been very happy with the ornamental fireplace that was there when they had bought the house; she filled it with candles and it looked fine. Andrew, however had insisted on opening up the fireplace and having a log burner fitted. She opened the small door on the log burner and began scrunching up some old newspaper, she lit the paper, then one at a time began placing the photographs; into the flames. They burned slowly, the flame delicately eating away at the picture. Each photo curled as it burned, emitting a blue glow within the flames. When the last photo had disappeared in front of her she took the poker from its stand and began poking at the charred and blackened remains. She poked and prodded until she was sure nothing remained, no small scrap that could expose her folly.

"What are you doing?" Nikolaas asked as he walked into the room. "I thought you'd packed those away."

Sandra was sitting on the floor with all sorts of paraphernalia strewn about her. They were her Dad's journals and papers, relating to the time he was involved with Karen.

"There must be something in here," she said. "Something that will tell me why he left it all to her."

"Does it matter? Tomorrow you will get it all back."

"Yes. It matters. Why her? What singled her out? She wasn't the only one you know."

"I know. You've told me. But truly Sandra it doesn't matter anymore. Let it go."

"I can't let it go," said Sandra. "I have to know. Don't you get that? My father bequeathed a sizeable chunk of his fortune to my school friend. I have to know why, I need to know why."

"You know why, look what he did to her."

"There has to be more," argued Sandra. "And can you not say it like it was all his fault. She's not the innocent you think."

"She was a child," shouted Nikolaas.

"She was a whore," countered Sandra.

He stared at her. There was no point arguing any more. When it came to her father there was no reasoning with her. She knew what he was, but nobody else was allowed to say it.

"If it bothers you that much, ask her."

"Ask who?"

"Karen."

"She won't tell me."

"She will if you make it a condition for handing over the photos."

Sandra looked at Nikolaas and nodded.

"Maybe," she said. "Maybe."

◉

Once it had cooled down Karen swept out the contents of the log burner into a dustpan and tipped it into the bin. The blackened scraps floated into the bin like confetti caught on the breeze; albeit black confetti. She lifted her foot and the bin lid closed, the relief was wonderful until she realised she would have to do this all over again once Sandra hands over the original photos. She sighed, today was going to be a long day. She needed to clear her head, get some fresh air. A walk, that's what she would do, go for a long walk. She rummaged through the basket in the cupboard under the stairs in search of her trainers.

She pounded the pavements, up one road and down another, striding in a military fashion. Marching but with no clear direction. She needed to walk and walk quickly as if her pace was the key to eradicating the ghosts that were haunting her once more. Before long she found herself at the park, she began walking across the playing field; now she had a direction. Karen had visited the park on numerous occasions with Charlie and Sebastian but she had never before felt the need to stray towards Bill's old house. The years had consigned memories of that time to the farthest reaches of her mind, hidden in a sealed box in a room behind a locked door. But now the door had been unlocked and the box ripped open in the cruellest possible way allowing the memories of that time to spill out and dance around in front of her; taunting her, tormenting her and threatening everything that she held dear.

Bill's house wasn't as visible as it used to be, it no longer had a view across the park. The garden had matured over the last thirty-something years, trees had grown to form an evergreen shield around the property. Karen got as close as she could and peered through a gap in the trees. It was just as she remembered it, even the summerhouse was still there, although on reflection this summerhouse did look much smaller, so was probably not the original one. The house looked the same, a bit dated, in need of some attention but still the same. So much had happened to her in that house. Karen blinked, her cheeks were wet again. She stepped back, wiped her eyes with the heel of her hand and continued her walk.

September 1978

"You're kidding me," said Yvonne.

"I'm not," said Sandra.

"But you said Karen was mad to leave home."

"I said she was mad not to go to college."

"Yeah, but you don't think much of her flat, do you?" said Yvonne.

"That's because it's not a flat. She lives in a room, one room, she doesn't even have her own bathroom. Mine will be a flat and you can move in with me if you want."

"Oh my God, yes. What about Karen?"

"What about her?"

"Aren't you going to ask her to move in too?"

"She didn't ask us."

"I know, but maybe we should"

"She probably didn't ask us because she wants to live on her own. She did say she liked having her own space."

"I suppose," said Yvonne "So when are you getting it?"

"Soon. Dad's working on it. He owns the lease on a few shops that have flats with them and some are empty."

"I can't believe you told your Dad you wanted a flat for your birthday. Won't he miss you?"

"Of course," said Sandra confidently. "But he also thinks it's a good idea as he is away a lot more these days and he'd feel happier knowing I wasn't on my own."

"I'm going to start packing tonight," said Yvonne excitedly. "This is going to be so amazing."

"Calm down," Sandra said laughing. "It may take a few weeks, which will give us time to find jobs."

"Jobs?"

"Yes jobs, we will have to pay for things you know."

"I know, but, I erm, I don't think I can leave college."

"You won't have to. We can get part-time jobs."

"Oh yeah, well that's okay then."

◉

"You look awful love. You feeling okay?"

Karen looked at Rita, her supervisor, smiled and nodded. Truth was she didn't feel okay, she was anything but okay. She hadn't eaten or slept properly since Sunday. She had dragged herself into work these past couple of days, in the hope that it would provide a distraction from her despair. It didn't. Her head was full of nothing else and even if there was a temporary moment of relief, when she had to deal with a delivery or serve a customer, something in the shop would soon remind her of her situation.

◉

Bill closed the file in front of him, stood up and strode over to look at the map on the wall. At first he couldn't see the Cayman Islands; they're so small, he thought. His accountant had suggested he look to invest in property in the Caymans. Benjamin had supported this view too:

"Willem, it's a good idea. You need to plan for the future, South Africa will change, it may take time but it will change. It has to. You need to put your money somewhere safe, where they ask no questions and where they will not take a huge chunk of it in taxes. There are no taxes on profits, capital gains or income charged to foreign investors. And no estate or death duties payable on Cayman Islands real estate or other assets held in the Cayman Islands."

He was right. Things were already altering in South Africa. The Soweto Uprising and its brutal suppression by the apartheid government had made the United Nations Security Council enforce the arms embargo. Of course this was actually good for business, for now. But Bill knew that eventually the arms embargo would be followed by economic sanctions, which would inevitably hinder the flow of money through South Africa. Botha had just become Prime-minister and although a little more liberal than his predecessor he was still against black majority rule. And it wasn't just South Africa that was changing, the Internal Settlement had just been signed in Rhodesia. The conflicts were still ongoing in the region, and Bill was sure there was more money to be made but the fact that the United Nations were becoming proactive meant that the risk was higher.

Bill walked back over to the desk and sat down. Perhaps a trip to the Caymans would be a good idea he thought. Get Sandra settled first though, he smiled to himself. He had been surprised that she wanted to leave home, but then she was very grown up and independent, as he'd always wanted her to be. She was strong and self-reliant, qualities he admired, qualities he had. Still, he had expected her to ask for a car, after all it was her seventeenth birthday. Maybe he'd get her a car too, as a surprise.

"What did your Mum and Dad say?" Sandra asked.

"Mum's fine. I haven't told Dad. Mum says I should go and then she'll tell him afterwards. She knows he's unfair on me," said Yvonne.

"Pity, she doesn't stick up for you more."

"Yeah, I know. But it's hard for her. She can't go against my Dad. He changed when Dean went you know."

"So is Saturday October 14th okay for you?" asked Sandra, keen to change the subject."

"Okay for what?"

"Moving."

"Yes, absolutely. Jason can bring my stuff round, he has a car now."

"I have a car. I can come and get your stuff."

"I know. Lucky thing. Can't believe you got a car and a flat for your birthday. You still can't drive it yet though, you haven't passed your test."

"So, Dad can sit next to me and it's probably best Dad doesn't see Jason anyway."

Yvonne was a bit put out, but she knew better than to argue. She didn't want to give Sandra the opportunity to change her mind. As long as Sandra didn't think she was going to stop him coming round once they had moved in, after all this was going to be her home too.

Sandra was glad Yvonne didn't argue. She'd have to make it clear to her that Jason wasn't welcome at the flat but she'd wait until they had settled in first. She didn't want to put Yvonne off as the only condition that her Dad had applied when she had said about moving out was that she had to have a flat-mate.

Karen was surprised to see Yvonne waiting for her outside work.

"Hello," she said. "What you doing here?"

"I wanted to see you. I have something to tell you," replied Yvonne.

"That's funny, I have something to tell you too." For Karen had decided to confide in her oldest friend.

Yvonne linked her arm through Karen's as they walked; "Go on, you first," she said.

"Wait till we get back to mine." Karen really didn't want to speak her truth out in the open.

Yvonne sat on the bed while Karen made them both a drink.

"Do you want something to eat?" Karen asked her.

"No, just a drink is fine. Hurry up and tell me your news, then I can tell you mine," said Yvonne excitedly.

"You go first." Karen could clearly see that Yvonne was desperate to tell her whatever it was and she also knew that after she revealed her secret Yvonne may have lots of questions for her.

"You sure? Okay then. I'm leaving home."

"Really? How? When?"

"Well," said Yvonne pausing. "Here's the thing, someone asked me to share a flat with them."

"That's great. You've been wanting to leave longer than I had. Can you afford it though?"

"I got a job; collecting glasses and washing up evenings at The Lion."

"Brilliant."

"It's okay for now. Luckily the flat is quite cheap."

"So who you sharing with, someone from college?"

"Yes, kind of." Yvonne looked at her friend. She hesitated before speaking, unsure what Karen would think. "It's Sandra."

"Oh... right, I see." Karen tried hard to retain her composure; she didn't want Yvonne to see how upset she was.

"You alright with this?" Yvonne asked her.

"Absolutely. A little surprised, that's all. Didn't think Sandra wanted to leave home."

"No, who'd have thought she'd ever leave Daddy."

"Exactly."

"I did ask Sandra if she was going to ask you to move in too, but she said you liked living on your own."

"I do, yes. So where is your flat?"

"Bridge Street. Other side of town, nearer college. It's one of Bill's flats. I tell you he has houses all over the place."

Hearing Bill's name was the sucker punch. She stood up and went to make another drink so she could conceal her face, she didn't want Yvonne to see how upset she was.

"So what's your news?" Yvonne asked.

"Oh. I, it's nothing really. Not as exciting as your news."

"So, tell me anyway."

Karen stuttered and stumbled over her words, trying to think of something to say. She wasn't going to tell Yvonne the truth, not now.

"I got a pay rise," she said.

"Oh. Well done," said Yvonne, although she didn't think Karen's news was that interesting. "I have to go soon," she said as Karen handed her another drink. "I'm working tonight."

After Yvonne had gone, Karen lay on the bed. She reached for a pillow, pulled it towards her, hugging it tightly as she wept. It was the middle of the night when she woke; she looked at herself, she was still dressed in her work clothes, even her shoes. She sat up and then she remembered. Remembered her conversation with

Yvonne, remembered her predicament. She needed help, but who to ask? Not Yvonne, not now. Her Mum, no way. There was only one person left, the only person she could ask and the one person she did not want to see.

2010

"Good God, you look dreadful this morning," said Andrew rubbing sleep from his eyes.

"Thanks," said Karen.

"Are you okay?" he asked. "Maybe you're coming down with something," he said answering his own question.

"I'm fine. Just didn't sleep so well."

"I slept like a log," said Andrew jauntily.

"I know," Karen responded through gritted teeth. She had always been jealous of Andrew's ability to sleep no matter what.

"The boys wore me out yesterday. You coming into the factory today?"

"Maybe this afternoon. I have a few things to sort out this morning."

Karen decided to drop the boys a little earlier than normal. She didn't want to be held up at the school gates by someone who had nothing better to do than stand and gossip. It was always the same old conversations anyway; mostly grumbles about the school. Whoever it was moaning only had to walk a few feet and they could take their complaints to whom it concerned and bother someone who gave a shit. Today Karen was only thinking of her own situation and the impending meeting rather than the petty gripes of fault-finding fathers and mal-content mothers. She also wanted to allow herself plenty of time for her rendezvous with Sandra for although she knew where she was going she had no idea what the traffic would be like or where she should park. Nothing could go wrong today, Karen could not afford to give Sandra any reason not to hand over the photographs; her life was at stake here. Well, maybe not her life as such, but the life she lived. The life she loved, with Andrew, the boys, everything she held dear. The thought of potentially losing it all brought a lump to her throat.

◉

"Come on Sandra. We need to be there before Karen. I want to check everything is as it needs to be," called Nikolaas up the stairs.

"I'm coming," she shouted. Under her breath muttering; "ongeduldig gat." (Impatient arse)

◉

Karen need not have dropped the boys so early. It took no time at all to reach the address that Sandra had given her, it wasn't even twenty to nine when she pulled into the car park. She reversed into a space and killed the engine. As she did she noticed another car come into the car park, it was Sandra and her friend, Nikolaas. Karen slid down in her seat hoping they hadn't spotted her, she wanted a few more minutes on her own to compose herself before facing Sandra. She watched as they got out of the car and crossed the road. Sandra was carrying a briefcase; they must be in there thought Karen, remembering the photographs, the reason she was here or maybe he has them. Sandra's friend was also carrying a briefcase. To anyone who saw them Sandra and Nikolaas looked like two business professionals on their way to work. Only Karen knew different, they were two people whose reason for being here was a lot more sinister than another day at the office. She looked at her watch, quarter to nine, almost. Time was moving very slowly.

◉

Nikolaas pushed on the door, it didn't open. He looked at Sandra.

"Try the buzzer," she said, sounding a whole lot calmer than she felt.

He did.

"Yes," a man's voice crackled through the intercom.

"Benjamin Vorster for Geoffrey Soppell," said Nikolaas. A loud buzzing followed and Nikolaas pushed the door, this time it opened.

"That's not your name," Sandra said.

"He doesn't need to know my name and besides he already knows Ben's name."

Sandra shrugged and walked through a small corridor that led to another door. The door opened as she reached it and she was greeted by an outstretched arm.

"Miss Davids, welcome."

The voice belonged to a rather short gentleman with very little hair. He was rotund with a cheerful, ruddy complexion. He brought to mind an image of a monk. He had a slight accent that definitely wasn't British but Sandra didn't believe it was South African either.

"So how is it you know Ben?" Sandra asked.

"I've known Ben for many years. I boarded with his family when I left Hobart."

So the accent is Australian, well Tasmanian, thought Sandra.

And he lived with Ben's family. Interesting. She wondered if he knew her father too.

"And you are?" he asked looking at Nikolaas. "For I know you are not Benjamin Vorster."

"I'm a colleague of Miss Davids," replied Nikolaas tersely, making it very clear he had no plans to offer his name.

"Quite," said the portly gentleman. "This way please," he continued, ushering them through to his office. Another man was already sitting in the office. "This is my associate and your witness and as we've already established, I am Geoffrey Soppell. My first appointment isn't until ten so I've told my secretary not to come in until half past nine. That should give us plenty of time to wrap this up. The other party should be here soon?" he said looking at his watch as he spoke.

"Yes," said Sandra.

"Splendid."

"Shall we deal with the payment while we're waiting?" asked Nikolaas.

"Splendid," said Geoffrey.

Nikolaas put his briefcase onto the desk, opened it, removed a large brown jiffy bag and handed it to Geoffrey.

"Splendid."

Geoffrey's use of the word splendid was beginning to grate on Sandra but she tried not to let it show.

"Aren't you going to count it?" she asked him.

"That won't be necessary." He paused before adding, "I'm sure it's all fine, after all we have an accord." Sandra was about to respond when they were interrupted by the door buzzer. "Showtime," said Geoffrey nodding at his associate who stood up and went to open the door. "Just to be clear, I want no interruptions or interjections from either of you. I shall conduct this matter within the bounds of the law. Anything either of you need to say or do, I do not want to be privy to, therefore your side of this deal has to be completed outside of this office. Is that clear?"

"Crystal," said Nikolaas.

"Splendid," uttered Geoffrey as the door opened and in walked Karen.

October 1978

"Penny for the guy."

Karen looked up, three young boys were standing in a shop doorway with a rather pathetic looking guy at their feet. The guy had very long legs; old jeans stuffed with newspaper, that were tied at the bottom of the legs with orange string. His body was a brown jumper unevenly stuffed so that one arm was significantly fatter than the other. His face was a brown paper bag with drawn on features. Karen continued walking up the street, followed by more shouts of 'penny for the guy' and the intermittent sound of exploding fireworks. The fireworks had been going off for several days now and it was still over a fortnight until bonfire night. When she reached the phone box there were two boys in it, they weren't on the phone they were just using the shelter of the phone box to light their cigarettes. Once they realised Karen was waiting they came out. As Karen stepped into the phone box the tobacco smell filled her nostrils making her feel nauseous. Karen leant on the side to steady herself and picked up the handset.

She tried his home number first, now that Sandra had left home it was unlikely she would answer, unless she happened to be visiting of course. Not that Karen was going to talk to him over the phone anyway. No she was using the phone to find out where he was. Nobody answered so she tried the office phone number, she hoped he was there, it had taken some time to find out the office number and she didn't want it to be a wasted effort. It rang twice then she heard Bill's gruff voice before the pips began. She hung up; he was at the office. Karen was glad, the office was nearer than Bill's house and there he would most likely be on his own.

It took her about ten minutes to walk to the office. She looked up at the window from the street, she could vaguely make out the silhouette of someone sitting at the desk. She walked up the side of the shop and round the back of the building, she hesitated at the bottom of the stairs. Slowly she climbed up the metal steps, slowly and silently. At the top she paused, her palm hovering above the door handle; now that she was here, she wasn't sure it was such a good idea after all, but it was the only idea she had. Her options were limited, the days were passing quickly; she needed help and Bill was the only one who could help her.

She turned the door handle, it was locked. Why wouldn't it be? He wasn't expecting her. Before fear forced her to turn and run Karen knocked on the door. It seemed an age before she saw Bill's shape walking towards the door. He pulled aside the blind that covered the glazed top half of the door. He stared at Karen, then let the blind fall and unlocked the door.

"What brings you here?" he asked her.

"I needed to see you," replied Karen.

"You'd better come in then." He stepped back and opened the door a little wider. Once she was inside he closed the door locking it again. "Come through." Karen followed him into the office, he pointed to the sofa and she sat down. Bill sat at his desk, swinging the chair round to face her. "So, how are you?"

"I'm fine," she said forcing a smile.

"Good, good. And why do you need to see me?" he asked.

"I erm, I, that is." Karen was wringing her hands. She had rehearsed in her head many times what she would say to him. But now she was here, face to face, she couldn't do it. She had to though, he would tell her what to do. He always told her what to do. Karen looked up at him; fear was winning. But not just fear, realisation too, for in that moment, that second, she knew what he would say. She knew exactly what he would say and it wasn't what she wanted to hear. Yes it would be an answer, it would solve the problem but actually, it wasn't the answer she wanted. She stood up and looked at him.

"I'm sorry, I disturbed you. It was a mistake coming here. Goodbye Bill." As she turned to go Bill stood up and took hold of her arm.

"Whoa, not so fast. Something brought you here. What is it?"

"I thought I needed you but I realise now I don't."

She tried to leave but Bill tightened his grip on her arm. She shook him free, but he took hold of her again.

"I've missed you and clearly you have missed me too. I can see you want me." He pulled her closer. Karen mustered all her strength to free herself from him.

"That wasn't why I came. I came to tell you something, to ask for help. But now, well now I've changed my mind and I'm going home."

"Like hell you are," he shouted. "You come here uninvited, stop me working, lead me on and then say I'm going home, it was a mistake." As he finished speaking he lunged at her, pulling her towards the sofa. "I know exactly what you want, what you always want." They fell onto the sofa, she could feel him fumbling with his trousers.

"Stop it Bill, please, stop it. I'm pregnant." He stopped and got up from the sofa, as he did Karen fell onto the floor. She looked up at him, he was staring at her, his eyes wide and angry. "I'm pregnant," she repeated.

"This has nothing to do with me," he spat. "This is one of your boys,"

"No Bill it is you, it's yours."

"Liar. I know your dates, remember. I'm not some imbecile you can trap."

"Bill, I swear. It was here, that last time."

He ran his hand through his hair, he went over to the desk opened a drawer, took out a bottle and glass and poured himself a very large whiskey. He downed it in one gulp, then poured another which he drank equally as fast. He sat down, heavily in his chair. This can't be so, he thought. He was careful, always. This wasn't his mistake, not this time. He looked at his diary that was open on the desk, trying to recall the last time he'd…. He flicked back through the pages. His mouth dried a little as he looked at the dates. Karen pulled herself up from the floor and went over to him. She lightly touched his arm, he flinched as though her touch burned.

"I should go," she said.

"Not yet."

"I'm going." She looked around for her bag, it was on the floor. She picked it up and turned to leave. Bill got up and stood between Karen and the door.

"You can stay here until it's sorted."

"I don't need to stay here. I can do this by myself."

"Do what exactly?"

"Have this baby."

"That's not going to happen." He paused before continuing. "Tomorrow I'll phone the clinic and arrange for… I'll make you an appointment, it'll be fine."

"I'm not getting rid of it," shouted Karen, instinctively clutching her abdomen.

"Yes, you are."

"No I'm not," Karen said reaching for the door. Bill side-stepped preventing her from opening it.

"You are," he said.

She tried again to reach the door handle but Bill stood firm. Suddenly Karen let out a scream and threw herself at him, scratching at his face. He grabbed her wrists and held them tight, shouting at her to calm down. She couldn't shake her hands free so kicked out at him instead, connecting with a shin. Bill dropped her arms and instinctively rubbed his leg. As he did this Karen tried to open the door, he pulled her back throwing her to the floor. Her leg stretched out again reaching the same leg as before. Bill pulled his leg back and let her have it, he was mad now. He kicked her three, four times, then bent down pulling her up by her clothes. He slapped her face with the back of his hand, her mouth filled with a metallic taste. He swung her round, pushing her towards the sofa but she missed the sofa and fell to the floor. She tried to curl herself up in a ball, but not before a perfectly timed foot landed on her stomach.

◉

Yvonne hoped she hadn't made a mistake agreeing to move in with Sandra. It had only been a few days and already it was apparent that Sandra didn't view their arrangement as entirely equal. She supposed she should have guessed as much, after all the flat did belong to Sandra's Dad, as did most of the furniture. He'd also given Sandra money for food to 'start them off' he'd said and the rent was nominal. At least she had been given a free rein to do whatever she wanted with her room; it was a great room, easily twice the size of her bedroom at home, if not bigger. At the moment is was a bit chintzy, her Mum would like it but it certainly wasn't Yvonne's taste. She preferred bold colours and abstract patterns; she'd get Jason to help her. As she thought of Jason, she realised that he may be an issue between her and Sandra. She knew that Sandra disapproved of him, as did Bill, but he was her friend, more than just a friend and she was going to invite him round. The weekend, she thought to herself, I'll invite him round at the weekend.

Sandra lay back on her bed, smiling. She loved having her own place, she didn't miss her Dad at all. That said he had visited every day. The phone was being connected today so hopefully after that the visits would be less frequent and she would get him to phone in advance. Yvonne was being quite amiable, which was a pleasant surprise. Sandra had been a little nervous about sharing with Yvonne but it was the one thing her Dad insisted upon, well that and no parties. Once upon a time she would have preferred to share with Karen, but she had changed. She was no longer fun and was frequently angry. Sandra didn't know why; there were rumours of drug taking and sleeping around, neither story Sandra had really believed until Yvonne had told her about Paul. That was a shocker, well initially it was, but the more Sandra thought about it the more it made sense. Karen had always been jealous of her and wanted what she had, so getting off with her ex wasn't that surprising. No, Karen probably wouldn't have made a good flat-mate.

◉

He hadn't meant to hurt her, but she had flown at him like a screaming banshee. He had to protect himself and now he has to make her see sense. She was on the floor, knees bent, arms across

BEWARE THE CUCKOO

her belly. She looked scared, helpless and scared. He bent down beside her.

"Why do you do this?" he asked softly, stroking her hair as he spoke. "It spoils all that we had."

Karen didn't respond. She looked at him, eyes wide with fear, but didn't speak.

"Come on, get up now and we'll talk about this erm, situation." He took hold of her and tried to ease her from the floor, she winced as he moved her. He didn't let go, instead he slipped his arms under hers and hoisted her onto the sofa. She was sitting on the edge of the sofa still holding herself. Bill went to the kitchen and got her a glass of water. "Here," he said, offering her the glass. "Have this, then we'll talk."

She lifted her hand to take the glass from him, but before she did, she let out a cry and bent forward.

"What is it?"

She didn't answer, not with words anyway. She emitted another cry and slumped further forward. Bill knew there was something wrong, he scooped her up and carried her into the bedroom. As he lay her on the bed he realised his arm was wet, he put the light on and looked in horror at the red streak that was across his arm. For a brief second he was unsure what to do, a feeling he was unaccustomed to, but then he took a deep breath and composed himself. He needed help, Karen needed help, medical help. He couldn't take her to a hospital or a Doctor's surgery, too many questions. He needed a Doctor to come here; one who wouldn't ask too many questions. He knew who to call, but he would still have to come up with a plausible story.

"Is she okay?"

"No Bill, she's not okay. She's had a miscarriage. Who is she exactly?"

"She's my daughter's friend."

"And why is she here?"

"She came to ask for help, she doesn't get on with her parents. She asked me for money, I said no. I told her I'd take her home and talk to her parents for her but she just started screaming and crying and punching herself. I tried to stop her and she fell over and then… well then I called you."

"Why ask you for help?"

"I don't know. She knows I have money I suppose, and I'm always nice to her, friendly."

"Define friendly."

"Whoa, she's the same age as my daughter for God's sake. What do you take me for?" said Bill feigning disgust.

"Sorry, I had to ask. She'll need to stay here, for at least tonight, maybe a bit longer. Do you have any painkillers?"

"I have some aspirin."

"Not aspirin, definitely not aspirin. Paracetamol."

"I'll get some."

"Go while I'm here. Get some paracetamol, sanitary towels and if your daughter has some clothes she could borrow, that would be good too. Something loose and comfortable that she can sleep in."

"Thank you, Veronica."

"Don't thank me. I'm not happy that you called me for this. I'm respected here, I don't want to do anything that jeopardises my life here and if I'm found to have treated someone in these circumstances I could lose my license to practise."

"I'm sorry, but let's not forget who enabled you to begin a new life here."

"I don't forget and I know I owe you everything. But I don't like it."

"I'll be about an hour."

◉

Karen opened her eyes and tried to take in her surroundings. Where was she? It was familiar, yet not.

"Good morning."

Karen looked to where the voice came from and was surprised to see Bill sitting in a chair at the end of the bed.

"Where am I?" she asked him.

"My office. You came here last night."

She sat up, gingerly. She didn't feel quite right this morning. As she moved she felt something between her legs, she lifted the bedclothes to look. What was going on? She looked back towards Bill.

"I'm sorry," he said.

His apology lifted the veil that was screening the events of the previous evening, as more details filtered into her consciousness she began to cry. Bill stood up and walked towards her. Karen pushed herself up the bed pulling the covers around her like a shield.

"I'm not going to hurt you, truly."

"The baby?" she asked, although already knowing the answer. He just shook his head, then left the room. He returned a few minutes later with a cup of tea and a couple of slices of toast. "I'm not hungry," she said.

"Try and have a little."

"I just want to go home."

"You need to wait until the Doctor has seen you. If she says you can go then I'll take you home."

"Doctor? What Doctor?"

"Karen, you needed a doctor so I got one. Now eat something. I'll be back in a bit."

As Bill left the room Karen picked up a piece of toast. She actually was a little hungry. She could hear Bill on the telephone, she stopped chewing and tried to listen to what he was saying:

"She seems fine. Yes I know. That's why I'd like you to come and see her. No of course she won't. Okay, see you in an hour."

Bill came back into the bedroom and Karen resumed munching.

"The Doctor will be here in an hour. We'll see what she says and then decide what to do."

"She?"

"Yes, she. Doctors can be female you know. Finish your breakfast then rest. I have some work to do and I'll come back when she's here."

Karen did as she was told and before long she was asleep again. Bill checked on her a couple of times and when he was satisfied she was sleeping he went and made a few phone calls.

Karen woke to the sound of voices, raised voices.

"I know I'm late. Sorry. But try and remember I'm doing you a favour here."

"Veronica, I think we all do favours."

The door opened and in walked Bill followed by a tall, elegant looking woman with long blonde hair.

"Doctor's here Karen," he said.

"Good morning," said the doctor. "How are you feeling today?"

Karen didn't speak, she just kind of shrugged her upper body. She was staring at the doctor, she recognised her but from where she wasn't sure. Veronica turned to Bill and told him he should wait outside. When he had gone, Veronica examined Karen and asked her a few questions. Karen's responses were very vague; this had more to do with her puzzling over where she had seen this woman before than her mental state, nonetheless it left Veronica a little concerned.

"Okay Karen, get some rest now. Goodbye"

"So, all good?" Bill asked Veronica.

"Physically yes, apart from being exhausted. Mentally, I'm not so sure. I wouldn't leave her on her own just yet."

"But she lives alone."

"What about her family? Can't you take her there?"

"Not really."

"Then I'd keep her here for a few more days."

"How many days exactly?"

"I don't know, two, three, a week. As long as it takes. It's the least you can do."

Bill closed and locked the door after Veronica left; things were beginning to unravel and he didn't like it. He liked to be in control and usually he was but this nonsense was a hindrance he could well do without. He was supposed to be going to The Cayman Islands to further his plans there and he had a couple of deals to sign off on. The last thing he needed was to have to babysit Karen. And why should he? He asked himself. But, Veronica's final comment had unnerved him; 'It's the least you can do.' What had she meant by that?

Karen heard the door close followed by the sound of someone in heels going down the back stairs; that was it, that's where she had seen her before. She was the woman Karen had seen coming out of the flat. Who was she to Bill, Karen wondered? Just then Bill came back into the bedroom, he explained that the Doctor thought it best she stayed here for a few days. Karen protested, she had no clothes and she had to go to work.

"Don't worry, I'll sort it. I'll phone the shop and I'll pick up some things for you. You just get yourself better," he said.

She knew her arguments were futile so she agreed to stay for a couple of days. She didn't fancy being on her own in that grotty room at the moment anyway.

"Is she your girlfriend?"

Bill paused in the doorway.

"Who?"

"The Doctor. Only I've seen you with her before."

"She is not my girlfriend. She is just someone I've helped, a friend."

"Is she really a doctor?"

"She is. She's my doctor. Now stop with the questions and rest."

Sandra shouldn't have been surprised to see her Dad at the door, but she was. Initially he'd turned up unannounced every day, then mysteriously didn't visit for over a week. She'd only spoken to him once in that time; to let him know the telephone was connected and to give him the number.

"Dad! Hi. You should've called to say you were coming."

Bill smiled, walked past her and went into the lounge. "Do you want a coffee?" she asked him.

"No, can't stop. Are you on your own?"

"Yes, Yvonne's at work."

"Is everything okay?" Sandra was suddenly concerned, her Dad looked terrible, unkempt; dark shadows hung under his eyes, he hadn't shaved and his clothes were creased, scruffy, almost dirty looking. So unlike him, Bill was a man who was particular about his appearance.

"Fine, everything's fine. I wanted to talk to you about your friend."

"Oh. Why?"

"I saw her and I'm a bit concerned. She doesn't look well."

Sandra thought his comment odd, especially considering how he looked at this moment in time,

"She looked fine to me."

"You've seen her? How? When?"

"Before she went to work." Sandra was confused.

"Not Yvonne, Karen."

"Karen?"

"She was waiting for a bus so I gave her a lift. She wasn't herself and where she lives is horrible. Not right for a young girl to live in that area."

"I know. I haven't seen her for a while. She's not at college and she doesn't have a phone so we have to wait for her to get in touch with us, which she hasn't done."

"Have you not been to see her?"

"Dad, you just said yourself how awful it is where she lives. Why would I want to go there?"

"True. It just doesn't seem right, that's all." Sandra wasn't sure what to say. Her Dad had always taken an interest in her friends, but his concern for Karen was unexpected. "No, it's not right, unfair even."

"What's unfair?"

"You and Yvonne living here; nice flat, right end of town." Sandra stared at him as he continued. "And you have a spare room."

"You want me to let Karen move in?" she asked.

"It would be a nice thing to do and well, I'd feel a little happier. You know, safety in numbers and Karen has always been a bit more reliable than Yvonne."

So that was it, despite all he had said he still had reservations about Sandra's living arrangements. She smiled to herself.

"I don't know Dad. Karen has changed, I'm not sure it would work and I think she likes living alone."

"I'm not sure that's the case. Think about it, it would make me feel happier and it makes good business sense."

"How so?"

"Karen will pay the rent to you, as Yvonne does. You then give it to me, but I'm not putting the rent up regardless that you may have an extra tenant. So that means your contribution will be less."

"Do you ever stop thinking about making money?" laughed Sandra.

"No, I'm a businessman,"

"Ever the businessman," she said as he left.

2010

"Good Morning, take a seat. Would you like a drink? Tea, coffee?" asked Geoffrey coming out from behind his desk to greet Karen.

"No thank you," said Karen politely; she wanted to get this over with as quickly as possible.

"Splendid."

Sandra raised her eyebrows at Geoffrey's limited vocabulary. She really thought him a tiresome little man and she too wanted this over with as quickly as possible.

"Right, introductions. I'm Geoffrey Soppell, Miss Davids and her... associate you know. This is Mr. James who is here as an independent witness. Everyone in the room acknowledged each other without actually speaking.

"Splendid. Then let's get on with it. You're here to sign a document relinquishing a bequest made to you by Mr. Willem Pieter Davids and to state that you will make no future claim on his estate. I shall read through the document that you're here to sign. If at any time you're unsure of something and want clarification, do stop me." Geoffrey looked at Karen, who nodded her understanding.

The whole process took little over ten minutes. When it was done she looked at Sandra and held out her hand.

"Not here," said Sandra. "Outside." Karen would've have preferred to have completed their arrangement inside but realised she was in no position to argue. She followed Sandra outside, who crossed the road and went and stood by her car. "Before I give you these there is something I need to know. Why you? You see you weren't the only one and you certainly weren't the first. My mother claims to have been the first."

"Your mother? I thought she was..."

"Dead, yes me too. But apparently not. No you were actually number five."

"Sorry?"

"I don't know if number five meant the fifth one or maybe it was a score; fifth best, fifth worst. We'll never know."

"I don't follow," said Karen.

"When I was sorting Dad's things I found some boxes, each with a number on the side. Each box contained souvenirs, mementos from each of his dalliances. You were box number five." Karen remembered seeing boxes like that in Bill's den.

"So, come on tell me. Why you? What did you do to make him think he had to leave you anything?"

"I don't know."

"Of course you know."

"I don't, now give me the photos."

"Maybe I don't want to give you the photos, maybe I need answers."

"You promised."

"Tell me why."

"Sandra, I don't know why. But what I do know is I've done as you asked. I've signed the form, you have your money so give me the photos and we'll never have to see each other again. If you don't I'll go straight back over there," she said pointing at the solicitor's office.

"And do what?" asked Sandra.

"I'll say I was forced into signing."

Sandra laughed; "You're pathetic. You know that, pathetic." Sandra opened her briefcase and took out a brown manila envelope. "Take them and I hope to God our paths never cross again." Karen took the envelope and left. "Finally," said Sandra as she got into the car. "We can go home."

"I've booked us into The Savoy," said Nikolaas.

"Can we afford it?" Sandra said with a hint of sarcasm.

"We can now. I thought it would be nice to have a couple of days of luxury before we leave."

"It'll be luxury all the way, now that I have my money back."

"Sounds good to me."

"I have an errand to run before we go. I'll drop you back at the house and you can make sure we haven't left anything behind, I'll be about half an hour."

The courier's office was exceptionally busy, Sandra had to stand in line for almost ten minutes before she reached the front of the queue.

"Good Morning, I have a package for delivery on Wednesday. I'd like one of your motorcycle couriers to do it please."

"Alright love, where's it going?"

"AL Plastics. Bounders Green Industrial Estate."

"I know it, we deliver a lot there. No need to hire a rider, we have vans out that way all the time."

"No. I'd like a motorcycle courier. I need the item handed to the recipient. It's a gift and I don't want it to get caught up with the business deliveries."

"Suit yourself, it'll cost you."

"Of course."

"Okay. Name of recipient."

"Andrew Lowther. For delivery Wednesday 6.30pm."

"There's an extra charge for out of hours delivery."

"I thought there might be."

"And most of them factories and offices finish up around 5 o clock. So what if he's not there?"

"He'll be there."

"Okay love. Pop it in that tray there."

"I'd rather you hang onto it and personally supervise it for me, I'll pay extra of course."

"As you wish love."

Sandra handed the package to the man behind the counter along with a handful of notes.

"Wednesday," she said.

"Wednesday love, no problem."

Before he could get any more details from her, Sandra turned and left. He looked at the package and the money, she'd given him way too much and she hadn't asked for a receipt. Quickly he slipped the money into his back pocket and put the package under the counter. He'd deliver it himself, after all she did ask him to 'personally supervise' it. He'd have to drop it today though, he was helping Clive and Sue move into their new house tomorrow and Wednesday was his day off. He was sure it'd be fine though, he knew Andrew Lowther well enough; he could just explain to him it was meant to come Wednesday. It's probably a birthday present or something, he thought.

Sandra had the broadest grin on her face as she drove back

to the house. She was imagining Wednesday evening, she would be settling into her seat in the first class cabin of a South African bound jet, sipping champagne; Andrew on the other hand would be viewing pictures of his wife in a variety of poses doing things she has probably never done for him while waiting for a prospective new client who was not going to show. The perfect revenge, two for the price of one, she thought. This made her laugh out loud. Ha, serves them both right; he'll wish he hadn't denied me and she'll wish she had not seduced my father and tried to steal my money.

November 1978

The fireworks seemed to go on all night. Just as she thought they had finished and she tried to settle down for some sleep they would start again. They were incredibly loud, but worse than that was the way they lit up the room. She got up and looked out of the window, there was a huge crowd of people standing on the mound. The 'Mound' was the name given to the large piece of ground that was left when they knocked down the old dance hall. It was supposed to have been replaced by a cinema, but that never happened. In fact nothing happened, even some of the debris from the old building was still left; a large pile of concrete and twisted metal that people had added their rubbish and unwanted objects to. It had all helped to make this end of town dirty and rundown. Decrepit and derelict and normally deserted, but not tonight. Tonight it was playing host to an impromptu firework display.

Karen hoped it would soon be over; she wanted to sleep, she needed to sleep. She had spent a few days with Bill, during which time she had hardly got out of bed, yet, she didn't feel rested. Being with Bill made her nervous, it always had, but more so now. After what had occurred between them, that was not surprising. He had looked after her well, although guilt was the motivation, nothing more. Karen recognised this and she finally realised there was no

BEWARE THE CUCKOO

future with Bill, not the kind of future she had once imagined. Maybe he did care for her; he certainly seemed concerned when he had dropped her back home. He had been quite horrified at where she was living and tried to persuade her to return to her family home. Karen was not interested; she didn't like where she was living either, but she liked the independence that living there gave her and to her it was still merely a stepping stone. Soon enough she would find somewhere better to live, an optimistic thought that she mulled over while waiting for sleep to find her.

◉

"Of course, I don't mind Karen coming to live with us," said Yvonne excitedly. "The three of us together that's how it should be."

"Okay, I'll ask her then," said Sandra.

"Brilliant. There's an added bonus too."

"What's that?"

"The rent will be split three ways instead of two."

"No it won't. Karen will have to pay the same rent as us."

Yvonne pulled a face at Sandra.

"Dad let us have this for less than he would normally ask for because we weren't using the third bedroom."

"Oh well, I'm no worse off," said Yvonne with a hint of disappointment.

"We'll be able to split the bills three ways. So we will be a little better off," said Sandra hoping that would be some consolation to Yvonne.

"True and the main thing is we'll all be together."

They went to see Karen at the shop the following day. When they got there they couldn't see her. They spotted Rita, Karen's supervisor. She lived a few doors down from Yvonne's Aunt so

Yvonne felt quite comfortable going up and speaking to her.

"She's sick?"

"Yes, has been for a while," said Rita.

"Thank you."

Yvonne told Sandra what Rita had said. Dad was right, thought Sandra, recalling him telling her that he didn't think Karen looked well.

"Let's go round and see her," suggested Yvonne.

"We haven't got time now, lunch is almost over. We'll call in on the way home."

The persistent banging was driving her mad, what is going on, she asked herself. Karen sat up, it was then she realised the banging was coming from outside her room, to be more specific it was someone knocking on her door. She was going to ignore it when she recognised a voice calling her.

"Karen, Karen are you in there?" Yvonne said to the door.

"Of course she isn't, she would've answered by now. She's clearly not that unwell if she's gone out." Sandra wished they hadn't bothered coming now.

Karen got out of bed and with a blanket draped over her went and opened the door.

"Jesus, you look shocking," said Yvonne as she pushed past her and went inside. Sandra followed and she had to agree with Yvonne's assessment. Karen did look shocking.

"What are you doing here?" Karen asked them.

"We came to see how you are," said Sandra. "Your supervisor said you weren't well."

"And we have something to ask you," interrupted Yvonne.

Sandra threw her a withering look and Yvonne decided best not to say anything more.

"You've been to the shop?" asked Karen.

"Yes. So what's wrong with you?"

"Bug of some sort. I'm getting better though. I'll probably go back to work tomorrow. Do you want a drink?"

Sandra declined, Yvonne wanted one and offered to make it herself. She'd leave Sandra to ask Karen about moving in with them.

"So what do you think?"

"I'm a bit surprised at the moment. I thought you were happy it just being the two of you."

"Well I actually thought you were happy living on your own."

"So why are you asking me now?" Karen was a little sceptical about Sandra's motives. She had a sneaking suspicion that Bill may have something to do with it.

"We don't get to see you anymore. You're not at college and you don't have a telephone so it's difficult to arrange anything. We have a spare room and... oh, it'll be fun. The three of us together."

"Say yes, please say yes," said Yvonne who'd been uncharacteristically quiet while Sandra was speaking.

Karen definitely wanted to say yes. She hated living alone. The room, this room was dark, damp and depressing. And bloody cold. Surprisingly the rent was less than she was paying now, she wouldn't have to share a bathroom with people she didn't know and she wouldn't be on her own. The only down-side was the probability of seeing Bill; she was sure he had most likely engineered this. But, on balance the pros outweighed the cons.

"Yes."

"Yay," shouted Yvonne. "When?"

"I have to give notice here first."

"You sort that," said Sandra, keen to take charge of the conversation once more. "Then let me have a date and I'll get Dad to move your stuff round."

"I can do that myself, I don't have that much to move. You don't need to bother your Dad."

"He'll be happy to do it."

After Sandra and Yvonne had left, Karen lay back on the bed and looked around her room, she would be glad to say goodbye to it. Bill may be a problem though, she resolved to keep him at arm's length – things would be on her terms now – after all, she was sure he wouldn't want his precious Sandra finding out about recent events.

◉

"Is that the last of it?" Bill asked her.

"Yes."

"I probably could have got in all in my car instead of borrowing this van."

Karen ignored him. Bill smiled at her. He was pleased she was moving in with the girls. He was still a little worried about her and it was difficult to keep an eye on her here, there was no legitimate reason for him to call round. But now it would be easy to watch her, he had every reason to visit. The flat belonged to him and his daughter lived there, yes it would be much easier. And who knows there may even be an opportunity to....

2010

The meeting hadn't taken long at all and Karen was home by 10.30, nevertheless it had been draining so she decided against going into the factory later, she didn't do anything vital there anyway. When she arrived home the first thing she did was destroy the photos Sandra had given her. They seemed to take an age to burn, longer than the first set, curling up and smouldering without completely disappearing. She prodded them with the poker, trying to stoke up the flames. Bill's face grinned at her before melting with the heat. When she was satisfied the pictures were no more than ash and once they had cooled down Karen cleaned out the log burner. She put the embers in a box, then into a bag and took the bag out to the car, she also took the bag from the dustbin containing the remains of the first lot of photos. She had decided against leaving them in the dustbin, it was going to be another few days before the bins were emptied and she wanted there to be no chance that Andrew might discover the ashes. The last thing she wanted was to answer questions about what she had been burning, she was a terrible liar and he would know she was hiding something. She drove to the supermarket, dumping the bags in one of the rubbish skips behind it.

When she got home she began cleaning; manically cleaning.

She had to scrub everything, she needed to as everywhere felt dirty and soiled. Which it wasn't, the house was always spotless. Karen was a frequent tidier and once a week she had a cleaner. But today it was tarnished, as if the house had played host to an uninvited guest who had contaminated anything and everything. When she had finished with the house it was her turn; she had a shower, an exceptionally hot shower. Far too hot, for when she finally emerged her skin was red. Red and sore, caused by a combination of hot water and heavy-handed scrubbing. She wrapped herself in a large towel and lay on the bed. She lay there curled up like a baby, swaddled in the towel. She wished it were possible to clean her mind too. Scour away all the memories that had been stirred up and were floating around in her head. The brain should come with a delete button, then she could delete every memory associated with Bill and Sandra, remove this whole sorry, tawdry affair. Erase them and reset her mind.

It was almost four o clock and despite only being Monday, Andrew was already tired. He'd finished most of what he had to do today so decided to go home early. He justified this by reminding himself he had a late meeting planned for Wednesday. He began shutting down his computer and tidying his desk when his assistant knocked on his door.

"Yes."

"There's a courier to see you," she said.

"You sign for it, I'm sneaking off today," said Andrew.

"Apparently, it's a personal delivery that has to be handed to you."

Andrew sighed, "very well, send him in."

"Hello, Mr Lowther. Have to put this one in your hand personally. Those were my instructions from a very elegant looking lady."

"No problem," said Andrew taking the package from him.

"It was meant to be delivered on Wednesday, so maybe you shouldn't open it yet. I think it's a gift of some sort. Birthday maybe?"

"Not my birthday. Thanks," said Andrew showing the courier out.

Andrew shut the door, his birthday was months away. He was puzzled as to who the elegant lady might be and what was in the package. He certainly wasn't going to wait until Wednesday to find out. He was too curious for that. He sat back down and peeled off the brown tape from the top of the packet. He pushed his hand inside and pulled out a large envelope. On the front of the envelope was the imprint of a pair of lips. A bright red imprint. The 'elegant lady' whoever she was had left her mark, she had kissed the front of the envelope. Across the pair of lips was written 'for Andy'. How curious, he thought. Nobody had called him Andy in years. He was very keen to see the contents now. He ripped open the top of the envelope and tipped the contents out onto his desk. Instantly he could see they were photographs, rather risqué photographs as far as he could make out. He picked up his glasses from his desk and put them on randomly selecting one of the photos as he did. What he saw made him recoil and he dropped the offending picture. It couldn't be, no it can't. He didn't want to look again, but he had to. Tentatively he gathered up a handful of the photographs, praying he was mistaken. As he looked through the images in his hand he realised he was not mistaken. It was Karen; every picture was of Karen. In some she was alone but in others she was with a man. That man was Bill Davids. Now he knew the identity of the elegant woman.

Karen was trying to broker a deal between Charlie and Seb regarding X-Box usage when her phone rang. She looked at the caller display, saw it was Andrew so decided to leave it and call him back once she had settled the boy's dispute. The phone stopped ringing, but immediately started again. She looked at the display once more, still Andrew.

"This had better be important," she said as she answered it.

"Oh it is," said Andrew. "I need you to come to the factory."

"When?"

"Now."

"Don't be ridiculous."

"I mean it Karen. You need to come here now."

"At the moment I'm trying to prevent the boys from killing each other and then I have to feed them. Whatever it is we can sort it out when you get home."

"No, we can't. Mum and Dad are on their way to look after the boys so I expect you here within the hour."

"What? I don't want your parents here."

"They're already on their way."

"Andrew, at least tell me what is so bloody urgent."

"You'll find out when you get here," he said ending the call.

Karen was completely bemused, she stared at her phone for a few seconds. What could be so urgent? She knew the business was in reasonable shape, they had a full order book. Andrew had said he had a meeting with another potential client this week, which he was quite excited about. She couldn't fathom what the problem was and more confusing was that they couldn't discuss whatever it was at home. Karen explained to the boys that she had to go out and that their Grandparents were coming over. Charlie was none too pleased but Seb was quite excited. So excited that he decided he no longer wanted to use the xbox as he'd rather do something with Grandad. One problem solved then, thought Karen.

She pulled into the car park of the factory and reversed her car alongside Andrews. The building was in darkness except for a single light towards the rear of the building; Andrew's office. Karen went to the side entrance that took her through the offices rather than the front entrance as she didn't wish to walk across the factory floor. The door was locked and she hadn't brought her keys, she banged on the door. She heard footsteps and saw a figure come towards the door, she hoped it was Andrew. It was, he threw open the door and headed back towards his office without speaking.

"So, what's the big emergency?" asked Karen.

"I had a delivery today," replied Andrew, who was now standing by his desk with his back towards her.

"Is that unusual?"

"This one was."

"And?" said Karen a touch impatiently.

"Take a look for yourself," said Andrew. "Over here." He nodded at his desk. Karen took a few steps forward so she could see what was on Andrew's desk. She lifted her hands to her face as she realised that neatly laid out across the desk were photos; the photos.

"Oh my God. She… I… I can explain."

"You don't have to."

"But… I."

"No Karen really, I don't want to hear about you and bloody Bill Davids." The two of them stood in silence for what seemed an age. Finally Karen spoke.

"What do you want to hear then?"

"I want to know why?"

Karen sighed heavily.

"I don't know why. I was young, impressionable and very stupid. He was someone who was hard to say no to."

"I don't mean that. I get that, you forget I knew him too. I remember how persuasive he could be."

"You do?"

"Oh yes."

Karen looked at Andrew, unsure what his last comment meant. Andrew could feel her looking at him, he knew he would have to explain; tell her he has known for years about her and Bill. She would have to hear how Bill warned him to stay away from her and that her future husband was so frightened by Bill's threats that not only did he stay away from her, but that he also abandoned his best friend and left his beloved football club.

He and Karen first met in 1977, the year of the Queen's silver jubilee and here they were over thirty years on. Over twenty of them as husband and wife and not once had they discussed Bill Davids. It was a conversation Andrew had never wanted to have, not least because he felt like a fool and a coward for allowing himself to be warned off all those years ago by an old man, but more because he did not want to be faced with the reality of what had transpired between Bill and his wife. But now there was no escaping it, he cursed Sandra in his head, every time she turned up trouble ensued.

Andrew motioned for Karen to sit down and then began recounting his story; his Bill Davids experience. Karen sat in silence, listening without interrupting. She never imagined that Andrew had always known about her and Bill and initially she was astonished he had never told her. Then he explained about the threat Bill had issued and she began to understand.

"I should've told you. I know that now, but I was embarrassed that I allowed myself to be intimidated like that." Andrew paused before continuing. "I was scared. There I've said it. He scared me."

Karen took hold of Andrew's hands.

"You were only young darling, not that much older than Charlie." She paused. "We were all so young. One thing though, we should've talked about this before now."

Andrew shook off her hands and stood up again.

"You're right there," he said angrily.

"Don't shout at me. Let's just get rid of these," said Karen pointing at the photographs, "and go home. I can't believe she's done this, she said she'd given them all to me."

"What do you mean?"

Karen didn't answer him, she started collecting the photos and putting them back into the envelope.

"You've seen her, again, recently. Haven't you?"

Karen stopped what she was doing and looked at him.

"I asked you not to, you promised me."

"And I wasn't going to, but she said she had something to show me and if I didn't see her then she was going to come to the house and I didn't want that, so I met her and she showed me those," Karen said nodding towards the photos staring up from the desk.

"You should have told me."

"I know."

"Really Karen, you should've told me. If you had this wouldn't have happened or at least the impact would have been lessened."

"I know that now," said Karen a little louder. "I never thought I would have to think about that time or him ever again and I didn't want you to know how foolish I'd been."

"But as I said, I already knew."

"I didn't know that because you had chosen not to tell me."

"So it's my fault."

"No."

"What I want to know now is; what does she want?" asked Andrew.

"I think this is what she wants, us two arguing with each other over this."

"There must be more than that."

"No, this would please her. I can't believe it though. After all I signed the papers for her. I did as she asked."

"Whoa… what papers?"

Karen told him that Bill had apparently left her some money in his will and that she had signed a document surrendering the money. Andrew wanted her to explain, in full, exactly what had happened. So Karen recounted the day's events to him. When she had finished she looked at Andrew who was staring at her, mouth open, clearly flabbergasted by the story.

"Well say something," Karen said when the silence had gone on long enough. She expected him to shout at her again, say something like, I can't believe you kept that from me. But what he did say, threw her into a tailspin.

"I'm calling the police."

"What? No. Why would you do that?"

"Karen, you have been blackmailed."

"I don't care. No police, I just want this over."

"That's the reason I'm calling the police."

"This is about the money, isn't it?"

"It's not about the money. But if we don't put a stop to this she may come back for more."

"She won't."

"How do you know that?"

"She has what she wanted."

"And still she sent these to me," Andrew picked up a handful of photos to emphasise his point.

"Well we have them now."

"You think she still hasn't got more copies. Next time she might send these to your Mum, my parents, the children."

Karen knew he was right, but she wasn't sure she had strength enough for a fight, because she knew that's what this would be. Sandra would not readily put her hands up to an accusation of blackmail.

"It won't be easy," said Andrew reading her thoughts. "But isn't it time you took control of this situation and drew a line under it. You've allowed yourself to be controlled and manipulated by Sandra and her father since you were, what? Thirteen, fourteen?"

"Not all the time, I haven't."

"Yes, you have. What Bill did has always been hovering over you. Mostly you get on with your day to day life and you're happy enough, I know. But it's always there."

"No it's not."

"It is and now it's time to say, enough."

"Andrew, I don't know. She has the money now. I'm sure we've seen the last of her."

"She'll turn up again. She's a duplicitous, under-handed woman with no scruples. You'll never be free of her or Bill unless we do this. Let me call the police. It's time to take control."

When Andrew finished speaking he picked up the telephone. He looked at Karen, telephone in hand waiting for her response.

"Okay," she said. "Call them."

◉

"You got us a suite," said Sandra as Nikolaas opened the door to their room in The Savoy.

"Only the best for you," he said holding the door open for her.

Sandra smiled at him, yet inside her irritation was growing. He seemed to forget it was her money he was spending. She also knew he was lining his own pockets with her money. She recalled the telephone conversation she had overheard back at the house. Once they were back home she may have to reassess the Nikolaas situation. He had been useful, he thought like she did and they'd had some fun together. But now he was becoming greedy and his temperamental outbursts were becoming more commonplace. He had a ruthless streak, she had always known that but he was becoming harder to handle. What she would miss about him though, was how he reminded her of her father. This wasn't surprising, not really as for a number of years he worked alongside Bill. Nikolaas regarded him as his mentor.

A knock on the door interrupted her thoughts. It was the hall porter with their luggage. Nikolaas tipped him and when the door had closed he took hold of Sandra's hand and led her towards the bedroom. Sandra was not in the least bit interested but she knew better than to say that; they had two days to spend together followed by a twelve hour flight, no point upsetting him. Not yet anyway. She would do as she often did, imagine it was someone else laying with her.

❦

Karen and Andrew were at the police station for over three hours. It was almost 10.30 by the time they finally arrived home. The boys were in bed, thankfully. After his parents left Andrew poured himself and Karen a large drink.

"What a day," he said, handing her a glass.

"I'm truly sorry, you know that don't you?"

Andrew sat on the sofa next to her and put his arm around her shoulders pulling her close to him.

"Stop apologising. You have nothing to be sorry for. As that detective said, in the eyes of the law you were a child."

"Do you think they'll find her before she leaves?" Karen asked.

"They will. They already know that she hasn't left the country yet, and once they get an arrest warrant she won't be able to."

February 1979

Karen woke to see Bill standing at the foot of her bed, initially she was startled to see someone standing there, but once she realised it was him her only surprise was that it had taken him so long. She pulled the bedclothes up towards her neck and let her eyes get accustomed to the light and his shape at the end of the bed.

"What do you want?" she asked bluntly.

"Now that's no way to speak to your landlord is it?" he replied playfully, sitting beside her on the bed as he spoke.

Karen moved up the bed a little pulling the sheets tighter around her.

"Where's Sandra?" Karen asked him.

"At college, I presume. It is almost 11 o'clock. No work today."

"Day off, because I went in at the weekend for the stock-take."

"I see," said Bill. "So are you going to offer me a coffee or something?"

"Yes, sorry. Would you like a coffee?"

"Why not."

Bill shifted his weight and Karen removed the covers from her, as she did he put his hand on her leg. Karen stiffened at his touch. He moved towards her, she went to say something but stopped as the front door opened, then slammed shut and a voice called out.

"It's me. My lesson was cancelled as the teacher is sick. Is Dad here? His car is parked up the road."

Karen stared at Bill, panic-stricken. Bill calmly stood up, removed his shoes, stood on the bed and reached for the light fitting and began playing around with it. Karen got up and put on a robe.

"I'm up here love, fixing the light in Karen's room."

Sandra came up the stairs and stood in the doorway.

"Hi Dad."

"Hi, Karen told me about the light a couple of days ago and as I was nearby I thought I'd drop in and take a look."

"I didn't realise the light didn't work," she said to Karen.

"I, I, erm," Karen stuttered.

"Flick the switch," Bill said to Sandra who was standing in the doorway. "All fixed," said Bill as the light came on. "I'll have that coffee now."

Bill and Sandra went downstairs. Karen closed her bedroom door and sat on the bed. Her heart was racing, that was close she thought to herself. She did not want the situation with Bill to start again, but how to avoid him now that she was living here. He clearly had his own key and was obviously aware of the comings and goings of her house-mates. She would have to try and make sure she was never home alone, not give him an opportunity. That wasn't really possible, maybe I'll put a bolt on the door. As if a bolt could keep Bill from what he wanted. Or maybe Karen it's time to use this situation to your own advantage, she said to herself. She wanted a coffee so headed down to the kitchen. Although it was technically a flat that the girls lived in, the kitchen was downstairs behind the shop. There had been a large storage room behind the shop that Bill had divided in half, one half was a kitchen and cloakroom for the shop, the other half provided the kitchen for the flat upstairs. This meant Bill could rent it as a three-bedroomed flat rather than a two bed, however it had stood empty for some time as most people wanting a three bed property wanted a house with a garden as opposed to a flat above a shop. One of his not so brilliant ideas; fortunate for the girls though.

As Karen walked down the stairs she could hear Bill and Sandra talking, she stopped halfway down and strained her ears to listen.

"She's always been a bit strange love," said Bill.

"I know, but I think it's more than that."

"Maybe she has boyfriend trouble." Karen leant over the stair-rail to try and hear more clearly what they were saying. She thought they could be talking about her. "Or maybe she's finding college hard. She's not as bright as you," continued Bill. "I wouldn't worry too much, she pays her rent on time."

They were talking about Yvonne, Karen continued down the stairs, as she neared the kitchen the conversation stopped.

"Right, I'd better get going," said Bill. "Unless you have anything else that needs fixing while I'm here?"

After Bill had gone Karen asked Sandra what was wrong with Yvonne.

"I heard you talking to your Dad," she explained. "If there's something wrong you should tell me."

"She's behind with her rent."

"But your Dad said she pays her rent on time."

"I've been paying it for her, but I can't keep doing it. I was trying to sound out Dad to see what he thought, but I think he would just tell her to leave if he knew she wasn't paying the rent."

"He wouldn't just throw her out?" said a horrified Karen.

"He's a businessman, that's how he thinks," said Sandra suddenly defensive. Karen decided not to say anything, she knew only too well how ruthless Bill could be. "I'll have to speak to her about it, but she's rarely here and when she is she just locks herself in her room."

"Maybe she's not getting enough shifts," said Karen. "I can help out a bit until she gets herself sorted."

"I think it's more than that."

"What do you mean?"

"I think she's choosing to spend her money elsewhere. You know she's seeing Jason again."

"Oh."

"Exactly."

"So what shall we do?"

"We'll have to talk to her. If Dad finds out he will make her leave and he may even make me go back home. He's already taking more of an interest in what goes on here than he used to."

Karen knew why that was. Bill's interest had more to do with her now living at the flat than whatever Yvonne was up to, or even Sandra for that matter, but of course she couldn't say as much.

2010

The two days passed by slowly, far too slowly for Sandra's liking. That was the downside of being in the company of someone who no longer appealed to you. It wasn't just that Nikolaas no longer appealed, she also realised that she didn't actually like him very much anymore either. For now, thankfully they were on their way to the airport, she would soon be home and then she could begin the process of extricating Nikolaas from her life, both personal and professional.

They checked their bags and learnt that the flight was on time. Once through security they headed towards the first class lounge. It was almost empty, which pleased Nikolaas. They sat down and ordered a drink each, Sandra drank hers very quickly.

"Steady on," said Nikolaas.

"I'm going to do a bit of last minute shopping."

"Alright, don't be too long. We only have just over an hour. I don't want to have to come looking for you," he chided.

Sandra left the lounge without replying, she hated it when he spoke to her like a child. He had always had a condescending manner, but now he was nothing more than an overbearing, sanctimonious arse. She didn't need anything from the shops and didn't particularly want anything either, but wandering around the terminal was preferable to sitting with Nikolaas for the next hour or so. At least on the flight she would be able to sleep. She ventured into a couple of shops, was tempted by a handbag but decided against it. However she did buy her favourite perfume before heading back to the airport lounge about forty minutes later. When she got there Nikolaas had gone, she looked around for him, then waited by the rest rooms for a moment in case he was in there. Maybe the flight had been called, although she hadn't heard it. She checked the monitors, no the flight time was the same, but there was a gate number now. She was surprised and incredibly angry that he hadn't bothered to wait for her. She strode out of the airport lounge and headed towards the gate, anger fuelling her steps. As she walked she thought of Andrew, who would be waiting in his office for a 'new customer' who wouldn't show, he'd be cross, of course, then he'd receive his 'special delivery' which initially may ease his mood until he saw its contents. Her anger subsided and her scowl was replaced by a surreptitious smile. She arrived at the gate, she couldn't see Nikolaas anywhere. He must have boarded already, she thought. Ahead of her a queue was forming, not for her though. First class travellers don't queue. She approached the desk and presented her passport and boarding pass. The girl behind the desk took them from her and opened the passport to the photo page, she looked up at Sandra, then handed the passport to a man standing next to her. He studied it carefully, then motioned to two men standing to the left of the desk. The two men stepped forward.

"Is there a problem?" asked Sandra.

"You need to come with us Miss Davids," said the shorter of the two men.

"Why?"

"We'll explain in a moment. If you'd just step this way please."

"I have a flight to catch, so explain now."

"You won't be getting this flight. Now, if you please, this way," said the other man holding his arm out to indicate where he wanted her to go.

"Excuse me," said Sandra. "I am taking this flight so if you have something to say I suggest you say it now."

"Sandra Evangeline Davids I'm arresting you on suspicion of the blackmail of Karen Lowther. You do not have to say anything; but it may harm your defence if you do not mention.........."

The words just washed over Sandra as she tried to comprehend the situation. How, why? Had Karen got a backbone after all?

"Do you understand?" said the detective. "Miss Davids, do you understand?" he repeated.

"Yes, of course," answered Sandra, adopting a sanguine tone.

She didn't understand. The weeks of meticulous planning were unravelling apace. Keep calm she said to herself. She knew it wouldn't do her any favours if she released the diatribe of insults that were sitting on the tip of her tongue. No, she needed to be polite and deferential and she needed a plan. As the police officers led her away a plan began formulating in her head. A plan that would see Nikolaas take the fall.

❧

The telephone rang, bringing Karen from her thoughts. She looked at Andrew who got up and answered it.

"Yes speaking. Hello. That's good news, thank you for letting us know." He was looking at Karen as he spoke and she knew it was the detective he was talking to.

"Well," she said impatiently as soon as he had put the phone down.

"They were both arrested at the airport a couple of hours ago."

"Good."

"Yes, it's over now," said Andrew.

"Actually I think it's only just begun," replied Karen wearily.

July 1979

"It's started again hasn't it?"

Karen stared at Sandra. She had no idea what to say, how to respond. She couldn't believe she knew, had she always known? Karen had not wanted to but Bill had made it very clear what he wanted and he was her landlord and Karen did not want to end up in a bedsit again. This time Karen had decided it wasn't going to be all one-sided though, so yes it had started again.

"Well I'm not paying her rent again, this time I will tell Dad."

Karen relaxed, it was a rhetorical question and she was talking about Yvonne, not her and Bill. She didn't know.

"What will he do?"

"He'll tell her to leave."

"And what about us? Will we still be able to stay here?"

"I hope so. Maybe not. It depends how much I tell him."

Karen knew Sandra was alluding to Yvonne's drug use. Although neither of them said as much they both knew that was why she never had money for her rent.

"Can't we try and talk to her? I'd rather not snitch."

"What do we say?"

"We'll tell her she has to sort herself out, pay her rent on time or she has to go. Give her an ultimatum."

"I suppose it's worth a go. I'd rather not tell Dad, but I'm definitely not paying her share of things anymore just so she can keep herself high."

"Agreed. Let's talk to her tonight."

It was almost three o clock in the morning when Yvonne finally arrived home. Sandra and Karen had fallen asleep in the lounge waiting for her. Despite her best efforts to come in quietly Yvonne did wake them up, the girls were glad she had for they were determined to speak to her. It probably wasn't the best time to challenge her as she was clearly under the influence of something, but eventually they managed to make her understand that they were serious and she had to start paying her way and no more drugs.

"Yeah, yeah. I hear you. Now don't go on," Yvonne shouted as she made her way to her bedroom. She slammed the door shut and put some music on, loud! Karen and Sandra looked at each other, both realising that dealing with Yvonne was probably going to be harder than they anticipated.

"We'll talk to her again in the morning," said Karen. "Let her know we're serious."

"It is the morning."

It was almost lunchtime before any of them woke. Sandra was the first to get up, followed by Yvonne who was in no mood for another lecture.

"Look, I'll give you the rent tomorrow, now give it a rest."

Sandra heeded the warning in Yvonne's tone and did give it a rest. She went back to her room and didn't come out again until she heard the sound of the front door closing.

◉

"Did she give it to you?" asked Karen.

"Threw it at me."

"Oh. Well at least she's paid it, hopefully things can get back to normal around here."

"I hope so," said Sandra. "I really do," she added when she saw the unconvinced look on Karen's face. "It's just... she's... "

"What?"

"She's no fun anymore."

Karen said nothing, what could she say. Not for the first time Sandra was right. Yvonne really wasn't fun anymore. She was miserable and morose and that was a good day. Very often she was aggressive and agitated. Karen longed for the return of her friend; Yvonne's humour and frank way of looking at things was something she missed.

2010

S andra could not believe they had put her in a cell. They had even taken her shoes from her. She had made it very clear they were Manolo Blahniks and God help them if they were damaged, but they were unimpressed. She was told she would have to stay in the cell until an embassy official arrived. She had not been allowed to call Benjamin; they had a solicitor available for her to speak to but she wasn't interested in speaking to him. She wanted her own lawyer, but as he was in Johannesburg and she was in London this had to be done via the South African Embassy and the Foreign Office. Sandra sat down on the bed, which was more like a shelf with a mattress on it. Well, not even a mattress, it was a piece of foam not much thicker than her Pilates mat. She hoped this wouldn't take too long. During her lengthy interview she had declined to answer any questions as was her right. Even when the police officer had informed her that Nikolaas had been quite vocal and revealing during his interview she still maintained her silence. The police seemed well aware of the facts; between Nikolaas' contribution and Karen's very candid admission of what had happened with Bill they had a good idea of what had occurred. Words like blackmail and fraud were bandied around, the police even tried insulting her father and accusing him of all manner of disgusting crimes to provoke a reaction from her, but Sandra did not rise to it. She stuck to her '*no comment*' response. No way was she taking responsibility for this, once she spoke to Benjamin and laid out her idea, she was sure she would be on her way home.

It was almost two hours before the man from the embassy arrived. A wait that did nothing to alleviate her mood. She told him exactly what she thought and exactly what she wanted. He listened to her patiently before explaining to her exactly what she should expect.

"But I don't want your lawyer. I want mine, or at the very least to be able to speak to him."

"As I've said, Miss Davids that isn't possible. I can however speak to him, inform him of your arrest and if he chooses to come to London he can then come and speak to you. In the meantime I suggest you speak to the lawyer from the embassy who will advise you how best to proceed. If you are released, then of course contact Benjamin Vorster yourself but for now avail yourself of our services."

"Fine," said Sandra. She had begun to realise that if she wanted to get out of here she would have to do things their way. "Get him here then."

Sandra was escorted back to her cell, much to her annoyance, where she had to wait for the lawyer to arrive. She didn't have to wait too long, little over forty minutes. They had a lengthy discussion during which Sandra constantly and consistently blamed all wrongdoing on Nikolaas. She in turn learnt that Nikolaas was in fact doing the same thing and laying all the blame squarely at Sandra's feet. He had also offered to reveal other details in exchange for his freedom, this had now led to the inquiry being widened.

"Widened?" queried Sandra. "In what way?"

"I haven't been given all the details, but I suspect they are now looking into business activity that either of you have been involved in. They are planning on questioning you a little more so I'll let them know we've finished and then we can get on with it. I would advise you to tell them what you've told me in relation to Mr. Venter rather than maintaining your silence, otherwise they may be more inclined to listen to what he is saying and follow that train of thought."

Sandra relayed her understanding.

The police interview lasted for an hour and half. She did as the lawyer had suggested and answered all the questions relating to Karen and the alleged blackmail, implicating Nikolaas as much as possible in her answers. What she did not respond to were the questions regarding her business activity and that of her Father. She said she could not see the relevance of their questions to the matter at hand. When the detectives were satisfied that they were not going to extract anymore information from Sandra they concluded the interview.

"I suggest you now need to either release Miss Davids or charge her," said the lawyer.

"You're absolutely right," said one of the detectives.

"Miss Davids, I am hereby charging you with the blackmail of Mrs Karen Lowther."

"No, you can't," interrupted Sandra.

The policeman continued reading the charge sheet, ignoring Sandra's persistent pleas. When he had finished the lawyer asked if he could be alone with Sandra.

"Right, we now need to look into the possibility of bail, although I think it unlikely the police will grant it so we'll have to apply for a bail hearing. In the meantime you will be held in custody, probably here."

"I can't stay here."

"I'm afraid you may have to, certainly until there is a hearing."

"How long will that take?" asked a shell-shocked Sandra.

"Hopefully we'll get one in the morning. That's the easy bit, the hard part will be convincing them to grant you bail."

"Why will it be hard?"

"Unfortunately you're a flight risk and… "

"How can I be a flight risk? I don't have my passport."

"And," continued the lawyer, ignoring Sandra's interruption. "You have no residence or family here."

"I don't have family anywhere," said Sandra. "Is that also a crime?" she asked sarcastically.

"You need to have somewhere to stay for the court to grant you bail. Do you have any friends here?"

"Karen is the only person I know here."

"Karen Lowther, the person you're accused of blackmailing?"

"Oh the irony," said Sandra alongside false laughter.

The lawyer wasn't amused. He explained that realistically she may have to face the prospect of being held in a detention centre for foreign nationals until a trial or being held on remand. "So you're really not much good to me, are you?"

"Miss Davids, I need to offer something to the court. Which needs to include an address that you can stay at. Hotels are not an option. If only you had a home here."

Sandra's face broke into a wide smile.

"Is rented accommodation okay?" she asked him.

"Yes, if you have a formal rent agreement or lease." She had meant to send the keys to the house back at the airport, but in her haste to have some space from Nikolaas she had forgotten to do that. She explained to the lawyer that she did in fact have a tenancy agreement on a property and that she had paid six months' rent in advance, of which there was still over three months remaining. "That's a start. But it may not be enough."

"Surely the fact that I paid six months' rent in advance proves I'm not a flight risk?"

"Miss Davids, you were arrested at the airport!"

"There must be something you can do."

"If there is nobody who could stay at the property with you, the only thing I can suggest is that you offer to observe a curfew."

"I can do that."

"We may have to offer another concession too."

"Okay. What else?"

"You should agree to wear an electronic tag."

"No way."

"I think the court will insist on it, so better if we voluntarily offer to do it in the first instance."

Sandra sat back in her chair. How had it come to this? Tagged like a common criminal. She weighed up her options, it didn't take long, not once she realised she didn't actually have any.

"Fine," she conceded.

"Good. I'll get on it."

❧

The hearing was brief and Sandra was very impressed with the lawyer's performance. The court accepted the suggestion of a curfew monitored via an electronic tag although they added a stipulation of their own and that was that Sandra had to report to a local police station on a daily basis. She accepted the conditions of her bail and once the tag had been fitted she was allowed to leave. She was pleased to learn that Nikolaas had in fact been refused bail. She was driven to her '*home*' and she was surprised at how pleased she was to see the dilapidated two up, two down, mid-terraced property that she had so despised the previous week.

BEWARE THE CUCKOO

September 1979

"Wouldn't your dad let you have the party at his house?"

"He said I could, but I just think hiring a club is easier. I don't have to worry about anything then. They do the food, drink and obviously the music and I don't have to worry about gate-crashers or people trying to bring in uninvited guests."

Karen knew that last comment was with reference to Yvonne's boyfriend, Jason.

"Do you think Yvonne will come?"

"I hope so, but I doubt it. She's still a bit off with me."

"Don't take it personally. I think she's off with everyone, she doesn't say much to me at all."

"Her loss," said Sandra. "She will miss the best party ever."

Karen wondered if she might be able to persuade Yvonne to come to the party. It would be so good if the three of them were together. Sandra may act like she didn't care but Karen knew she really wanted Yvonne there. She resolved to talk to her, next time she saw her, after all eighteen is an important birthday.

"I'm sure she doesn't care one way or the other if I'm there," said Yvonne.

"She does care and so do I. It'll be so good if we're all there. Go on say you'll come, please."

"I'll think about it."

"Pretty please??"

"I said I'll think about it, now leave it," snapped Yvonne.

Karen left it. She had learnt not to push it with Yvonne these days. She was always so tightly wound, the slightest thing could set her off. Her thoughts were interrupted by the telephone ringing, she knew Yvonne wouldn't answer it so she did.

"Hello."

"Ah, I'm glad you answered," said a voice Karen knew all too well. "No work today?"

"Day off," she replied, then immediately regretted answering honestly. She wished she had it in her to lie.

"On your own?"

"No Yvonne's here."

"Oh. Can you get rid of her?"

"Not really, she does live here."

"I'll meet you at the office then."

Karen did not want to go to Bill's office, she hadn't been back there since... If she had to see him she would prefer it if he came here.

"I'll find out what her plans are and call you back."

"Don't be long."

Karen recognised the impatient tone in his voice so quickly went to find Yvonne. She was coming out of the bathroom as Karen came out of the lounge. It was then that Karen noticed how awful she looked. Her eyes were sunk in her head with huge dark circles around them. Her lips were chapped and sore, the lower lip looked like it had been bleeding. There was also a strange smell about her.

"Are you okay?"

"Yeah."

"What are you up to?"

"What is it with the questions?"

"Just wondered what you're doing."

"Not that it's any of your business, but I'm going to meet some friends."

"Okay, have fun."

Yvonne scowled at her, then left. Karen called Bill back. She wanted to say Yvonne's staying here and so am I, but what she actually said was, she's gone. I'm alone now.

He didn't stay long, he got what he wanted and then went to work. "I'll see you Saturday," he said as he opened the door to leave.

"Saturday?"

"Sandra's eighteenth."

"Oh yes, see you Saturday."

Once he had gone Karen had a shower. She wanted to wash him away, she shuddered at the thought that once upon a time she thought she loved this man. His touch repulsed her now but still she could not turn him away, the control he still exercised over her was scary and Karen didn't know how to escape it. There were advantages too; the gifts were lovely, but still not enough to make her feel totally relaxed about her situation. She sat on the edge of the bath with a towel wrapped around her, cursing her inability to fully take control of her life. If this affair was going to continue it needed to be on her terms. Once upon a time Karen saw a future with Bill, but that was before... As she sat there, pondering, she noticed something on the floor down by the toilet. She bent down to pick it up, it was a plastic bag, a very sticky plastic bag filled with some sort of liquid. It smelt awful so she threw it in the bin and washed her hands, then went to get dressed. The ghastly smell lingered, no matter what she did. She tried spraying some perfume around to mask the smell, but all that did was add sickly floral notes to it. It reminded of her something, she wasn't sure what and then she remembered; not something, but someone.

❧

The party was a great success. Sandra had the best time, there were so many people there, although there was one notable absentee. Neither Karen nor Sandra mentioned it until they returned home.

"I knew she wouldn't bother."

"Maybe she's not well."

"She's well enough to go out," snapped Sandra referencing the fact that Yvonne was not at home.

"Her loss," said Karen. "She missed a great night."

"She did. Didn't she?"

The next morning the girls were woken by someone banging on the front door. They both came out of their rooms at the same time.

"What's the time?" asked Sandra.

"Err, just after eight," said Karen looking at her watch that she had forgotten to take off before going to bed.

"Who knocks on the door like that at eight o clock on a Sunday morning?"

"Answer it and find out."

"You answer it."

Karen started walking down the stairs when she heard shouting coming from the other side of the front door.

"Hurry up will you."

"It's Yvonne," shouted Karen up the stairs. Sandra came running down, pushed past Karen and opened the door.

"What are you playing at?" she screamed at Yvonne. "Not satisfied with missing my party, you have to wake us up at silly o clock."

"Drop dead," said Yvonne pushing past her and then Karen.

"No, you drop dead. I've had enough of this, you can just go."

Yvonne ignored her and went up to her room, slamming the door behind her. Sandra was furious with her and ran up the stairs after her. She tried Yvonne's door, it was locked. She began pounding on the door with her fist, screaming insults and demanding to be let in. Karen had never seen Sandra like this; yes she got angry occasionally, but this was something else, she had completely lost it. Karen tried to pacify her.

"Just leave it, talk to her later."

"I'm done talking. She has to leave," said Sandra, loud enough so Yvonne would have heard her comment through the locked door.

"I'm going back to bed," said Karen just as the sound of music, very loud music came from Yvonne's room.

"You can sleep through that can you?" asked Sandra. "I'm going to Dad's. Come with me if you like."

Sandra was right, neither of them would sleep anymore. Karen decided she would go and visit her Mum, she hadn't been home for a while and Sandra's offer didn't appeal to her.

◉

Karen had a pleasant day with her family, she did not find herself getting irritated or wound up as she used to when she lived with them. The day was relatively quiet, well certainly in comparison to the events of this morning. She played board games with Debbie and the boys and enjoyed a delicious roast dinner before heading home. It was quite a nice evening so she decided to walk. As she crossed the High Road she saw someone walking just ahead of her who looked familiar, he turned and looked at her, recognition on his face. He walked a few more steps then stopped, turned and smiled at her.

"Hi. I thought it was you," he said.

"Hello," replied Karen. "What brings you this way?"

He laughed. "I live round here, don't you remember?"

"I thought you moved away."

"No. What made you think that?"

"I think Sandra or Ryan said, long time ago now. I forget."

"I moved to a different football team, not a different house." His voice softened as he spoke, as if embarrassed.

"Oh. I just thought…" An awkward silence fell before Karen said she had to get home.

"Yeah, me too. See you."

Karen continued on her way.

"Hey," he shouted after her. "Fancy going out sometime?" He ran a few steps to catch up with Karen. "Well?"

"Yes, ok."

"Give me your number."

"It'll be easier if you give me yours," said Karen.

"You got a pen?" Karen rummaged in her bag for a pen and handed it to him. "Paper?" All she could find was a screwed up till receipt and an old bus ticket. She gave him the bus ticket and he scribbled his number on it. "You free Wednesday?"

"Yes," said Karen.

"We could see a film," he suggested.

"Okay, I'll meet you outside the cinema about seven."

"I can pick you up. I drive now."

"No, I'll meet you there."

"See you Wednesday then."

Karen walked away feeling quite excited about her impending date. She was glad it was Wednesday as that was half day closing so she would have plenty of time to get ready. What shall I wear? She wondered. Her thoughts were rudely interrupted by the sound of a siren, the sound was getting closer. Karen looked up as an ambulance screamed along the road. Blue lights flashing, siren wailing. The noise bounced off the houses, as it raced up the street leaving a lingering echo long after it had disappeared. As Karen turned into the road she lived on, she was surprised how busy it looked. The shops weren't open as it was a Sunday so Karen was surprised there were so many people about. There was a police car too and an ambulance, she wondered if it was the one that passed her. As she got nearer to home she realised all the activity was right outside where she lived. She spotted Bill's car, then she saw him and Sandra. He had his arms around Sandra and they were talking to a policeman. Karen started to walk quicker, then run. She pushed her way through bystanders who didn't seem to have any reason for being there other than being nosey. As she passed the police car she saw Jason sitting in the back of it. Sandra must have told her Dad about Yvonne; she must have told him everything. As she made her way towards Sandra another policeman stopped her.

"Sorry miss, you can't come through here."

"But, I live here," she protested.

Sandra recognised Karen's voice and turned to look at her, Bill turned too. Karen knew instantly something wasn't right. Sandra tried to speak but couldn't, she buried her face in Bill's side as Bill reached towards Karen and pulled her towards them both.

"Karen, something terrible has happened."

2010

S andra was still reeling after her discussion with Benjamin. She had been allowed to have a video call with him at The South African Embassy. He had been a big player in South Africa and still had a lot of contacts and was well respected in high circles. When Sandra learnt she was able to speak to him she was convinced her situation would be resolved and she would be on a flight home very soon. What she did not expect was for him to advise her to change her plea.

"But I'm not guilty."

"Yes you are Sandra. Believe me when I tell you this is the best way."

"I did not want to do it like this. It was Nikolaas."

"Then tell them that, claim coercion. They are already aware of his past."

"This is so unfair, that money belongs to me. I was only trying to get back what is rightfully mine."

"I know."

"Why did he do it Ben?"

"Who?"

"Dad. Why did he leave it to her? I don't understand."

"I truly don't know. I didn't draft the amended will. He told me there were changes, he said he had seen a different lawyer as he was also leaving me something, as you know."

"You were also his friend. What do you think of all the things they are saying about him?"

"Sandra darling, everyone has a dark side. Even Willem."

"He had a weakness, I accept that. But they preyed on his weakness, the girls, they are just as much to blame, if not more. Especially Karen, she was the worse; I've said it before, she's nothing more than a damn cuckoo."

"Cuckoo?" enquired Benjamin.

"Yes, she always wanted what I had, my clothes, my house and even my Dad. She was so jealous of me, she wanted it all. Well she is not getting my money."

"You are just making yourself angry, an emotion you can do without at the moment. You must show contrition. Show you are sorry, display your wounds and hurt. The court will like that. If you appear broken and remorseful you may avoid prison."

"Prison?"

"Blackmail is a serious offence."

"Yes, but prison?" Sandra was horrified, the thought of going to prison was not something she had contemplated at all.

"It's possible. Which is why you really must take my advice. And there is something else."

"What?"

"Your assets and the undistributed portion of your father's estate have been frozen."

"Why?"

"Two reasons. First, the court needs to establish the rightful beneficiaries."

"You mean Karen."

"Second, thanks to Nikolaas, officials here and in the United

Kingdom are going through both yours and your fathers business dealings to establish if any illegal activity has taken place."

"Will they find any?"

"Not if you and he have always followed my advice. However, we are learning that your Father kept secrets from us all."

Sandra changed her plea. This meant the case would be brought forward which was a good thing as the lease on the house was almost up. Her lawyer was glad she had changed her plea, it meant Karen would not have to testify. He told Sandra the court would look favourably at this. He was also going to emphasise that Nikolaas was a domineering bully with a violent history and he would make them aware at how acutely Sandra felt the loss of her Father and how shocked she was at discovering the relationship between him and her oldest friend.

"Altogether, it provides a strong case for mitigating circumstances."

"So I should be okay?"

"I cannot predict the sentence, but I believe we will elicit leniency."

👁

"She's changed her plea?" queried Andrew.

"What does that mean?" asked Karen.

"It means neither of you will need to testify," said the prosecutor.

"Thank God." Karen's relief was palpable.

"So what now?"

"Well, the hearing has been set for next week. You aren't obliged to attend anymore as you're no longer witnesses. If you wish to still go that is perfectly acceptable."

"Too right we'll go," said Andrew enthusiastically.

Karen gave him a hard stare. She didn't like the fact that he seemed to be enjoying himself.

"What will happen to her?" asked Karen.

"Miss Davids?"

"Yes."

"Who knows? Prison is a possibility. It depends if they enter a plea of mitigation."

"I don't think she deserves prison," said Karen to Andrew as they were driving home.

"I do. They should throw away the key after what she's done to us. But, knowing our judicial system she'll get a proverbial slap and told not to do it again. Especially now we won't get our say."

"Yes, I noticed you were a little disappointed at us not having to appear as witnesses."

"I am a bit. Still I shall make the courts aware how we have suffered with my victim statement."

"My victim statement."

"What? Yes, your statement, but I'll write it for you. I'll make it have more of an impact."

"No Andrew. I am going to write it."

"But I'll be able to…"

"I will write it." Karen said this with such vehemence that Andrew knew better than to argue with her.

◉

"Are you going to sulk all day?"

"I'm not sulking."

"You are and you need to stop. We need to put this whole business behind us."

"Exactly, which is why we should ensure she gets what she deserves."

"The court will decide what she deserves, not us. We just need to draw a line now. Remember?" she said, quoting Andrew's own words.

"My worry is she'll get off and then try and make her peace with us and you being the soft touch you are will let her back in our lives."

"That's not going to happen. Besides, I'm sure she'll go back to South Africa."

"You can't be sure of anything that woman does... or says."

"Look whatever happens I will never have anything to do with her again. I promise."

"I seem to recall you making that promise once before."

"That was when you didn't know about Bill and... well when I thought you didn't know. Oh come on Andrew, I've told you everything now, you know more than she does. We have no more secrets. Do we?"

Andrew turned away, avoiding her gaze but as he did Karen saw something in his eyes, something that disconcerted her?

"Do we?" repeated Karen.

"You're right," said Andrew. "It's up to the courts now. We need to stop letting her come between us."

"What don't I know?"

"Do you want a drink?"

"What don't I know?"

"Is it too early for wine?"

"What is it?" asked Karen, her voice rising. "There is something you're not telling me."

"There's nothing darling, truly."

"I don't believe you."

"That's charming, I must say." Andrew's disgruntled tone didn't dissuade Karen from probing more.

"Then tell me."

"There's nothing to tell."

"Andrew. What is it I don't know about you and Sandra?" As she asked the question the penny dropped.

"Oh God, that's it, isn't it? You and her?"

"No, no. Well not like... Karen, it was..."

"She was telling the truth, all those years ago. You and her you did."

"It meant nothing,"

Karen emitted a pained cry.

"Please I'm sorry. It's you I love, you. It's always been you. You know that."

Karen went into the hallway and put her coat on.

"Oh God. Please don't leave me. It's not what you think. We can sort this."

She ignored his pleas, saying nothing as she put her shoes on.

"Karen please, I'm sorry. It was such a long time ago, years."

"I need some fresh air, I need to think."

She returned almost an hour later.

"I'll have that drink now," she said to him. She hung up her coat and sat at the table, she drunk a large amount of her wine before speaking again.

"I don't want our marriage to end. I'm not doing that to the boys and I do love you and our life together. But for years you have let me believe that Sandra was making up malicious lies, when all the time it was you, you was the one lying. I need to know the truth, everything. Do you understand? I don't want any more surprises." Andrew did understand, completely. He knew if they were to move on he had to tell her the truth; the whole unpalatable truth.

November 1979

It had been almost two months since Yvonne died and both girls were still struggling to come to terms with it. Friends and family tried to help but they didn't understand how they felt. Only they knew what each other was going through. It wasn't just shared grief, it was also shared guilt. They both knew if they had done something, said something then Yvonne might still be here. She probably would've hated them, wouldn't have spoken to them ever again, but she would still be here. She would be alive. This mutual guilt was what bound them to each other for they had little else in common anymore. Neither of them were able to acknowledge that they were both different people now so they continued seeing each other. They met once a week at the coffee shop on the High Street.

"Hi," said Sandra as she walked in. Karen was already sitting in one of the booths nursing a hot chocolate.

"Hi. How are you?"

Sandra just shrugged in response. When the waitress came over she ordered a hot chocolate too.

"You still at your Mum's?"

Karen said she was adding that she hoped it wasn't for long. Although things were a lot different from when she lived there before it was still not where she wanted to be. Sandra felt the same about her living arrangements and suggested not for the first time that they get a place together, a different place of course and as she had done on previous occasions Karen declined. "Maybe I'll go back to South Africa when I finish college."

"Really, I thought university was the next step?"

"It is, but maybe in South Africa. You still looking for another job?"

"Yes. I need to earn more money and I wouldn't mind having…" Karen stopped mid-sentence.

"Having what? Karen, having what?" Sandra followed Karen's gaze. She was staring at a group of guys who had just come in. One of them was staring back at her. Karen smiled at him but he just turned away and sat with his friends. "I recognise him, I think he goes to my college."

"He doesn't."

"Oh," said Sandra, slightly affronted as she did not like being wrong and more than being wrong, she did not like being told when she was wrong. "Well I know him from somewhere."

"He used to play football with Ryan. We went to that disco with him and Ryan a couple of years back."

"Yes, I remember him now. I thought he moved?"

"No, he didn't. I need to speak to him," mumbled Karen.

"Why?"

"I was supposed to meet him, but then with Yvonne and everything I forgot."

"You stood him up?"

"Yes, but I didn't mean to. That's what I need to explain."

"Then go and explain."

"Not in front of his friends."

"I wouldn't bother," said Sandra. "If he was still interested he would come over."

"Maybe. Actually I..." Karen began rummaging in her bag.

"What you looking for?"

"This," said Karen pulling out a scruffy scrap of paper.

"What is it?"

"A bus ticket with his phone number on it. It was all I had at the time."

"Are you going to call him?"

"I am."

"And say what?"

"I'll tell him what happened."

"He probably won't be interested anymore."

"Maybe. Come on let's go."

As they walked out of the door Sandra noticed he was watching them. He's quite nice, she thought. What is his name? I'm sure it began with A: Anthony, Alan, Andy. That's it, Andy, his name is Andy.

2010

The days were passing at an alarming rate and the hearing was racing ever closer. Sandra was becoming more and more fearful of losing her liberty. As tough as she was, prison was something she knew she wouldn't survive, she was barely coping with the restrictions imposed on her at the moment but at least she had the freedom to come and go albeit within time constraints. As she dwelled on the idea of prison, her fear became anger. She screamed and with a violent sweep of her arm drove everything off of the kitchen table on to the floor. The sound of breaking china and metal clanging as an array of objects hit the tiled floor brought her back to her senses and reminded her of Benjamin's advice. 'Anger is an emotion you can do without. You must show contrition. Contrition and remorse.'

He was right, of course. It was her only option. So how best to display *contrition*. It was not a quality that came naturally. She decided to write a letter; a letter to Karen.

Dear Karen

As I begin this letter my heart is filled with profound sadness at the loss of a childhood friendship that meant so much to me. I know that is my fault and I am truly sorry. On discovering your relationship with my father I allowed myself to be consumed by anger; anger and even jealousy. I was upset to realise my place in his affections had been shared by another and what made it harder was not being able to ask him about it for as you know this discovery was made after losing him. The first hint that something had happened between you and Dad was at the reading of the will. I was surprised to find you were named as a beneficiary, surprised and confused. It was when I began sorting through his things that I learnt in graphic detail what had occurred between you. My grief was replaced by a rage, a rage that burned and deepened. A rage that grew in intensity as time passed. I needed answers, explanations, but more than that I needed someone to blame for the way I was feeling. That someone was you. Alongside this discovery, I also had to deal with the fact that the business was not in the best state, cash-flow was a problem. Then on a personal level I was trying to cope with a relationship that was becoming increasingly volatile. I grouped all these issues together and laid the blame for them all squarely on your shoulders. I believed all my problems were a direct consequence of what passed between you and Dad. My anger and bitterness along with encouragement from Nikolaas decided that retribution was the solution. I know my actions have caused you great distress and I am sorry, truly sorry. I hope that once the formalities of the court case are over you will be able to move on from this and be happy. This letter is not looking for forgiveness, just understanding.

Best wishes

Sandra

She signed her name hoping this was contrite enough. It had been hard trying to convey false emotions through words. She would give this to her lawyer, who in turn would ensure copies were delivered to all relevant parties, including the judge.

July 1980

Karen laid the dress she was planning to wear across her bed. She had mixed emotions about tonight. She was looking forward to going to the restaurant as she had fancied going there for a while, but it was way out of her price range. Tonight, however was a party that had been paid for by the hosts, the hosts being Sandra and Bill. It was their farewell party as they were both returning to South Africa. Karen hated goodbyes which was one of the reasons she wasn't looking forward to this evening, the other reason was Bill. She hadn't seen him since Yvonne's funeral. This hadn't been deliberate, their paths just hadn't crossed. Karen was living back at the family home and after eventually calling the number scribbled on the back of the bus ticket she had started going out with Andrew. He was going to the party with her tonight, although initially he was reluctant to come. Karen was pleased she had managed to persuade him as she did not want to walk into the restaurant alone and she wanted Bill to see her on someone's arm. And not just Bill, she wanted Sandra to see too. She finished touching up her make-up, pulled on her dress and went downstairs. She could hear Andrew in the kitchen chatting to her mum.

"Hey, didn't realise you were here. You been waiting long?"

"No, five minutes or so. You look nice."

Karen blushed, she was always embarrassed when anyone paid her a compliment. She was never quite sure if they were being serious.

When they arrived at the restaurant it was quite busy, Sandra was standing by the bar with a group of people who appeared to be listening attentively to whatever she was saying to them. Sandra caught sight of Karen, excused herself from her admiring audience and went over to her.

"I was starting to think you weren't coming."

"You knew I wouldn't miss it," said Karen.

The three of them went over to the bar and Sandra ordered Karen and Andrew a drink.

"We'll be sitting down to eat shortly," said Sandra. "I've put you two in between Dad and I as you don't really know anyone else. You sit next to Dad," she said to Karen, "and you can sit next to me," she said to Andrew.

"Where is your Dad?" Karen asked, not wanting to be surprised by him.

"Over there," nodded Sandra towards the other end of the bar, "talking to Veronica."

Karen looked up, she didn't see Bill at first but she saw Veronica; the Doctor. Veronica sensing someone was watching her looked towards Karen, she raised her glass in acknowledgement when she saw her. Karen blushed for a second time that evening. Bill followed Veronica's gaze as he had noticed her raise her glass, he too spotted Karen. He smiled at her and then continued his conversation with Veronica. Karen turned her attention back towards Sandra and Andrew who were giggling away at something.

"What's funny?" she asked them.

Andrew went to speak but was prevented from doing so by

someone asking them all to take their seats for dinner. Sandra and Andrew continued giggling together as they walked to the table. Andrew sat in between the two girls and Bill sat down next to Karen.

"Hello Karen," he said. "I haven't seen you for a while, how are you?"

"Good, thanks. I can't believe this time next week you and Sandra will be gone."

"Yes I know it's come round rather quickly. You must come out and visit us."

"Thank you," said Karen. "I don't actually have a passport though."

Bill laughed. "Well you will need one."

Karen turned to Andrew who was still laughing with Sandra. She leant forward to try and get his attention but a waiter appeared alongside her.

"Prawn cocktail?"

"What?"

"Would you like a prawn cocktail?"

"Thank you," said Karen.

The waiter placed a starter in front of her and then continued along the table.

"This looks good," said Andrew, also leaning forward so he could speak to Karen. "Sandra said we can go back to hers after we've finished here."

"Oh really, I don't know. Maybe."

"I said we would. May as well make a night of it.

Not everyone went back to the house but there were sufficient numbers to fill the large, almost empty rooms. There was some furniture remaining which would be put in storage or redistributed among Bill's other properties that he was leaving in the hands of a property management company but most of the good stuff was already on its way back to South Africa. The space created by the absence of furniture in the lounge left a large area for them to dance in, Sandra was in the mood for a dance and tried to get Karen to dance with her. Karen wasn't much of a dancer, so declined blaming tiredness. Sandra decided Andrew would dance with her instead and he happily accepted. Karen stood in the doorway watching them, Andrew's reticence about this evening had been replaced by a desire to party all night. Karen was unaware that she too was being watched and when she went to get herself a drink she was followed.

"Hello," said Veronica. "You look better than the last time we met."

"I, I er, I am," stuttered Karen.

"Don't be nervous. I'm not going to talk about it. I'm just pleased you're okay."

Karen relaxed a little. "Are you going to South Africa too?" she asked.

"Good heavens no. There's no way I'd go back."

"Oh sorry. I thought…" Karen's voice trailed off.

"What did you think?"

"I thought being Bill's girlfriend you'd be going with him."

"Karen, I'm not his girlfriend." She paused before adding, "And we both know why that is."

"I don't know why that is."

"I'm too old," whispered Veronica with a knowing smile. "It's nice to see you Karen, take care of yourself."

Karen watched Veronica leave, studying her carefully. She didn't think she looked that old. She got herself a drink and went back into the lounge. Andrew and Sandra were no longer in there, but someone had opened the patio doors so Karen assumed they'd gone outside for some fresh air. She was going to look for them when someone caught hold of her arm.

"Having fun?" asked Bill.

"Yes thanks, its good."

"Come with me a minute," he said leading her along by her hand. He took her into what was his den. It was empty apart from several boxes stacked up against one wall. He closed and locked the door behind them.

"What do you want Bill?"

"I just thought it would be nice to have a moment alone, you can say goodbye to me properly."

As he came towards her she side-stepped and dodged out of his way.

"Bill, I shall say goodbye to you just as I shall say goodbye to Sandra. Which will be at the end of this evening along with everyone else who is here. Now unlock the door and let me go."

Bill stood and stared at her, her feisty demeanour and refusal to do as he wanted surprised him. She was certainly different, as was Sandra. Yvonne's death had altered them all but there was more to it. Maybe she had grown up, maybe it was the boyfriend. He'd been surprised when Sandra had told him that Karen was bringing someone this evening. Whatever it was, this new-found confidence wasn't unappealing and he liked a challenge.

"I will, but give me one kiss first," he said to her, not wanting to be fully defeated. She allowed him to kiss her, but she didn't respond. He tenderly stroked her face. She just stood there, firm and rigid, conveying nothing. He stepped back and opened the door, Karen left without uttering a word.

2010

Karen and Andrew drove in silence to the court house. She had told him to give her time, she was still reeling from his revelations. She didn't want it to be over, she knew that, but at the moment her heart was heavy and her head was a muddle. When the court case is over then we can start to fix 'us'. That's what she had told him, so for now he had to be patient.

They were greeted at the door of the court by the prosecutor's assistant. She told them that the prosecutor needed to speak with them prior to the case beginning.

"Is everything okay?" Andrew asked. "We thought we were here just to observe."

"It's nothing to worry about, he'll explain," said the assistant holding open a door to a small side office. "He'll be along in a moment." Karen and Andrew sat down at the desk and waited. Both were a little concerned that there was a problem.

"Hello. I'm sorry to have kept you waiting," said the prosecuting lawyer, sitting down and at the same time depositing a large pile of files onto the desk. The files began to slide towards Karen who placed an arm out ready to catch them. "Sorry," said the lawyer a second time as he tidied up the mound of paperwork. "It's been a hell of a morning already."

BEWARE THE CUCKOO

Karen smiled at him.

"So, is there a problem?" asked Andrew a little impatiently.

"No, no. No problem. As you know Ms Davids has changed her plea and alongside that she has written a letter. A letter to you Mrs Lowther."

"I knew it. Didn't I say to you this is what she would do? She's…"

Karen put her hand on Andrew's knee which stopped his rant. The lawyer handed the letter to Karen for her to read.

"What does she want?" Andrew asked.

"I don't know, I haven't read it yet." Karen was becoming a little irritated with Andrew and her tone let him know that. He sat back in his chair and waited for her to read the letter. When she had finished she handed it to him so he could read it too.

"Does this have any bearing on the hearing?" asked Karen.

"Well, a little. Ms Davids' lawyer has filed a copy of this letter as evidence."

"Evidence of what?" said Andrew.

"Her regret, I suspect."

"Her regret. Only thing she regrets is getting caught. She's just trying to avoid what's coming to her."

"Very possibly," said the lawyer. "However, it is perfectly legal for her to write to you and for her lawyer to make the court aware of such a letter. It's evidence of remorse and adds weight to their plea for leniency. What I need to know is how you feel about the letter and the sentiments contained therein?"

"It's nonsense," said Andrew, "and we see it for what it is, a false statement by a proven liar."

"Actually," interrupted Karen. "I believe it took a lot for her to write this letter. Sandra has never been one for apologies and yes it may have been written to keep herself out of prison but," Karen paused before continuing. "Look I don't think she deserves to go to prison. What she has done has been horrible, but we've all made mistakes." Karen was looking at Andrew as she said this.

"Karen, just think of the lengths she went to," protested Andrew. "The elaborate charade that was supposedly Bill's funeral, pretending to be a new client of mine and intimidating you with that thug. This is a woman who would stop at nothing to get what she wants."

"No, this is a woman who's hurting and not a woman who should go to prison." Karen looked straight at the lawyer who had been sitting patiently and quietly while Karen and Andrew had been debating the nature of Sandra's letter. She spoke to him very directly. "I would like you to convey to the courts that I accept Sandra's apology and believe the remorse shown in her letter. Although Sandra and I will never be friends again, I have no desire for her to be sent to prison."

Andrew stood up quickly, his legs pushing his chair back noisily as he did and he left the office. He strode along the corridor before finding a quiet spot where he stopped and leant against the wall. He wasn't sure who he was angrier with: The solicitor for giving them the letter, Sandra for writing it or Karen for reading it and foolishly accepting it. In his mind he had no doubt that Sandra deserved to go to prison. Over many years she had manipulated them all.

Karen thanked the lawyer before exiting the office too. As she looked for Andrew she mulled over what had just occurred. She wasn't wholly convinced of the sentiment in the letter, but by accepting it she hoped it may assuage a little of her own guilt.

June 1985
The Wedding

S andra took in some welcome shade beneath a huge tree and watched Karen and Andrew pose for the photographer. A call went up for the bridesmaids to join them, a posse of giggling girls varying in age and height, all clad in a hideous peach hue dutifully went and stood alongside the bride and groom. Seeing them, confirmed to Sandra that she had been correct in turning down Karen when she had asked her to be one of the bridesmaids. With the exception of the youngest among them, who looked a little bit cute, the girls all resembled one of those hideous dolls with the knitted dress that people used to disguise the extra toilet roll in the bathroom. Sandra wished the photographer would hurry it up, he was rather ancient, so consequently very slow. She was desperate for a drink, weddings were not her favourite thing at all and she was getting a little fed up looking at Karen and Andrew's almost identical smiles. Of course they should look this happy and maybe they are, but she also knew the fragility of those smiles. What she could reveal would certainly alter those expressions, this thought filled Sandra with a perverse feeling of power.

The wedding breakfast and speeches dragged on late into the afternoon. Sandra longed for it to be over, at least during the evening part of the celebrations she could move around so wouldn't be limited to making small talk with Andrew's ageing aunt and her small-minded husband.

"So how long is the flight from South Africa?"

"Almost twelve hours," replied Sandra, without any attempt to hide her boredom.

"Did you hear that Malcolm? Twelve hours, her flight. That's a long time."

"It is. Don't know that I would've bothered myself."

Sandra was beginning to wish she hadn't. Then just when she thought she could stand it no longer, it was over. People began standing up and moving around, most of them gravitating towards the bar. She decided to join them. It took a while to actually reach the bar, so when she did she ordered herself a double. She was mindful of someone standing behind her, turning slightly she was surprised to see that it was Andrew.

"Ahh, the erstwhile groom," she said with amiable alacrity.

"Sandra, how are you? Having fun"

"Absolutely, are you?"

"I am. I really am. I'm so incredibly lucky."

"Yes you most certainly are." Sandra moved closer towards him and whispered in his ear, "I think it's called having your cake and eating it." She picked up her drink from the bar and walked away. Andrew followed her with his eyes before being accosted by his best man.

"Getting them in are we Andy? Jolly good."

Andrew watched nervously as Sandra went and spoke to Karen.

"You look beautiful Karen," lied Sandra.

"Thanks. Look I'm sorry I haven't had time to see you this week. It's been manic. The only evening I was free was Wednesday. Andrew was visiting an old friend and stopping with him so he could have a drink so it would've been perfect, we could've had a sleepover. Like the old days."

"I know, it's a shame but I already had plans for Wednesday that I couldn't get out of."

"Never mind. At least you're here today. I'm so glad you came. I really appreciate it, I know it's a long way."

"It's no big deal, I always come over this time of year anyway."

Karen shook her head. Why couldn't Sandra just accept her gratitude?

"What?"

"Nothing, do you want another drink?"

"Yes, rum and coke, a double."

"It's a long night Sandra,"

"I know, but I'm not fighting my way through that more than I have to," said Sandra highlighting the crowded bar area. "Who are all these people?"

"To be honest, I don't actually know. Most of them are Andrew's parent's friends and as they are paying for most of today I let them invite whoever."

"What are his family like?"

"They're okay, a little over-bearing at times, but they mean well. Come on let's get that drink."

As they fought their way up to the bar Andrew continued watching them, Sandra being here made him nervous, especially as she seemed to be drinking rather a lot too. He decided to introduce her to some of his friends and then try and prise Karen away from her.

"Sandra we'll have to leave you in the capable hands of my best man as there are some people I need to introduce Karen to."

"Yes, you should do that. Not exactly right that the bride doesn't know half of the guests at her own wedding," said Sandra. "Still how well do we know anyone," she added with a wink. Andrew looked at her, Sandra blew him a kiss then turned her attention to the best man.

"What did she mean by that?" Andrew asked Karen.

"Nothing really. She asked me who someone was and I couldn't tell her. You know how she likes to stir things up a bit."

That's what worries me thought Andrew but kept that thought to himself.

Before long the best man wasn't the only one vying for Sandra's attention. Many of Andrew's friends were still single and Sandra was by far the most attractive woman at the wedding, it was no surprise that they were hovering around her like moths to a flame. And she so knew how to work this sort of situation, many women would have been overwhelmed by such attention, but not her. She knew she could have her pick of any of them, unfortunately for them none of them interested her. Her interest lie with another who was, for today at least, unavailable. Still, she would not let that stop her from enjoying herself.

"So, who's going to get me a rum and coke?" she asked.

Before long Sandra had a row of drinks lined up for her. She had endless dance partners and was actually having a great time. The tempo of the music changed and she found herself dancing very slowly with someone called Matt who apparently had been at school with Andrew. As they were dancing she noticed that the bride and groom were also on the dancefloor. She took the lead and began moving towards the newly-weds.

"Hey," she called to Karen. "I think we should swap partners, just because you married him doesn't mean you can keep him all to yourself."

Karen laughed and willingly switched places with her.

"Hello gorgeous," said Sandra as she hooked her arms around Andrew's neck. "Have you missed me?" she asked pressing herself close to him.

"Sandra, behave."

She started laughing.

"Actually you're the one who needs to behave."

"I know and I will. Wednesday really was the last time."

"We'll see."

"No Sandra, it really was. I love Karen and I'm not risking what I have with her."

"Scientia potentia est."

"What?"

"Knowledge is power."

Andrew stopped moving and stared at her.

"And what exactly does that mean?"

"Don't stop dancing Andy, Karen is watching us. Andrew started moving again, he adopted a false smile as he's eyes linked with Karen's. "That's good," said Sandra. "Things are better when you do as I say." The music ended and Andrew let go of her. Sandra leant forward and kissed his cheek before relieving Karen of Matt and heading towards the bar, again.

"I think she's had too much to drink," Andrew said to Karen.

"Don't worry about Sandra. She can look after herself. I don't think I've ever known her to lose control."

Andrew nodded, but he was anything but reassured.

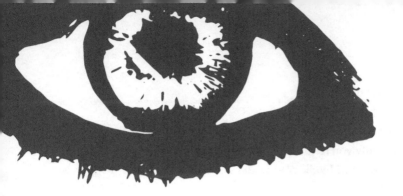

2010

"A suspended sentence, can you believe it. A bloody suspended sentence."

"I'm just relieved it's all over," said Karen.

"It was your acceptance of her letter and liberal attitude that let her off the hook."

"For God's sake Andrew, give it a rest."

"The woman is a manipulative liar and deserves to be behind bars."

"And you are also a liar so where do you deserve to be?"

Andrew gripped the steering wheel tighter and stared straight ahead, a great quiet filled the car. There was nothing he could say to that. She was right, he had lied. But he had done it to protect her, protect their life together and maybe himself, a little. At least that's what he thought. He felt his lies had been justified unlike Sandra who was absolutely in a league of her own. Andrew's biggest failing was that he was weak. His weakness had allowed him to be intimidated and pushed into situations. He was intimidated by Sandra and by Bill and others. Dishonest or weak? Neither adjective was very flattering. He was guilty of both and he knew it.

Karen massaged her temples with the tips of her fingers. Her head hurt, it had been hurting for a long time. It had probably been hurting ever since that day in The Melrose. She pulled down the sun shade and slid open the small mirror, she looked dreadful. The lines on her face seemed deeper, the shadows around her eyes dark and aging. Stress had done what time had not; made her look substantially older than her years. She closed the mirror and clipped the sun shade back where it should be and looked out of the window. She tried to lose herself in the ordinariness that was continuing all around her. Ordinary people with ordinary lives going about their day to day business. She watched a woman trying to hold onto a toddler while pushing a pram laden with shopping bags. She watched people marching along shouting into their mobiles and observed a bus stop queue where each person was staring expectantly up the road hoping to be the first to spot the over-due bus. Sandra used to say, 'I will never settle for ordinary,' right now that was all Karen wanted, the mundane would be a luxury. They stopped at traffic lights and she spotted a man pushing a cart along the pavement, he stopped and with a litter picker began removing crisp packets and take away cartons from the grass verge, disposing of them in the bag that hung on the cart. He was singing as he was doing this and he was smiling, Karen realised that his was the first smile she had seen today. He turned and caught Karen's eye, jokingly offering her a half-eaten burger that was stuck on the end of his stick before dropping it into the bag. As the lights changed and they drove away he gave her a mock salute and flashed her another big smile. Maybe that's the answer, a simple life, mused Karen. It was certainly true that the more you had or busier you were the more complicated life became. But surely he can't really *enjoy* picking up other people's rubbish. The more she thought about this man, the more she wanted to know about him. Why did he look so happy and why did he share his smile with her?

"Andrew, can you turn around and go back to the supermarket, I could do with getting a few things."

"We'll stop at the shop near us."

"No, I want to go to the supermarket. I'm not paying the prices they charge and besides they don't stock what I want."

"I'd rather just get home."

"So would I, but if I don't get them now I'll have to come out later."

"Fine," said Andrew braking hard and doing a u-turn. The car behind hooted and its driver gesticulated angrily at Andrew, who responded in kind with a gesture of his own. "I'll drop you at the supermarket then I'll nip over to the factory to see if there's anything I need to deal with. I'll pick you up in, say forty-five minutes."

"Fine, just drop me here at these lights then you haven't got to go back through the one-way system."

Karen jumped out quickly as the filter light was already green. Andrew turned the corner, heading towards the factory; she looked across the road and there he was, still picking up litter, still singing.

"Hi," said Karen as she approached him.

"Hello," he replied.

Karen stood just looking at him for a moment, not sure what to say, not really sure why she was standing here.

"Are you alright?" he asked.

"Yes, fine. I'm sorry, I just, we drove past you and I, erm, well I wondered…"

"The lady in the Range Rover. Right?"

"Yes. I, you know you look so happy despite, oh dear, what I mean is you look happy…"

"Despite picking up other people's rubbish for a living."

"No. Well actually yes. What's your secret?"

"Ha, no big secret but it's not this. This doesn't make me happy," he said waving his litter picker. "People make me happy."

"Yes, of course," said Karen. "Sorry to bother you."

Karen walked towards the shops, feeling more than a little embarrassed.

"Hey lady." Karen turned around. "You know, the best way to cheer yourself up, is to try to cheer somebody else up."

"I like that idea, said Karen. "well said."

"Don't quote me," said the street cleaner. "That one is courtesy of Mark Twain." A street cleaner quoting Mark Twain, who'd have thought; she chided herself as she realised she was making assumptions regarding peoples' intelligence without even knowing them.

As she walked around the supermarket she kept thinking about that phrase. The obvious person for her to cheer up was Andrew. She knew it was in her hands to do this. She just had to forgive him. Forgive him for cheating, forgive him for lying; she wanted to, she really did, but wasn't sure that she could, not completely. If only it had been anyone other than Sandra. Sandra had always had everything that Karen wanted and now, as it turned out, she had also had what was Karen's. She paid for the shopping and went outside, Andrew was already waiting for her.

"Everything okay at the factory?" she asked as they loaded the shopping into the car.

"Yes, all good. Shall we pick the boys up on the way back?"

"I thought your parents were getting them?"

"They are, were. I just thought as we're back earlier we could get them."

"No, let them get them, or have you already cancelled them?"

"No, I haven't."

"Then leave it as it is. We need to talk."

❧

Sandra exhaled deeply as judgement was passed. A suspended sentence, what a relief. Benjamin was right, contrition was a powerful emotion and the letter, well that had surely sealed the deal. Once the judge had finished speaking her lawyer asked for travel restrictions to be lifted so that she could return home and the judge readily agreed. She was free, sadly she would be going home without the money that she had come here for but at least she was going home. Once she was back in Johannesburg she'd discuss with Benjamin the best way forward; for she fully intended to continue her pursuit to reclaim what she knew was rightfully hers.

❧

"Sandra, there is nothing left for you here. Your business account has been frozen and property registered with your business or mortgaged to finance the business has been seized by the state and you will not get it back no matter how many lawsuits you throw at them. Your father made some very dubious business deals in the past; things I knew nothing of, I hasten to add."

"Why should I pay for what he did?"

"Because everything you have started with money from him. Money that the government says was illegally made."

"I knew nothing of any illegal deals, it's just so unfair Ben."

"I know, but now these things have come to light they will pick through everything he or you ever did. The money will be tied up in the system for years and truthfully, I don't think it will ever be released to you. It is gone and you should go too."

"Go where?"

"The Cayman Islands. You have a property there and plenty of money, neither which can be touched by this government even if they do locate it."

"Not all of the money is mine, not yet."

"There is enough even without the portion your father put aside for Karen."

"You talk of her as if she is a deserving family member."

Ben ignored her comment and just pressed his case for her to start a new life.

"The Caymans are fine for a holiday, but I don't know if I really want to live there."

"You may not have a choice. Not if you wish to maintain your lifestyle. Look, why not go for a holiday, an extended holiday. You may grow to love it there, your father did."

"Even he didn't stay there."

"No, but I think he would have done, if he hadn't got sick."

"Do you think that was the only reason he returned to England?"

"Yes, well and maybe guilt." Sandra raised her eyebrows. "He was a dear friend but we both know some of the things he did were not right and maybe as he got older he regretted them. A diagnosis like his may have made him look at his life and want to make amends."

Sandra stared at Ben, she was shocked at his admission but also pleased as he had inadvertently given her a glimmer of hope.

"So Dad amended his will following his diagnosis."

"Yes."

"I never realised that." Sandra smiled.

"No, I see what you're thinking and it's unlikely to change anything."

"If his will was changed after his diagnosis then surely I can challenge it on the grounds of diminished health or whatever the legal term is."

"I will not help you do this."

"You don't have to, there are plenty of lawyers who will take this on. I just wished you had told me this before."

"It was better to get Karen to relinquish the bequest. Your Father was my friend and I did not wish to have his health and reputation torn apart in the courts."

"Well unfortunately that has happened anyway, if I'd foreseen all this trouble I would have just challenged the will."

"Hindsight is a wonderful thing Sandra. But please heed my advice and let it go. I feel no good will come from pursuing this."

"Benjamin, I have to do this, it is probably my last hope."

"But the chance of victory is small and it could take years before a judgement is reached. Go to The Caymans. Build a new life."

"Maybe I will go to The Caymans, but only when I have the rest of my money."

"Don't waste more time on this. Time is the one thing you can never get back," said Ben sadly, shaking his head.

October 1994

"So why are we meeting here darling?" she said as she entwined herself around him. "I do so prefer the hotel."

He pulled her arms from around his neck and gently pushed her away from him.

"I'm not staying, this is not happening anymore."

"You say that every time, it's rather boring. Haven't you learnt yet darling. I always get what I want."

"Not this time."

"Must we really play this game?"

"Sandra, I mean it. Do you know you haven't even asked me about Karen yet?"

"I shall see her next week before I go back, so I'll ask her myself."

"You won't see her. She's not seeing anyone at the moment. She miscarried again."

"Andy, I'm sorry. It must be hard for you too."

"It is, but it's worse for her."

"I'm sure I can make you feel better," she said reaching for him.

"Sandra, I meant it. No more. I'm going home now; my wife needs me."

"What your wife needs is to hear the truth about you and she will. If you leave I swear to God I will tell her about us."

"Do you know what Sandra? Do it, tell her. But this is over."

As he left he could hear Sandra screaming after him. He hoped he was right to call her bluff. He loved Karen, he always had, despite his dalliances with Sandra. Whenever Sandra came over to the U.K. she called him and every time he tried to say no, but he believed her threats that she would tell Karen. He was a coward, he knew that and maybe there was a part of him that enjoyed it too, but it had to stop. She won't tell Karen, he thought to himself, after all she would be risking a friendship that had endured for many years.

Just over a week had passed since the day he had left Sandra, the sound of her screams and threats had rattled around in his head for a few days but now he was beginning to relax. Andrew was sure that Sandra was not going to say anything to Karen after all. Had that been her intention she would probably have done it straight away, she certainly wasn't the sort of person to let the grass grow, no she had thought better of it. Andrew regretted not showing this strength much sooner. He picked up the photograph of Karen that sat on his desk; he was a lucky man, he knew that. The only cloud in their life was the absence of children. He knew they would have to investigate this further and look at other options in their quest to become parents, he had always been the one who had dismissed that idea but now he knew he owed it to Karen to at least look at other possibilities. His thoughts of her were interrupted by the sound of his telephone.

"Hey, I was just thinking about you."

"That's nice, what time are you coming home?"

"Another hour or so. I have a few things to sort out before I leave. Everything alright?"

"Yes, well no."

"What is it? Shall I come home now?"

"No, its fine, don't panic. I'm just in an incredibly bad mood, actually I'm furious."

"With me?"

"No, not with you. Really its fine I shouldn't have bothered you at work, I'll talk to you later."

"Tell me now, you must want to otherwise you wouldn't have called me."

"I've had a row with Sandra."

Andrew froze momentarily at the mention of her name.

"You two always bicker, I wouldn't worry about it."

"No, this time she's gone too far, you won't believe what she said, she made the most outrageous claims and quite frankly I'm done with her. Look I can't talk now I'm getting wound up again. I'll fill you in when you get home. Don't be late."

Andrew said goodbye and put the phone down. She couldn't have, no it must be something else. He finished up what he needed to do and headed home, unsure of what awaited him but slightly comforted that Karen didn't seem to be angry or upset with him.

"She said what?" said Andrew trying desperately not to convey any emotion and hoping his face wouldn't give him away.

"I know, it's farcical. I think she's just, I don't know lost it. I told her you don't even like her."

"I've never said I don't like her."

"Oh Andrew, you really don't have to pretend. I know you only ever tolerated her because she was my oldest friend."

"She was your best friend."

"Well not anymore."

"Are you sure you're okay?"

"No, but I will be."

He decided not to say anything more, he didn't want to give himself away. The only thing he wished was that he had been a fly on the wall when Karen had dismissed Sandra's accusations as nonsense.

2010

"Is it too early for a drink?" asked Andrew.

"Yes it is. And besides what I have to say I want to say with a clear head."

"Karen please, you know I love you and I'm sorry."

"I know that."

"Then please don't say we're finished."

"Andrew..."

"I made a mistake, a big one, granted but,"

"Andrew, shut up and listen."

"Okay, sorry."

"We're not finished, that's not what I want, but there is no quick fix. This is going to take time. The trial has exhausted me, then finding out about you and her and the lies,"

"I never lied."

"Excuse me."

"No, I didn't lie, you just didn't believe Sandra."

Karen bristled.

"You didn't correct me though, did you?"

"I..."

"Defend it if you want Andrew, but as far as I'm concerned you lied. And what about when you met her? You never told me that's what you were doing, you claimed to be going somewhere else. More lies. I'm sure I could go on."

"No, you're right. I'm sorry, carry on."

"Thank you. I don't want this to be over, we have too much to lose. But it is not going to be sorted overnight, as long as you understand that and if we take our time. I think maybe we'll be okay. I want us to be okay."

Andrew's face said it all, the relief was visible as was his joy at getting a second chance. His smile matched that of a child on Christmas morning. He swept Karen into his arms amid declarations of his love. Karen thought of her conversation earlier, with the road sweeper, he had been right for Andrew's joy did please her, for a moment anyway. She hoped they could make it work and she would try, for the boys, for Andrew and for herself. However, she knew that her decision had been made based not only on her feelings for Andrew but because of how she felt about Sandra. She may not have wanted to see her in prison, but she damn well wasn't going to give her the satisfaction of thinking she had finally come between her and Andrew.

Sandra was not going to win that battle.

May 1995

It had been a year since Nelson Mandela had become South Africa's President, a year that had seen the pace of change quicken. Although apartheid was abolished in 1991 it wasn't until the country saw its first black president that things truly began to progress. The rate at which his country was changing rang alarm bells for Bill. He was someone who had profited from apartheid, profited from those on both sides for Bill held no views. The only thing that swayed him was money, although if his dealings were studied in detail it would reveal that he traded more with white nationalists and the AWB* than any other organisation. He had always felt it was safer not to visibly align himself with any political persuasion but now he was realising that playing both sides may have been a dangerous move.

He had handed over a large portion of his business to Sandra; the legitimate side. Which had been a shrewd move as she had already substantially increased their profits. Her business degree was showing its worth. He had been alarmed however, at her decision to sell the properties that they still owned in the United Kingdom. He had in the end, convinced her to keep one residential and two commercial properties. The commercial holdings had long-term tenants in, so to sell those would be folly as they would not have realised their full value and he thought it was worth keeping a residential property there, who knows in the future either he or Sandra may want to go back for more than just a short visit. She had agreed to this as long as he was the one who dealt with any issue arising from those properties. He had tried to find out what it was that had suddenly made her anti-England, for clearly something had irritated her on her last visit there, but she wasn't forthcoming and he knew better than to press her. The remainder of his South African based business, Bill kept control of. Mostly, the deals looked legitimate, on paper anyway. The majority of the time he had taken Ben's advice and therefore the transactions that Ben helped him with were not going to bother him in the future. However, there were a few instances where he had not heeded Ben's warnings. Sometimes the prize on offer was so great that he had deemed it 'worth the risk'. Like so many others he had not thought he would see such change in South Africa within his lifetime, well at least during his business lifetime. He had been sure he would have long since left South Africa before the political climate altered. But now that change was here and it was rapid so he made the decision to bring forward his planned retirement to Grand Cayman. He already owned property there and had substantial assets in an off-shore account, therefore he could go whenever he liked, but first he knew he had to make sure he didn't leave any trace of his more unsavoury dealings, although he would be out of reach, his daughter would not.

"So, the transfer is complete. Your home here is now in Sandra's name as is the business and the office suites. Is there anything else I can do for my friend before he leaves these shores?"

"Benjamin, don't be so dramatic. You make it sound like we're never going to see each other again."

"That may be the case."

"Never. You are my oldest friend and I expect you to visit me often. The Caymans are a great place to have a vacation."

"Very well. And rest assured I will always be here for Sandra."

"Thank you. I appreciate that."

"I know it must be hard to leave her."

"It is, but with you looking out for her and Nikolaas by her side I know she will be fine."

"Nikolaas Venter?"

"Yes."

"You trust him, Willem?"

"Completely. Why do you ask?"

"His family have, let's say, erm, dubious connections."

"Elaborate please."

"His father and Uncle were, probably still are members of the AWB. His uncle was very much an active member of their para-military wing."

"I have heard this, but I understand they are engaging in dialogue now with the new government and the para-military wing has been dissolved."

Bill did not want Ben to know that he actually knew Nikolaas' father and Uncle. He had done business with them both; that was how he had met Nikolaas, who had proved himself very useful when Bill had conducted business that he wanted kept off the radar. He in turn introduced Nikolaas to Sandra.

"Yes, that is the official line, but I'm not so sure. Who knows? Our country is changing, so maybe everyone has to change, even the hardliners like the Venters."

"Well you can keep an eye on both of them for me," said Bill rising from the chair. He held out his hand but Ben stepped out from behind his desk and embraced his oldest friend.

"Take care Willem."

*Afrikaner Weerstandsbeweging (Afrikaner Resistance Movement – a South African far-right separatist organisation.

2010

S andra was right, there were many lawyers prepared to take her case. She trawled the internet to find suitable candidates; lawyers who had previously handled inheritance disputes like this and more importantly lawyers who had been successful. As she studied web pages displaying lists of lawyers and league tables relating to their successes she couldn't help but marvel at the wonderful tool that was the internet. She was able to gather all the information required and communicate with those she may potentially hire from the comfort of her home, over five and a half thousand miles away. Eventually, following hours of research and several emails she decided on three possible candidates. All were based in London so she scheduled appointments for the following week; she would see them each in turn, make a decision then fly on to Grand Cayman.

❦

Sandra saw each of the lawyers on the same day, it was a tiring and draining process; repeating her story over and answering the same questions, but it had been necessary. Each of them had emphasised the difficulty in a case like this and that the outcome could not be guaranteed to go in her favour, however they all believed there was a legal basis for her challenge. Of the three, it was the first one who impressed Sandra the most. Typical really, like going shopping for a dress for that special occasion; you try on several but it's almost always the first one you tried that you go back to. The first lawyer she had seen was a woman, a ballsy woman who completely sympathised with her. A woman who, like Sandra had also done her research and was well aware of the trial and Sandra's conviction. When Sandra called her later that day to appoint her she wasn't surprised, despite the fact that Sandra had been honest and told her she was also seeing other lawyers. She sounded as though she expected to be the choice.

"I have been able to move my day around tomorrow so you can come back in and give me the relevant information I need to proceed."

"Thank you," said an impressed Sandra.

"Well I'm aware you are only in London for a limited time. Bring with you as much documentation as you have relating to your Father including personal information like his Doctor's details etc."

◉

"So let me explain, for a will to be valid the maker of the will, the testator, must have what we call testamentary capacity. People often refer to this as 'being of sound mind'. Wills can therefore be contested on grounds of mental incapacity. A very common situation is where the testator is/was suffering from an illness such as Alzheimer's disease as your Father was. However, the presence of Alzheimer's or similar degenerative conditions does not automatically mean that the person lacks mental capacity.

So contesting their will is not easy. Each case has to be looked at individually, there is no assumption simply due to the presence of an illness. In cases like this medical evidence will be required, which is why I need the details of your Father's doctor. Now, sometimes when a solicitor draws up a will they may take the precaution of getting written confirmation from a doctor to confirm that the testator has testamentary capacity. This isn't the case here and I suspect that the solicitor in question was not even aware of your Father's condition, which could be to our advantage. We have to show that at the time of the new will being made your Father's state of mind was impaired. If we can prove this, it is likely that a court will declare the will to be invalid and therefore a previous will, if there is one, will come into effect. With me so far?"

"Yes."

"Good. A few questions for you now. Veronica Meyer; she was your father's only physician?"

"Yes."

"He wasn't registered with a G.P?"

"No."

"Hmnn."

"Is that a problem?"

"No, I don't think so. It's unusual."

"My Father was a private man, especially regarding personal matters like his health. Veronica was a friend of his from South Africa so she took care of all of his medical needs."

"So she diagnosed his Alzheimer's?"

"In the first instance yes, and then she arranged for him to see an expert in that field to have the diagnosis confirmed."

"Privately?"

"Yes."

"Self-funded or through insurance?"

"Self-funded."

"Do these things have any relevance?" asked Sandra.

"Probably not, but I like to have a complete picture of the people involved with any case I'm working on. Did Veronica Meyer benefit from your father's estate?"

"No."

"Right. I think that's it. I need you to sign these documents then we can begin. As I said before it is not a quick process, so it may take some time. I shall keep you apprised of our progress. Now go and enjoy the Caribbean sunshine."

"Thank you. I will."

Sandra was looking forward to escaping and on Grand Cayman she could do that; escape and hide from the circus her life had become of late. The islanders allowed you to enjoy your privacy if you so wished, however she was equally apprehensive about the trip too. The fact that she wasn't sure when or even if she would ever return home filled her with a profound sadness. She did like Grand Cayman and the house on the island was beautiful; she had spent many happy times there visiting her Dad. Although she did recall one such visit that wasn't so happy. The first time it became apparent to her that Bill's health was deteriorating and not just his physical health. She wished now that at that time she had stepped in to take over the finances completely. Maybe then she wouldn't have to fight Karen for the money as it never would have become an issue. Ah well, no good having regrets now, she thought. Let's just focus on getting it back.

1999

S andra was exhausted, it took all her energy to muster up enough strength to pull her suitcase from the luggage carousel. She hated having to change planes and was amazed that there was still no direct flight from South Africa to Grand Cayman. The layover was only meant to be two hours but actually ended up being almost double that. She hoped Dad was here, last time she came out he had gone fishing and completely forgot he was meant to be picking her up. She walked through the small arrivals hall and scanned the people all eagerly waiting for friends, loved ones or whoever they were meeting. She didn't spot him at first and began cursing under her breath, then she looked up again, there he was standing by a phone booth. She made her way towards him, calling as she neared. He didn't seem to be able to hear her. She called again, he looked up. She smiled and began waving; he was looking straight at her, but didn't smile. He didn't do anything, his face was devoid of expression entirely. Something must be wrong, she quickened her step.

"Dad, hi. Why are you waiting way over here?" Bill stared at her. "Dad? Is everything ok?" Bill turned around, looking behind himself. He turned back at looked at Sandra again. "Dad. What's wrong?"

"Are you looking for someone?" Bill asked her.

"Dad, its Sandra."

"I know you're Sandra. Here give me your bag." Bill picked up Sandra's suitcase with one arm, the other he slipped around her pulling her closer. "How was your flight?"

"Long," said a confused Sandra. "Have you been in the sun Dad?"

"Car's over here," said Bill leading her outside and ignoring her question.

It took about twenty minutes to reach the house. When they got there Isaac came to meet them.

"Miss Sandra, how good to see you."

"And you Isaac. Everything okay?"

Isaac glanced at Bill before answering.

"Yes. Everything is fine."

"Good." Sandra turned to face Bill. "I think I'm going to unpack and have a nap then I'll come and have a swim."

"Okay, a cocktail will be waiting for you."

"Sounds perfect."

Sandra lay down on her bed and within seconds she was asleep. She had been asleep for well over an hour when she was suddenly wakened by banging and crashing coming from outside. She jumped up and ran outside, stubbing her toe on her unopened suitcase as she did. She was confronted by Dad sorting through a large wicker chest that sat on the terrace by the pool. He was throwing the contents of the chest all over the place. Isaac was running around picking up the items which included: flippers, snorkels, old fishing reels, an array of deflated inflatables and oddly an old tea tray. Bill suddenly stopped and reached deep inside the chest and pulled out a string bag containing buckets, spades and a small watering can. It was the bag that Sandra used to take to the beach back home when she was very young, she was surprised it still existed and even more surprised that it had made its way over here. She assumed it must have just got packed up with items from the boat. He spotted Sandra and held up the bag waving it at her before going inside the house. Sandra didn't know what to make of the scene she had just witnessed but decided that whatever it was it would have to wait until later. For now, she needed to unpack and freshen up.

Sandra and Bill had a lovely dinner on the lower terrace; Sandra's favourite spot on the estate. The terrace wasn't far from the water's edge and she could hear the water as it gently lapped against the rocks. The view across the bay was stunning, the sea a heavenly azure occasionally turning pink when the evening sun caught the delicate ripples that played on its surface.

"I thought we could go down to the beach tomorrow," said Bill.

"The beach?"

"Yes, you love the beach."

"I think I'd rather stay here, slap on some cream and let myself fry by the pool."

"I've got your beach bag ready." Sandra looked at her Dad, she didn't say anything. "It took me forever to find it. You know the one I mean, the old string bag?" continued Bill.

"Yes Dad, I know the one you mean. But I don't think I want to go to the beach.

"Of course you do."

"No, I don't. For God's sake, I'm 38 years old. I don't want to sit on the beach building sandcastles!"

Sandra stood up and ran up the stairs leading to the house. Isaac was on his way down, he had overheard her shouting. He stopped her.

"Don't be mad at him, it makes it worse."

"Makes what worse?"

"This thing, he must tell you and he will, tomorrow. Mostly it's okay, but if he gets upset or worked up it can be problem. I think he was looking forward to seeing you too much, that is all. Go and sleep now, I will look after him."

"Thank you Isaac."

A horrible combination of worry and jet-lag meant she did not sleep well. The next morning she was greeted by Aya, Isaac's wife. Together they looked after the house and Bill. Cooking, cleaning, gardening, driving and anything else that needed doing. Bill paid them well and housed them in a guest cottage in the grounds.

"Morning Aya."

"Good morning Sandra. Your father is sitting by the pool having coffee. Would you like some?"

"Yes, thank you. Is Isaac around?"

"He's in the vegetable garden. Would you like me to fetch him for you?"

"No, I'll go round and find him."

Sandra walked the long way round to the vegetable garden, she did not want Bill to see her before she had spoken to Isaac. She walked under the archway of intertwined bougainvillea and hibiscus; delicate pink and purple petals paraded before her eyes and the glorious scent made her pause for a moment. Some things in life were very special and deserved to be appreciated, fully enjoyed. Dad had taught her that. As she came out from under the archway Isaac was walking towards her.

"Good morning."

"Isaac, tell me about Dad."

"It is not my place, he will tell you."

"Isaac please. I'm a little afraid to ask him about last night."

"No, don't do that. That would not be good. He will not recall last night, which is for the best. If you try and tell him that will upset him and make him bad again."

"I need to know what to do."

"He will tell you. Today he is fine, most days he is fine. He only gets... upset, when the routine is changed."

"So my being here is not a good idea."

"No, it is fine idea. Most days are good, now go. He will tell you when he is ready."

❦

"Alzheimer's disease?"

"Yes."

"How can you be sure?"

"I'm sure."

"Have you had a second opinion?"

"Second and third."

"So what are they doing about it?"

"There is nothing they can do. Medication helps the symptoms but there is no cure."

"Somewhere in the world there must be. The U.K., America, Canada even."

"Sandra, do you not think I have asked these questions."

"I refuse to believe there is nothing we can do. I will find something, I have to, we have to."

"What you can do is keep doing what you are doing. Working hard and making me proud. I am transferring the rest of my assets over to you, well most of them. You have the business already, the title deeds to our home and the land in Cape Town are now in your name, Benjamin has seen to that. You can sell the two commercial properties in England at any time now. There is also some money due from some outstanding arrangements, Nikolaas will oversee that and then deposit the money with you. I am keeping the house in the U.K. and of course here."

"You're not coming home?"

"No, I plan to stay here for as long as I am able. Then when, things change. I am going to the house in England. It is being modified as we speak so that it is suitable for any care I may need."

"Who is arranging that?"

"Veronica."

"Why Veronica? I could sort that out for you."

"She is a doctor, my doctor and she knows better than anyone what I may need in the future."

"You seem to have it all planned."

"As best as I can, yes."

"What about money?"

"What about it?"

"For your care, modifying the house. Shall I wire some when I get back?"

"No I have more than enough here. Right enough of this. We are going to enjoy ourselves while I am able, which may be for a while yet."

"I'm sure it will Daddy," said Sandra putting her arms around him and holding onto him as tightly as possible.

2010

K aren picks up the mail from the doormat, flicking through the assortment of flyers and envelopes, one envelope catches her eye. It's from the solicitor. She goes into the kitchen, dropping the mail onto the table, except the solicitor's letter which she opens and reads. It is not what she expected to hear; although it is about the money. She knew it would be about the money. The solicitor had been quite certain once the trial was over the money would be released to her. Karen hoped this would be done quickly and with minimal fuss so she could press ahead with her plans. But this, she didn't expect. As far as she was aware Sandra had returned to South Africa and she never expected to hear from her again. The last thing Karen expected was that Sandra would still try and take the money.

The letter detailed that Sandra had mounted a legal challenge to have the will declared invalid due to Bill's failing health at the time the will was written. The court had agreed that there were adequate grounds for a hearing. As this was the case the solicitor asked Karen to get in touch so they could prepare to contest the challenge if that was what she wished to do. She would have to talk to Andrew now, she couldn't keep this from him.

He had sat and listened patiently, he had resisted interrupting her, but now she had finished and it was his turn to speak, but there were no words; just astonishment. Astonishment that Sandra had the nerve to come back and continue to press her claim for the money. Astonishment that a British court actually thought she may have a case and astonishment at what his wife intended to do with the money should the judgement go in their favour.

"Are you just going to sit there and stare at me?"

"Karen, I'm flabbergasted."

"At what?"

"At what?" he repeated. "At the absurdity of it all. I suppose we shouldn't be surprised at Sandra's action, I've never known a more audacious woman, but the courts allowing it is quite ridiculous and then to top it all, if we win…. Well, it's utterly ridiculous."

"And what is bothering you the most? I sense it's my decision more than anything else."

"Yes actually, it is. Do you not think something like this at least merited a discussion?"

"No I don't. At the end of the day it is my decision."

"It's not just your decision."

"Andrew, you make all the decisions regarding our finances and the factory and I've been happy to go along with that. But now it's my turn to decide."

"Just think what we could do with that money. We could have the most amazing holidays, the boys would love that."

"Don't you dare bring them into this…"

"Well they've had to put up with a lot lately. They've had to go backwards and forwards to my parents and put up with you being stressed."

"Don't Andrew. You are not being fair. For a start, you've been just as stressed as I have and to be honest I don't think it's touched them at all."

"Alright, what about us? Don't you think a break would do us good?"

"We don't need Bill's money to do that."

"This money could change our lives forever."

"I don't want to change our lives. I like our lives, well I did before all this business with Sandra started."

"There you go, this money will go some way to repairing the damage."

"We have to repair the damage."

"For God's sake Karen, don't you think you've earnt that money?"

"I can't believe you just said that."

"What?"

"Of all the words you could use."

Andrew looked at her blankly, he was confused.

"What?" he said again.

"You think I've *earnt* the money."

"Yes."

"Earnt?"

"Deserve, that's what I mean. You deserve it. We both do. Look, think of it as compensation. What he did to you, was wrong. You were still at school, for God's sake and then there's, you know the other thing." He paused, expecting a reaction from her, but she said nothing.

It was clear that her mind was set, but he wasn't happy. It was not what he had wanted to hear. It was a life-changing amount; he could sell the business, they could get a bigger home, a second home. Why can't she see what this money would mean?

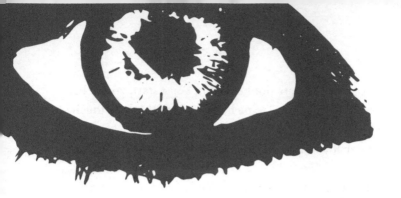

2002

He walked from room to room, they all looked the same: cold, clinical, cheerless. Each room resembled that in an institution. His eyes moistened as he realised this may be home one day. It was a stark reminder of what was on the horizon. He probably shouldn't have come to see the house yet, he should have listened to Veronica; she said although the modifications were complete, it did not look like a home; it had yet to be decorated and furnished, personal touches had not been added so it may not be a pleasant experience. But he wanted to see where his money had gone, he was still in control; for now.

Bill hadn't just returned to view his future home. He also had a few things to organise himself while he was able. The first of which was to make amendments to his will. Benjamin had always taken care of any legal work that Bill required and he had been the one who had drawn up Bill's original will. Bill knew his old friend would come to him if he asked, even though he hated to travel beyond South Africa's borders these days, but he wouldn't ask him to do that. Ben may notice changes in him and more importantly he may question the changes Bill was making to his will. It was easier to get someone else to undertake this, so he asked Veronica to find someone for him. Ben would remain as executor and he too would receive a bequest. Bill wanted to leave something to his friend who had always remained loyal to him. He also intended making a greater provision for Isaac and Aya, they had proved invaluable of late and he hoped they would continue to maintain the house in Grand Cayman for Sandra after he had gone. He was to allow them to have the cottage on the estate for life. However, if Sandra did decide to sell the house - although he hoped she wouldn't, he hoped she would love it as he did – then Sandra would have to buy them a home of their choosing. The final change, was the addition of Karen as a beneficiary. He had not seen or spoken to her for several years, but lately she had never been far from his thoughts; he didn't know why. It was just her he thought of, only Karen, none of the others and there had been a few. Sometimes his mind wandered back and he thought of her and recalled the time they spent together, he never felt it was wrong; but at night these thoughts became dreams, then the dreams became nightmares. His dreams saw him lying with Karen, caressing her, having her. She was smiling at him, eager to please him but then, the dream gave way and the nightmare began. Karen's smile would fade and her face became dark and full of anger; she would shout and cry but then when he looked closely it wasn't Karen's face any longer. It was Sandra's face, and she was screaming at him. Why did Karen haunt him? Was it because of that night, the night she came to him for help and he was less than kind? He had heard she had suffered miscarriages, was that a consequence of that night, was that his fault? At the moment his memories were slowly slipping away, sliding from his consciousness to a place he no longer had access to. But that night, well, that was one memory he couldn't erase. Why won't the bad memories fade? Why are they harder to forget?

Each morning he would wake, the shame and guilt on his shoulders pinning him to the bed. The shame and guilt that had robbed him of another night's sleep. He knew he had to try and make amends; atonement and reparation might rid him of this nightmare. The only way he could do that was with money, he knew no other way. Money was the only medium he understood.

Still he puzzled over what made Karen different? Was it because of that night at the office or had he loved her after all and never realised. She had such power over him, even now. Her image taunted him, thoughts of her teased him, still. Why though? It made no sense to him. He had never cared this much for anyone other than Sandra. Maybe that was it, perhaps it was because Karen's life had always been so entwined with his daughter's.

2011

S he would only have to answer one question. A simple question, the answer, a simple yes or no. But to answer it truthfully would deliver the wrong outcome, of that she was sure. Facing a dilemma was not something new to Veronica. There had been several occasions where she had been presented with choices, very often they were tough choices, but this was something else. She had never been in a situation where she actually contemplated lying. Especially on oath.

◉

Veronica arrived in England in 1977, alone and afraid. Mourning not just her lover, but her homeland too. She had never wanted to leave South Africa but following Makalo's internment and apparent suicide there was nothing to keep her there. Disowned by her family and most of her friends, shunned by the medical profession she had worked so hard to be part of and all because she fell in love.

She hadn't been looking for love, her career was all that mattered to her at that time, but love found her. It found her and descended upon her like long overdue rain on an arid wasteland, soaking every inch of her. The intensity of her feelings surprised her, she had never felt this way. They came upon her like a door being flung open, fast and instant.

The joy Makalo brought to her was immeasurable but it was twinned with sadness, a sadness as profound as their love; for theirs was a love that had to be hidden. Veronica could not express her delight and happiness to anyone. Her joy could not be shared, not with her closest friends or even her mother. Their relationship had to be conducted in secret for the eyes of those around them would not see love, they would see sin, wrong-doing, behaviour so shameful they would seek to end it. And not just end it, punish it too.

They were always careful, aware of the dangers should their relationship be exposed, but as time passed they began to relax. They relaxed just a little too much, became careless and they did not notice that suspicions had been aroused. Neither saw them come, as they lay together as one, contented and blissfully happy. Not until they were suddenly and violently wrenched from each other's arms. Makalo was dragged to his feet, spat at and beaten. Veronica screamed as he pitched forward following a blow across his back. She too was dragged away, but they spoke to her as a victim, presuming she was not there by choice. Ignoring her protests, dismissing them out of hand, she was delivered back to her parents; her father refused even to look at her. It was left to her mother to make her aware of the shame she had brought upon them. Veronica was told she must speak against Makalo, maybe her career could be saved and the family honour restored. A black man descended from tribesmen and a white woman, a doctor from a respected family; it was clear to see where the blame lie. But she would not comply, she would forsake her career and reject her family as they had rejected her. But it would not be enough to save Makalo, the law was clear. He was imprisoned and within six months he was dead, found hanged in his cell, by his own hand they said, although Veronica never believed that.

She could stay in South Africa no longer, her disgrace was absolute that was clear. But where should she go, where could she go? Everyone she knew lived here, she had never known anyone to leave. Well except an old friend of her brother's. He had gone to England with his young daughter. He had come back for her brother's funeral and had kept in touch with Veronica following this, although she had been rather remiss in replying to his letters of late. At the funeral he had said if ever she needed anything, just to ask, almost as if he had assumed her brother's mantle. Maybe he could help her. Her brother used to talk of him as someone who was able to arrange many things. Well it couldn't hurt to ask, she thought, after all she had nothing to lose.

Her brother had been right, Willem Davids was able to help her and quickly too. Eight weeks after contacting him she was on a plane bound to London. Not only did he sort out the flights and relevant paperwork for her, he also arranged for her to have somewhere to live and money to live on until she was able to begin working again. She promised to repay him every penny but he said it was not necessary.

"I'm sure one day I may need you to help me," he said.

And she did help him, although she never felt entirely out of his debt, for what he did for her was immeasurable. He gave her a new life, a fresh start, something she could not have achieved without him. He was a flawed man, she knew that. His wealth was dubiously earned, he had a violent temper and his predilection for young girls left her feeling uncomfortable, yet she still saw him as her saviour for he helped her when no one else would or could.

When he had finally returned from Grand Cayman, she had spent a lot of time with him. He had asked her to make sure Sandra was okay when he'd gone. He would talk of her as though she were still a child. Veronica promised him she would look out for Sandra, and she did try. However, Sandra made it clear that she was a capable woman who could take care of herself and besides she lived in South Africa and Veronica in England. She saw her just twice following Bill's death and since then she hadn't heard from her, until now.

The letter began with thanks for the care she had shown Bill and apologies for not keeping in touch. It went on to say how much Sandra missed her Dad and she would sacrifice all she had to see him again. As that was not possible, she felt it important to continue in his footsteps by working hard and maintaining all that he had strived to achieve. By this she meant not just his business but also his reputation. Sandra then wrote how a third party had influenced her father when his health was failing and convinced him to change his will. She was contesting this change on the grounds that he was not able to make such decisions due to his condition, something which Veronica as his Doctor was sure to agree with. She added that the new beneficiary was someone who had made scurrilous and salacious claims about her father and that 'anyone who was a true friend of my father's would surely want to defend him against such invectiveness.'

Sandra is her father's daughter alright, thought Veronica. The letter was pleasant enough at the beginning but by the end there was a definite hint of menace, very subtle, but it was there.

She already knew about the impending court action as she had received a letter asking her to attend a hearing which would seek to ascertain the validity of the will; she would be asked about Bill's diagnosis and health at the time his will was changed. Veronica was aware he had done this for it was she who had arranged the visit to the solicitor; a visit that did occur after his diagnosis. He was deteriorating at this time, his recall was not what it was and he was finding it hard to concentrate for any length of time. If she revealed this it would be highly likely that the will would be declared invalid, but was that the right outcome? She didn't think so. She was acquainted with the fact that Karen was the beneficiary and she knew why. She remembered clearly the young girl she had met many years earlier; a girl who had suffered unnecessary trauma because of Bill.

Veronica was torn, she had always told the truth. But to tell the truth now seemed wrong to her. How could that be?

The day of the hearing loomed large but Veronica tried to concentrate on matters at hand and not think about it, almost hoping if she didn't acknowledge it, then that day would not arrive. But it did arrive, as surely as night follows day.

She would tell the truth today, she knew that. It wasn't a conscious decision on her part to do that, she just knew she did not have the ability to lie. And then she saw her. She recognised her instantly, despite the passing of over thirty years. She was with a man, who appeared to be fussing over her a little too much. Veronica watched, discreetly as she told the man to leave her. He sat down, deflated. She looked as vulnerable as the first time they had met. The recollection of that meeting was instantly clear; Karen was just a girl, barely out of school. A frightened innocent girl, who was innocent no more. Her innocence had gone, long before taken by a man old enough to be her father, of this Veronica had no doubt. The thought disgusted her. She was the same age as his daughter, his daughter's friend. Worse still he had impregnated her and Veronica thought he was most likely responsible for the miscarriage that followed.

Veronica wondered how Karen's life had turned out. It looked like she had married. Had she gone on to have children? A career? She couldn't tell. Was she happy? She didn't appear to be today. Her observations were halted by someone calling her name.

"Veronica. So nice to see you. You look well," said Sandra coming towards her in a strident manner. Sandra put her arms out, embracing her rather exuberantly. Veronica hid her embarrassment, she was aware of people looking at them, including Karen and then, their eyes met. Veronica acknowledged her and Karen responded with a smile, a slight smile that could so easily have been missed for it was loaded with sadness. That smile changed Veronica's mind, it was a smile that made her realise just because something is true, doesn't necessarily mean that it is right.

◉

"How much did you offer her?"

Karen ignored her and kept walking.

"Oh come on Karen, you can tell me now," said Sandra as she ran in front of her forcing her to stop.

"Tell you what?"

"How much money have you offered Veronica for her lies?"

"I haven't offered anybody anything."

"You expect me to believe that."

"Frankly, I don't care what you believe. Me, I'm just glad it's over."

"I'm sure you are, especially now you have my money."

"Sandra, I didn't ask for the money I never wanted the money."

"You wanted everything and as usual you got everything."

"What?"

"You wanted it all, you always did. Never satisfied that was always your problem. You always wanted more, greedy, selfish and jealous of everybody else." Karen stared at Sandra as she continued her rant. "I remember when we first met, you wanted my clothes and my house. You wanted to be like me, I know. You were so jealous, that's why you went after my Dad. You were always at mine, I thought you were my friend, but it was him you wanted. You tempted him, then seduced him. He was my only family and now he's gone and because of what happened between you I don't even have my memories of him, they are all spoilt, tarnished and tainted by you. I think of Dad now and I just see you, you and him. You had your own family, including a Mum, which I never had. And now you have your children and him." Sandra nodded at Andrew. "I have no one, not even a brother or sister to share my grief."

Andrew had been listening patiently to Sandra's diatribe but now he'd heard enough.

"You could have had a brother or sister."

"Andrew don't," said Karen.

"No, she needs to know."

"Know what?" asked Sandra.

"She was pregnant. Your father made her pregnant. So you may well have had a brother or sister if your father hadn't beaten her until she miscarried."

"You're a liar," spat Sandra.

"Ask the Doctor, Bill's doctor. She was the one who looked after Karen when it happened. She knew what a bastard he was." It was Sandra's turn to stare at Karen. "Now, we are going home. I suggest you do the same, hopefully your home is still overseas because the idea of living in the same country as you sickens me," said Andrew taking Karen's arm and steering her away.

Sandra followed them outside and watched as they walked up the street.

"I have nothing because of you," she shouted. She didn't think they'd heard her but then Karen stopped walking and turned around. Andrew was trying to pull her along. She wrested her arm from him and walked back towards Sandra.

"You should have called me when he died, when you first knew. You should have called then."

"Why?" asked Sandra.

"If we'd spoke about it, we may have avoided a lot of unpleasantness."

"You think it would have been any less unpleasant for me? For God's sake, you had sex with my Dad and then he left you my inheritance."

"Not all of it."

"Enough of it."

"Then I guess he screwed us both."

"It's not funny."

"I know and I'm not trying to be funny. But this whole business, we could have bypassed it all if you'd just spoken to me."

"And said what exactly?"

"You could have started by asking for the money."

"Oh and you would have given it to me just like that?"

"Maybe. We're not all motivated by money."

"You really expect me to believe that?"

"Believe what you like Sandra. I don't care anymore, I never asked for the money and to be honest I don't even know that I want the money."

"Feel free to give it up then."

"Perhaps I will."

Sandra was dumbstruck, just for a second.

"You're going to give it back."

"Give it up, not give it back. I don't want it, but I'm sure as hell not going to give it to you. Not after the things you've done to me." Karen turned on her heels and walked away as she did she threw one last comment Sandra's way. "You stupid fuck."

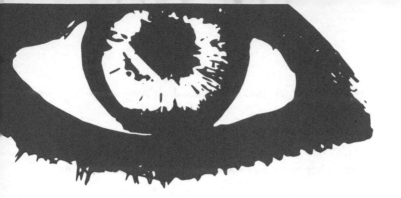

2015

Karen poured the remaining coffee into her cup and continued perusing the headlines on her iPad. It was clearly a slow news day, the headlines really didn't amount to anything much in the way of new news. She drained her cup and went to get ready. She so enjoyed these leisurely mornings; no breakfasts to make, no school run, in fact nothing to do at all. So often her mornings were fraught with issues like unwashed football kits, lost ties, overdue homework and that was just the boys. Andrew was worse, rushing around barking out instructions for things that needed collecting or delivering and blaming everyone but himself when he was unable to find whatever he may need for that day. She didn't feel guilty anymore either, certainly having some time away had made her more tolerant when she was back at home.

When the money from Bill's estate had finally been released to Karen it was a shock. Not just actually receiving it, but the amount; interest had been accruing on the money since Bill's death and even after the relevant deductions it was far more than she had expected. She hadn't told Andrew exactly how much she had received, she'd told him a figure, a believable amount, which he accepted without question. There was enough money for Karen to press ahead with her plan and to buy this place; her

BEWARE THE CUCKOO

bolt-hole, her sanctuary. Karen had never had anywhere that was just hers, a place that offered calm and solace when she needed it. Andrew wouldn't understand, he didn't grow up in a house that was constantly noisy and offered you no privacy. He had never had to share a bathroom with strangers and he probably didn't feel that his life was beyond his control. He wouldn't be the only one, she imagined not many people would understand her need for her own space. A refuge, somewhere to do as she pleased because everything belonged to her. But more than that it was also somewhere to be who she pleased. No, nobody would get that, well Sandra might, Karen grinned at the irony.

Her phone vibrated alerting her to the fact that she had a text. It was Andrew. *'Morning darling. Hope you slept well. Looking forward to seeing you later. What time? xx'*

Karen began typing a reply then deleted it, deciding to call instead. He answered immediately.

"Hey."

"Hi. All good on the home front?" she asked.

"Yes, all went like clockwork. Charlie even managed to get up in time to get the bus today."

"Wow, I need to stay away more often."

"Please don't, we've missed you. How did it go?"

"Good, although I'm not sure the building is right."

"Well, I'm sure you'll find the right place. There's no hurry, the first one only opens today. Remind me what time?"

"Four 'o' clock. But get there before then if you can."

"Will do. See you later then. Love you."

"You too, bye."

Karen sighed as she disconnected the call, she didn't like lying to him, but it wasn't like she was cheating on him. She just hadn't been visiting potential new sites. She had been on her own, here, the entire time. She'd had a long soak in her own bath, watched an old film, had a couple of drinks and gone to bed, alone. It had been heavenly. She glanced at the clock on the oven, time to get ready.

She walked into the second bedroom that she used as her dressing room. A beautiful room, all white with cupboards along one wall. It was her favourite room, because this is where she kept all her wonderful things. It was her equivalent of a child's play room except her 'toys' were clothes and jewels and other trinkets. She opened one of the cupboards to choose something to wear. So much choice; she had enjoyed several shopping trips of late and had a lot of clothes, many still unworn. Some she knew she would never wear, well not outside of here. She loved trying on the different outfits, contemplating her reflection in the ornate full length mirror, but some of them were far too flamboyant, sparkly or risqué to ever wear anywhere else. Karen selected a conservative outfit that would suit today's occasion, nothing ostentatious. She added a scarf and looked in the mirror. Something missing, earrings. She looked on the dressing table, then recalled a pair of earrings that would perfectly compliment her outfit.

The box had to be dragged from the back of the cupboard, she knelt beside it and opened it. A treasure trove of jewellery and lace and ornaments greeted her. Although some of the things were dated and some a little juvenile now, there were some things like the earrings she was searching for, that were ideal. He had bought her many presents and he had such good taste, well mostly she thought, as she pulled out a rather hideous looking brooch. She rifled around in the box a little more before she found what she was looking for, a small velvet box, inside were a beautiful pair of earrings, blue and violet at the same time. She had never worn these before, what were they again - tanzanite. They were perfect. She admired herself in the mirror then held up the camera and pressed the button, almost instantly it delivered a photo of her. She gently waved the picture through the air. When she was sure it was dry, she stuck it on the inside of the cupboard door with the others.

Karen clapped as Ben Jackson snipped the red ribbon and declared the building officially open. Initially she was going to approach the Mayor to do it but Charlie had told her in no uncertain terms that wasn't cool. Most of the staff - all quite young themselves - had agreed with him. Apparently, Ben Jackson was an up and coming singer/songwriter, the next big thing and he was a local lad, so in the end a good choice. She still couldn't quite comprehend that she'd done it; a drop-in centre for young people. Somewhere they could relax and chill out but also somewhere that offered comfort and counselling should they need it. There was nothing like this in her day.

"Well done you," said Andrew slipping an arm around her waist.

"Thank you."

"You know I think this place will make a difference, especially around here."

"I hope so. It's taken a lot to get to here. Blood, sweat and tears all the way. As well you know."

"I do know, but it's been worth it. There's a difference in you these days."

"Really, how so?"

"You're clearly happier than you have been in a long time, even before all the trouble you weren't properly happy."

"Was I always miserable then?"

"No, it's just that… well there was always a kind of sadness. Like something was missing. I think this project has filled that void."

"Maybe. You're not sorry we aren't jetting off on some exotic holiday then?"

"No. I'm sure exotic climes are overrated."

"So you won't be wanting this then," she said handing him an envelope.

"What's this?"

"Open it."

Andrew opened the envelope. It contained the itinerary for a trip to Florida and The Bahamas.

"When?"

"It's not booked yet, I need you to tell me when you can take the time off. We can work it out later."

Andrew drew her close and kissed her.

"I really am so very proud of you and I'm so glad that we've been able to move on."

"Well," Karen gently twisted one of her earrings as she spoke. "Moving on was easy once I realised I had no desire to live a life dictated by the past."

Once everyone had left Karen walked through the building, tomorrow they would be open for business. She hoped it would be a success. Time would tell. As she walked towards her car Karen stopped by the sign, she brushed away the stray leaves that had attached themselves to it so it could be clearly read.

Cuckoo House

BEWARE THE CUCKOO

ACKNOWLEDGEMENTS

Many people have helped me as I worked on this, my first novel, too many to list but you know who you are and I'm incredibly grateful to you all. Some however I need to single out. First and foremost, I would like to thank Matthew Smith of Urbane Publications, without his willingness to take a chance on me, this book would be nothing more than an idea languishing on my laptop. Matthew's unique style has created a wonderful environment at Urbane; it is the publishing home of a family of talented and supportive authors that I'm proud to be a part of. I am indebted to my dear friend Maddy Butcher for her advice, encouragement and friendship. She was also an endless source of prosecco when required! A big thank you to Sheree Murphy who read Beware the Cuckoo prior to publication and went on to pen some wonderful comments about it. Thanks also to photographer Louise Reed.

It is with boundless love and thanks that I mention my husband Richard for his unstinting love and support. To my beautiful children, Tom and Hayleigh thank you so much for filling my life with love and joy and for saying, go on Mum, you can do this.

Finally, thanks go to you for picking up this book. I hope it doesn't disappoint.

Author photo courtesy of Louise Reed
www.louisereed.co.uk

Julie was born in East London but now lives a rural life in North Essex. She is married with two children. Her working life has seen her have a variety of jobs, including running her own publishing company. She is the author of the children's book *Poppy and the Garden Monster*.

Julie writes endlessly and when not writing she is reading. Other interests include theatre, music and running. Besides her family, the only thing she loves more than books is Bruce Springsteen.

The Kindness of Strangers is Julie Newman's new novel publication spring 2018:

She should have listened.

That was all she had to do; it had nothing to do with her anyway. She may have brought them together, but what happened thereon was not her business. She knew this, but she also knew what was right. And she always had to do what was right.

But she should have listened.

That was all she had to do; it had nothing to do with her anyway. She may have thought she was helping, but she wasn't. She knew this, but she also knew what was right. And she always had to do what was right.

Still, she should have listened.

That was all she had to do; it had nothing to do with her anyway. She may have known the truth, but it wasn't her truth to tell. She knew this, but she also knew what was right. And she always had to do what was right.

Bet she wished she had listened…

Urbane Publications is dedicated to
developing new author voices, and publishing
fiction and non-fiction that challenges, thrills and
fascinates.

From page-turning novels to innovative
reference books, our goal is to publish what
YOU want to read.

Find out more at
urbanepublications.com